THE
CREEK

Also by LJ Ross

THE SUMMER SUSPENSE MYSTERIES

1. The Cove
2. The Creek
3. The Bay
4. The Haven

THE DCI RYAN MYSTERIES

1. Holy Island
2. Sycamore Gap
3. Heavenfield
4. Angel
5. High Force
6. Cragside
7. Dark Skies
8. Seven Bridges
9. The Hermitage
10. Longstone
11. The Infirmary (Prequel)
12. The Moor
13. Penshaw
14. Borderlands
15. Ryan's Christmas
16. The Shrine
17. Cuthbert's Way
18. The Rock
19. Bamburgh
20. Lady's Well
21. Death Rocks
22. Poison Garden
23. Belsay
24. Berwick

THE ALEXANDER GREGORY THRILLERS

1. Impostor
2. Hysteria
3. Bedlam
4. Mania
5. Panic
6. Amnesia
7. Obsession

THE CREEK

A SUMMER SUSPENSE MYSTERY

LJ ROSS

PENGUIN BOOKS

PENGUIN BOOKS

UK | USA | Canada | Ireland | Australia
India | New Zealand | South Africa

Penguin Books is part of the Penguin Random House group of companies
whose addresses can be found at global.penguinrandomhouse.com

Penguin Random House UK,
One Embassy Gardens, 8 Viaduct Gardens, London SW11 7BW

penguin.co.uk

First published by Dark Skies Publishing 2022
Published in Penguin Books 2026
001

Copyright © LJ Ross, 2022

The moral right of the author has been asserted

Penguin Random House values and supports copyright. Copyright fuels creativity, encourages diverse voices, promotes freedom of expression and supports a vibrant culture. Thank you for purchasing an authorised edition of this book and for respecting intellectual property laws by not reproducing, scanning or distributing any part of it by any means without permission. You are supporting authors and enabling Penguin Random House to continue to publish books for everyone. No part of this book may be used or reproduced in any manner for the purpose of training artificial intelligence technologies or systems. In accordance with Article 4(3) of the DSM Directive 2019/790, Penguin Random House expressly reserves this work from the text and data mining exception.

Cover artwork by Andrew Davidson
Cover layout by Stuart Bache

Set in 12.8/18.25pt Minion Pro
Typeset by Riverside Publishing Solutions
Printed and bound in Great Britain by Clays Ltd, Elcograf S.p.A.

The authorised representative in the EEA is Penguin Random House Ireland,
Morrison Chambers, 32 Nassau Street, Dublin D02 YH68

A CIP catalogue record for this book is available from the British Library

ISBN: 978–1–804–96040–0

Penguin Random House is committed to a sustainable future
for our business, our readers and our planet. This book is made
from Forest Stewardship Council® certified paper.

CHAPTER 1

Kate Irving slipped into her son's bedroom like a silent shadow.

She crossed the room quickly and opened his wardrobe, pausing to listen for any sound in the hallway beyond, before shoving aside his clothes to reveal a holdall she'd packed the day before.

"Wake up, Jamie."

The little boy heard his mother's whisper through a haze of sleep and rolled over, tucking himself into the foetal position.

Looking down at his tiny form, at the rounded curve of his cheeks and the long sweep of his lashes, Kate experienced a fierce wave of maternal love that was followed by another, even stronger wave of guilt.

It wasn't too late to change her mind.

Maybe things would get better...

She stood there for endless moments while tears pooled in her eyes and fell onto Jamie's pastel-blue bedspread. Through her clouded vision, she looked around the room and her eye fell upon a series of framed pictures she'd hung on the wall, one taken at each of Jamie's four birthday parties. In every one of them she was smiling broadly—smiling so hard that her cheeks ached.

Happy families, she thought, and her heart shattered.

She stared at an image of the three of them, her eyes tracing the contours of the man she'd married.

Until death do us part, the registrar had said.

Beneath her clothing, she wore a thick, homemade bandage around her left wrist and, unconsciously, she reached for it, rubbing the ache that still troubled her.

No, she thought. *It was already too late.*

She must stay strong.

Kate helped Jamie into his jacket, tugging his arms through the sleeves with gentle hands, casting the occasional glance over her shoulder towards the door and what lay beyond it.

"Mummy…"

Jamie's eyes struggled open, and a small frown crinkled his young brow.

"Why are you wearing a jacket?"

"We're going on an adventure," she whispered, and hoped it would turn out to be the truth.

"But...it's night-time," he said, and his voice sounded impossibly loud in the quiet house.

"*Shh,*" she said, while fear turned her blood cold. "It's a secret, Jamie, so we have to be very, very quiet. Okay?"

Her son's eyes lit up with the promise of fun and, for a painful moment, she wondered whether Will had ever looked that way, as a boy.

"*Okay,*" Jamie agreed, in a stage whisper.

"We have to be like mice," Kate said, zipping up his jacket before strapping the velcro on his shoes.

"You mean we have to squeak?"

She smiled, despite it all. "No, sweetie," she murmured. "I mean we have to be very, very quiet."

"Oh," he said, with a hint of disappointment. "Where are we going?"

"Somewhere nice."

"Will Daddy be there?"

Her chest contracted with pain. "Come on," she whispered, tugging him up into her arms so she held him securely against her chest. "Time to go."

"But—"

"*Quiet*, remember?"

Kate grabbed the backpack, which held only the bare necessities, then cocked her ear to the door.

Silence.

"M—"

"Shh, Jamie," she whispered, before stepping back out into the darkened hallway.

With one final, lingering glance towards the door at the very end, she turned and walked slowly and carefully, avoiding any creaking floorboards that could give them away. Her heart hammered against her chest in time with her footsteps and she felt suddenly light-headed, fearful that she'd collapse or fall down the wide staircase to the hard marble floor below, taking Jamie with her.

"I need a wee-wee," her son whispered, as they reached the bottom.

The front door was tantalisingly close.

"You'll have to wait," she told him. "Hold on a little bit longer."

"I need it *now!*"

There was an urgency to his tone that couldn't be ignored, but panic was a living thing inside her and the urge to run grew stronger with every passing second.

"Quickly," she muttered, and hurried to the nearby cloakroom.

"Why can't we put the light on?" Jamie asked, as she helped him out of his onesie, cursing the time it was taking.

Because the light activated an extractor fan, and that was noisy, she wanted to say.

"It's all part of the fun," she told him, and hated herself for telling him yet another lie. "Hurry up, now, sweetheart."

She waited, using a hand towel to wipe the sweat that caked her brow, while her mind conjured up all the things Will would say…all the things he would *do,* if he discovered them.

"All done," he said, wriggling back into his onesie.

"Good," she said. "Now—"

Jamie reached for the flush and tugged at it, as he'd been taught to do. A moment later, the sound of gushing water filled the hallway, echoing around the walls of the house.

Horrified, stricken by a fresh wave of fear, she reached for the boy and peeped out into the empty hallway. She stood there listening intently and was about to move again when she heard it. Faint, little more than a breath of sound, but instinct told her she was right.

A door opening, somewhere upstairs.
He'd heard them...

Her breath came in short and fast gulps now, and she cast wide eyes towards the front door, and the freedom that lay beyond it.

Go! her mind whispered. *Go, now!*

"Mu—"

Kate ran towards the front door, clutching her child against her hip. Her fingers fumbled with the latch but finally it opened, and she surged outside into the chilly night air, wincing as the security lights blazed all around them. She didn't stop but kept running towards her car, bundling Jamie into his seat.

In her peripheral vision, she saw each of the windows in the house illuminate, one-by-one.

He was looking for them.

"Kate! KATE!"

She heard him calling to her inside the house, and knew there was no more time. Having secured Jamie into his car seat, she ran around to the driver's side, ignoring her son's cries of confusion, all pretence of adventure now gone.

As she shut the driver's door and reached for the key, she glanced up to see her husband's tall figure framed inside the front door, no more than a dark silhouette.

Hyperventilating now, she turned on the engine and jammed the car into gear, watching as Will sprinted barefoot from the house towards them.

"KATE!"

He trained his body like an athlete, a man used to speed and endurance, and it took him no time at all to reach them.

But she was faster.

When he would have thrown himself into the path of her car, she surprised him by reversing in a wide semi-circle.

It didn't stop him for long.

Enraged, he chased her again and, as she looked through the glass windshield into the eyes of the man who'd once said he loved her, Kate knew she'd been right to leave.

If she'd stayed, he would have killed her.

Resolved, her face a mask of grief and resignation, she accelerated down the long driveway and out of the gates she'd left open in preparation for their flight.

This moment had been months in the planning.

Maybe, years.

"Mummy, you forgot about Daddy," Jamie said plaintively, and she felt the emotional punch to her gut as strongly as if he'd taken a fist to it.

"No," she said softly. "I haven't forgotten a thing."

But I will, she added silently.

CHAPTER 2

It took three hours to drive from Edinburgh to Newcastle, where Kate abandoned her car at a service station on the outskirts of the city and boarded an early bus into the centre with Jamie fast asleep in her arms. She watched the sun rise as they reached the train station, where they stopped briefly in the ladies' room—in her case, to don a blonde wig and beanie hat, and, in Jamie's case, to complain about the over-large baseball cap she insisted he wore.

Kate had imagined her son would protest much more during their journey but, after the first ten or fifteen miles on the motorway, he'd fallen into silence and then to sleep, for which she'd been grateful. With her nerves shredded and their future still uncertain, she'd needed the silence of pre-dawn twilight to recover herself. Now, she stared back at a different woman in the mottled train station mirror, one with a new sense of purpose.

She looked across to her son, who stood barely to her hip and, at just four years old, was already possessed of dark, soulful eyes.

Her eyes.

"Are we nearly there, yet?" he asked.

She wished she could say 'yes' but, in truth, they had many more hours of travel ahead of them.

"A little while longer," she said, tugging his cap. "Are you hungry?"

Jamie nodded.

"How about a bacon sandwich?"

His face split into a grin, and it warmed her from the inside.

"Let's go and find one," she said, taking his hand. "After that, we'll be getting on a train."

"Where to?"

"To London."

"To see the Queen?"

Kate's lips quirked. "Not quite," she said. "To catch a bus."

He groaned. "Another one? My legs are tired…"

"You've hardly done any walking at all!"

"They're still tired."

"A bacon sandwich will be just the ticket, then."

Hours later, after they'd passed through the smoggy streets of London, melting into the crowds that swarmed its grey pavements as they made their way to the bus depot, Kate finally allowed herself to breathe. It was true that the coach smelled faintly of stale vomit, and the man in the seat behind theirs snored more loudly than a ship's foghorn, but she held her child securely in her arms and, for now, they were safe.

There was little to see through the grubby window except motorway, but, as day gave way to night and the coach joined the smaller A-road that ran through Cornwall like an artery, the scenery changed, and Kate remembered the many times she'd travelled that road before.

Not far to go, her mother would say, after they passed the sign for Truro. *Another forty minutes and we'll be in Helford.*

As a child, she'd loved their yearly trips to the hidden landscape surrounding the Helford estuary, so different to the usual Cornish scenes of golden beaches, sand dunes and surfboards. The towns and villages that peppered the creeks and inlets on either side of the estuary were populated by those who loved the river life; where sailing boats were as common as cars and those who inhabited its lush, verdant hills moved from place to place by water as often as they moved by land. It was a rarefied, secretive world of botanical gardens and grand summer houses, of quaint, pastel-painted fishing cottages and bronzed, barefooted children trailing their kayaks behind them.

Kate had been one of them, once.

Every summer, she'd joined their merry band and accompanied the children who lived there year-round, accepted as one of their own. The process had been accelerated by the fact she had family living in that part of the world—as the local ferryman, life-long fisherman and artisan carpenter, her grandfather, Ben Carew, was a pillar of the small community clustered around Helford village and its sister village across the water, Helford Passage. At eighty-one, he still motored his little red ferryboat back and forth across the river three hundred and sixty-four days of the year, resting only on Christmas Day which was spent snoozing in front of the fire following a traditional roast lunch and a glass of cider raised in the Queen's honour. It was a simple life, one that had made Ben and his late wife, Deborah, very happy. They'd raised Kate's mother, Alice, in a stone cottage on the banks of Frenchman's Creek, within walking distance of Helford village, and had considered themselves the most fortunate of families.

As time passed and the village children had grown, so Kate had grown with them. Some of her old friends suspected she'd lose interest in their quiet world, especially as she was a city girl all the way from London.

But, she hadn't.

If anything, her love for the water grew stronger as she grew older. Perhaps, if life had turned out differently, she would never have left…

If her parents hadn't died.

"Mummy?"

Kate's reverie was interrupted by the sleepy sound of Jamie's voice, and she dragged herself back to the present, where a little boy demanded her attention.

Yes, she thought. *A great many things might never have come to pass, but there was at least one thing she would never regret.*

"I love you, Jamie."

"Love you too, Mummy," he said, and then added, "I'm hungry."

Shaking her head, Kate reached for the bag of provisions she'd paid for in cash at the last service stop.

"Not far to go," she said.

CHAPTER 3

Two days later

"She's back, y' know."

Nick Pascoe didn't look up from his task of rubbing down an upturned wooden dinghy, his arm flexing in rhythmic circles as he sanded the wood in preparation for re-sealing.

"Who?"

"Kate Ryce," his friend said, leaning back against the harbour wall to enjoy the late morning sunshine. "Course, it's Kate *Irving*, now, isn't it? Came in the middle of the night, so they say."

Nick's hand stilled briefly, before restarting with harder strokes than before.

Kate Ryce.

There was a blast from the past.

"You remember her, don't you?" Pete tagged on, when no reply was forthcoming. "Tall and leggy, with long, wavy red hair, as I recall."

Of course, Nick remembered.

If he closed his eyes, he could still see a reed-slim girl of eighteen with hair the colour of spun gold, and deep, dark brown eyes he'd almost drowned in. They'd been summertime friends every year, picking up the friendship when her parents came to spend July and August with Kate's grandparents—until everything changed, and there had been no more lazy summers… and no more friendship, it seemed. As far as he knew, it had been years since Kate had been back to Helford, and he knew Ben Carew must have been deeply hurt by her prolonged absence—though, he was far too proud to say as much. Most people thereabouts assumed there'd been some sort of disagreement or estrangement, but they respected the old man too much to ask him about what was, after all, none of their business.

All the same, he wondered what had changed to bring Kate back to the neighbourhood.

Unable to shake her image from his mind's eye, Nick straightened up, chucked his sanding block into a nearby bucket and stretched, easing out the kinks in his back.

"I remember her," he said, at length. "Finally decided to pay her old grandad a visit after all this time, has she?"

"Seems that way," Pete said. "Been keepin' herself to herself. Might never have known she was back in the neighbourhood, if it wasn't for ol' Fred Lorne having caught sight of her on the road to Frenchman's Creek after midnight—on foot, no less. Says he offered her a lift, but she turned him down, flat."

Nick frowned. "Midnight? I won't ask what Fred was doing on the roads at that hour, because he'd be on his way back from Friday Night Poker with Cam and Ernie. But what's a young woman doing walking around alone in the dark?"

"Hardly dangerous, around these parts," Pete pointed out, fairly. "The worst we ever see is an occasional underage drinker down at The Ship's Mate, or maybe a time or two when Bill Hicks forgets himself and does somethin' silly—"

"That's not the point—"

"In any case, she wasn't alone," Pete continued, yawning hugely. "Apparently, she had a kid with her."

Kate was a mother, now?

After the initial shock, Nick was incensed.

"What kind of *idiot* drags a child around country lanes in the middle of the bloody night?" he raged. "Anything could have happened!"

Pete risked a glance at his friend, smiled privately, and then closed his eyes again.

"She's stayin' with her grandfather, so maybe you should pay them a visit and find out the answer for yourself?"

The hell he would, Nick thought.

After Kate had left for good, he'd made a fool of himself writing letters to her uncle's house in London, where she'd gone to live after the funeral—*letters*, for God's sake—long, rambling pages about how much he missed her, how they were all thinking of her... how *he* was thinking of her.

And for what?

She'd never once bothered to reply.

"Where's her man?" he found himself asking. "I thought she married that bloke from the telly—the one who plays a baddie in that North-East crime drama."

"Yeah, *The Hacker*," Pete said. "Good bit o' drama, that. Will Irving's the name of the actor. Dunno where he is—probably on some film set or another."

Nick pulled a face and folded his arms across his chest. The only reason he'd known about Kate's marriage had been thanks to a double-page spread in a glossy magazine, which had sent the local busybodies into a feeding frenzy for a while. For his part, he'd never imagined Kate would get married so young…

Or to an actor.

"I guess they've been too busy and important to check in with Ben," he said, not bothering to conceal his contempt. "The man's eighty-one and deserves to have some family around him, especially after losing his wife and child. Kate was all he had left of them."

"Aye, it was a shame, that," Pete said, sombrely. "Ben's wife was a good soul, and I was sorry for Kate when she lost her parents, too. It's a lot for one family to bear."

Nick turned to look out across the water, which shimmered like molten silver in the morning sunlight, and raised a hand to shield his eyes from its glare. Across the estuary, nestled amongst undulating layers of green forest, lay a cluster of pretty cottages and a white-painted gastropub perched on the edge of the water, known as The Ship's Mate. Its owner, Joanne, had given Nick his first job pulling pints, and Kate had worked there for a couple of summers, too, alongside Joanne's daughter, Lucy. During their break-times, the three of them had often perched on the harbour wall to watch the sailing boats come and go, munching on a sandwich while they talked or, in Kate's case, while she painted. Her dream had been to go to art school, and he'd indulged her time and again as she'd sketched his face, trying to capture its changing expression.

He remembered Kate had been sketching when the bad news had come, her hand flying across the page as she spotted a swan gliding on the water below. He remembered the expression on her face, focused and lovely, just as he remembered the light in her eyes dying when the death knell had sounded.

"Kate, there's been an accident," Joanne had said, rushing out from the pub. *"You need to go home to your grandfather, now. Nick? Walk with her—"*

"What? Why? What's happened?"

"Kate..." Joanne's voice had trembled. *"It's your parents..."*

Lost in thought, his mind far away in the past, Nick heard the chug of a boat's engine and realised belatedly that it was Ben's ferryboat coming into shore. His eyes scanned the water and saw that, rather than Ben, it was Danny, one of his part-time helpers, who steered the rudder and guided the boat towards the floating pontoon. Soon enough, he brought it neatly alongside, before securing the line so his passengers could disembark. Nick watched them without much interest, counting one family with a toddler and an older child, another couple with their dog, a woman with a walker's backpack, and then...

Then, a tall, slim woman with red hair that shone like the sun.

She gave Danny a quick, shy smile of thanks and then reached for a dark-haired little boy who stood by her side. Without realising it, Nick began to walk across the sandy beach, pulled towards her despite all that had gone before.

He waited on the sand, watching the way her body moved gracefully along the bobbing pontoon, noting the quick, furtive glances she gave to either side, and the tight hold she kept on her son's hand.

She didn't notice him, at first.

Then, her eyes locked with his, and time simply fell away.

CHAPTER 4

A salty breeze whipped Kate's hair across her face, briefly obscuring her view of the glistening water that spread out across the channel separating each side of the estuary. It had taken two days for her to pluck up the courage to leave her grandfather's house but, thanks to his nonchalant mention of a beach where ice-creams, buckets and spades could be found, Jamie had no longer taken 'no' for an answer and his enthusiasm had propelled them both from the house and down to the ferryboat landing.

So it was that she found herself on her grandfather's boat, albeit crewed by a young man named 'Danny', while he went off for his annual 'MOT' at the doctor's surgery.

"Just checkin' my ticker's still tickin'," he'd said, with a wink for Jamie.

It had been a shock to find her grandfather so much older than she remembered, but nobody could stay the hand of time and the guilt she felt at not having been able to visit him sooner was another weight to add to her already laden heart.

If you ever think of leaving me, Kate, remember that I'll find you. There isn't anywhere you could run to, anywhere you could hide...you know that, don't you? I don't want to hurt you. I never want to hurt you. I never want to hurt anyone...but I will, to protect what's mine.

Will's words replayed like a crackling reel in the back of her mind, and she shivered, no longer able to enjoy the breeze, nor the view.

"Look, Mummy!" Jamie cried, pointing towards the approaching shoreline. "I can see the sand!"

The beach was hardly a sweeping vista, consisting of a brief arc of sand and shingle at the foot of the village, but it was undeniably quaint, and she'd spent many happy times digging around for shells and sea glass in the shallows.

"Nearly there," she said, and ruffled his hair.

Her eyes narrowed as they approached the landing spot, scrutinising every face for one she might recognise, but finding none. Her gaze passed over families with toddlers and young children paddling in the water, over groups of what she'd have called 'sailing types' dressed in their ubiquitous garb of chinos, rubber-soled shoes and polo shirts with collars turned up against the sun which was beginning to beat down more ferociously as it rose higher in the sky. There were crowds of chattering friends and families sitting on the tables outside The Boatman pub—Joanne's only major competitor in those parts—and a few other scattered groups lining the shore, bronzed men rubbing down boats or leaning back against the wall to enjoy the sunshine.

There were no men with film-star looks, hair the colour of the sky at night and a heart just as black.

"Here we are," Danny told them.

Kate was startled to find the boat tethered, and she reached for Jamie's hand to help him onto the pontoon.

"Boat runs there and back with the tides," Danny told her, and pointed towards a large board displaying the tide times for that day.

Kate remembered. "Thanks, we'll see you later."

"Right y'are." He nodded politely, smiled at Jamie, then turned his attention to the short queue of passengers waiting to step onto the boat and make their return journey.

"Can I have an ice cream, please, Mummy?"

To her shame, Kate didn't reply immediately, and realised she was waiting for Will to answer on her behalf. Somehow, over the years, decisions had become his sole remit, no matter how big nor small, while she'd been conditioned into silence.

Not any longer, she vowed.

"Yes, sweetheart," she replied, softly. "You can have whichever flavour you want."

Jamie's face lit up and he skipped along beside her as they made their way towards the ramp that connected them to the beach. As they approached, she looked up to find a tall, tanned man standing a short way off, obviously waiting to meet someone off the ferry. He wore khaki shorts, a loose-fitting t-shirt over an athletic physique and a well-worn baseball cap which cast half of his face in shadow. His feet were bare, his thumbs were tucked loosely into his pockets, and the ghost of a smile played around his lips. Good-looking, she acknowledged—but then, she'd been fooled by a pretty face once before and had paid a harsh price for that folly.

Never again.

She was surprised when he took a step towards them, and turned to look over her shoulder in reflex.

"Kate?"

She spun back around.

"It *is* you, isn't it?" His voice was warm and rich, and tugged a memory at the back of her mind.

"I—" She peered beneath his cap, and he smiled again before reaching up to remove it, running an absent hand through thick, wavy brown hair lightened by long hours in the sun.

"It's been a long time," he said, with a note in his voice. "I shouldn't have expected you to remember—" He swallowed, bright blue eyes passing over her face, searching for the girl he'd once known.

"Who're you?"

Nick's attention turned to the little boy who clung to his mother's leg like a limpet—whether from a desire to hide from him, or to defend her, he couldn't tell. He dropped down onto his haunches so he could be at the boy's level and gave him an easy smile, thinking the kid was cute as a button with his big brown eyes and hair so dark it was almost black.

"I'm Nick," he said, and held out a hand. "What's your name, then?"

"Jamie," the boy replied. "It has an 'ie' on the end, not a double 'e'."

"Pleased to meet you, Jamie with an 'ie'."

Above his head, Kate's lips curved into a smile. "Nick," she murmured, and wondered why she hadn't seen it before.

"Are you Mummy's friend?" Jamie asked, forthrightly.

Nick glanced up at Kate, a question in his eyes.

"Yes," she replied. "Nick's a very old friend."

He looked away again, back into the boy's curious, all-seeing eyes. "We used to play together when we were your age, but we haven't seen each other for…a long time," he added.

"My daddy's an *actor*," Jamie blurted out suddenly, with just a touch of defiance. "What do *you* do?"

Nick hid a smile. "This and that," he said, with a twinkle in his eye. "I like music, mostly. I like ice cream, too, and there's a stall right over there. How about we go and get ourselves a scoop?"

Jamie grinned, but looked to his mother for approval.

"Go ahead," she said. "Lead the way."

Nick straightened his long body and they walked behind the little boy, who ran on ahead towards the ice-cream kiosk, his feet making prints in the sand.

"It's—"

"I—"

They laughed awkwardly, and Nick gestured that she should speak first.

"I was going to say, it's been a long time," Kate said. "I'm sorry, I didn't recognise you at first."

Nick thought back to the last time they'd seen one another, when he'd been a gangly youth of twenty with floppy hair and a penchant for Nirvana. He still had the floppy hair and an appreciation for Kurt Cobain's music, but the rest of him had probably filled out a bit, and there were a few more lines around his eyes than there'd been before.

"I've changed a fair bit," he admitted.

"We've all changed," she said, distantly.

Nick thought the biggest change he could find in the woman standing beside him was more subtle than mere skin and bone; it was something intangible in the way she held herself, in the tone of her voice and the air of sadness that surrounded her.

"What brings you to Helford?" he asked, turning to face her.

"I—" Her tongue caught on the lie she was about to tell, but she told it anyway. "Um, Will is working away and we—um—we thought it was a good chance to come and visit my grandfather."

"Ben will appreciate that," he said.

Kate stole another glance at his face, which was bland and unreadable.

"I know it's been a long time," she said, and wished she could explain. "I had my reasons for staying away."

Nick looked across at the little boy, who was gesturing wildly for them to catch up with him, and then down at the cap he still held in his hands.

He tugged it back on his head.

"I'm sure you did," he said. "Well, I'll leave you to enjoy the rest of your day. See you around, Kate."

He raised a hand briefly to wave to Jamie, then turned away, striding back down the beach towards the boat and his friend, who'd been observing their exchange with interest.

Kate watched Nick's retreating back and told herself she didn't need to explain anything to anybody, nor lament the loss of a friendship that had once been steadfast. She wouldn't demean herself by asking why he'd never kept in touch or why he'd forgotten her as soon as she'd moved away; she supposed it had been a case of, 'out of sight, out of mind'. Besides, it made no sense for them to try to rekindle a friendship now, not when she didn't intend to stay in the area more than a few days.

Every day she lingered there was another day Will could discover them.

For some, out of sight was never out of mind.

CHAPTER 5

"I told you to *find* them."

"I've got my best men looking into it as a priority, Mr Irving—"

"I don't want any half-wit underlings handling this, Charlton," Will snapped. "I want you to manage this personally."

Andy Charlton thought of the holiday he'd been promising his wife for the past three years, and of the divorce she'd threatened if he should let her down again. But, when he looked into Will Irving's dark eyes, he saw an opportunity, and those were not to be missed.

He cleared his throat.

"Well, if you want me to take this case on exclusively, I'm sure you understand this puts me in quite a predicament. I have several cases running, and it isn't my habit to ditch one for the sake of another. My clients rely on me—which is why you came to me in the first place, after all."

Will eyed the man sitting opposite him with a degree of grudging admiration. Charlton of 'Charlton's Confidential Services' was a bloodhound, a private investigator who sold his wares to the very highest echelons of society for princely sums. Now, it seemed his superior nose had detected the prospect of a king's ransom and, though it pained him to admit it, the man was not wrong in his assessment. He'd shown his hand, his desperation, his need…whatever he should call the all-consuming, visceral drive he felt to reclaim his property, which he would do at any cost. That left little room for negotiation and so, with that in mind, he cut to the chase.

"How much do you want?" he asked.

Charlton wet his lips and thought briefly about eking things out a bit more. But then he sensed the danger that lurked beneath the cordial, polished surface of the man sitting before him, and thought better of it.

He named his price, and watched Irving flash a smile, baring a set of perfect, pearly-white teeth.

"Done," he said, without hesitation.

"You understand, my expenses are on top—"

"Whatever," came the reply. "Money is no object, Charlton, but I want my wife and child found within the next twenty-four hours. Is that understood?"

"Perfectly," Charlton said, and wished he'd asked for double.

"No credit or debit card transactions have been made on any of her accounts in the past three days," Irving remarked. "She won't be able to survive for long without funds."

Charlton was about to ask how he could be sure his wife had no money, before assuming correctly that the man kept a tight stranglehold on his wife's financial affairs and could likely tell him her bank balance to the nearest penny. A small corner of his heart was sorry for Kate Irving, but he dismissed the feeling. He hadn't become the best of the best by harbouring weak emotions such as *empathy* or *guilt*, and, the way he saw it, she'd made her bed by marrying the man in the first place. As for invading her privacy, tracking her down like an errant dog…well, he told himself he was helping a husband who was concerned for his wife and child and that was a worthy-enough cause.

Besides, Will Irving was a film star.

How bad could he be?

"I contacted the bank to tell them that her cards had been stolen," Irving continued, answering Charlton's unspoken question. "Her accounts are now frozen, and any attempt to use them or access the funds will alert the bank to her whereabouts."

Charlton reminded himself that he was not in the business of judging his clients, however ignoble they appeared to be. "Ah, well now. If your wife has no immediate access to funds, can I ask how she is likely to have been able to travel?"

Will had given the matter serious thought. "She might have saved some money, here and there, from petty cash we keep around the house," he said. "Our son was given some cash for his birthday, lately, and she might have pocketed that rather than adding it to his ISA account."

Paltry sums, but they added up.

"Might your wife have kept a private bank account?"

The possibility that Kate, whom he'd groomed and moulded into his vision of the perfect wife, would ever have struck out on her own was anathema to Will Irving.

"I would have known if she'd transferred funds into another account," he said, decisively. "There would be a paper trail."

Charlton nodded. "What about private earnings?" he persisted. "Is your wife employed?"

"My wife doesn't need to work," Will snapped. "Being my partner and mother to my child was occupation enough."

And then, some, Charlton thought.

"I understand, Mr Irving, but...I wonder if Mrs Irving might have taken it upon herself to run a little enterprise, where her earnings could go directly into a private account, in anticipation of...ah..."

"*Leaving* me?" Will growled. "You're suggesting she planned and schemed to abandon her husband and steal a child from its father?"

Charlton was careful to avoid eye contact. "I only mean that, in cases such as these, when a spouse leaves the marital home it's seldom on the spur of the moment."

Will thrust back from his chair and stalked to the edge of the terrace to stare unseeingly across the manicured lawns. He thought about Kate's behaviour recently and acknowledged that, with hindsight, she'd been far more rebellious than usual. For instance, when he'd given her his dinner preferences at the start of the week, as he did at the start of every week, she'd had the nerve to suggest that *he* might like to cook, for a change.

He'd laughed that one straight out of the park.

As his father had always told his mother, some tasks were a woman's domain and always would be. He supposed that, with his income, he could have hired a private chef, but it gave him a little thrill to see Kate in the kitchen.

Sometimes, he watched her, just because he could.

Then, there'd been her willingness—or lack, thereof—in the bedroom. He supposed it had been a very long time since she'd demonstrated genuine enthusiasm, but she put on a decent act and that was good enough for him, most of the time; after all, it wasn't *his* fault if she was one of those cold, asexual women, was it? He knew plenty of other willing candidates who were far more adventurous than his dutiful wife, and he could have his pick of them any day of the week.

Still, he didn't want them.

He wanted Kate, and he expected obedience, which she'd shown a remarkable lack of, even up until the very night before she'd abandoned him.

She'd fought him…

Will touched a finger to a long, healing scratch on the side of his neck, and thought briefly of that short, unsatisfying interlude. She'd cried, of course, and claimed he'd hurt her wrist, among other things...he couldn't remember the ins and outs but, if she hadn't made so much of a fuss, she wouldn't have hurt herself—would she?

He turned back to the man sitting on his terrace, sipping his fine Italian coffee.

"My wife has no particular talents," he said. "If she's surviving without my money, it's because somebody's taken pity on her. That makes them an accessory to kidnapping, and no friend of mine."

Charlton felt a ripple of something unexpected while he listened to a voice that he'd heard many times on stage and screen.

Something like fear.

"Do you have a list of her family and friends?"

A self-satisfied smile spread across Will's face, and, despite his symmetrical features, he became ugly.

"I can count their names on the fingers of one hand," he said, wriggling them, for effect. "Her grandfather, Ben Carew, is the only remaining relative on her mother's side—both of Kate's parents died, and she's an only child. Her father's parents are both living, but they live abroad, in New Zealand. As for friends, she hasn't any."

Charlton blinked.

None?

"Are you...quite sure about that, Mr Irving? How about another mum, from Jamie's school or former nursery?"

Will shook his head.

"Jamie hasn't started school yet, and he didn't attend nursery. There was no need, since Kate was at home—it isn't as if she was *working*, is it?"

Charlton made no comment, but scratched a note in his book.

"Neighbours?"

"Out here?" Irving laughed, and gestured to the acres of gardens and pasture surrounding the beautiful country home where they lived, twenty or so miles outside of Edinburgh. "I hardly think so. Our acquaintances were carefully chosen and vetted by me, as you know, since you're the one that vetted them."

Charlton inclined his head. "Indeed. All the same, there is always a chance that Mrs Irving struck up a friendship with any number of people, so I'll look into it," he said. "Coming back to her family...does she have any aunts, uncles?"

"Her mother was an only child, but her father has a brother," Will said, pensively. "His family live in London, but Kate hasn't seen them in years."

He'd made sure of it.

"It's amazing how people can...grow apart, isn't it?"

Charlton eyed him over the rim of his notepad, and said nothing but, amid all the wealth and finery, felt dirtier than if he'd been sitting in a rat-infested outbuilding.

"So, her uncle's family is a possibility, shall we say?"

Will gave a tight nod, and scribbled down all he knew of Kate's uncle, Oliver Ryce.

"Thank you," Charlton said, and prepared to ask another, explosive question. "I have just one more thing to ask, at present..."

He paused to gather his courage.

"Well?" Irving snapped. "What is it?"

"Could...that is, could it be possible that Mrs Irving met a...ah, that she met a *special* friend?"

The look Will Irving levelled in his direction would have terrified a lesser man.

And, let's face it, Andrew Charlton *was* a lesser man.

"She wouldn't dare," Irving said.

He'd kill whatever poor sap looked at her twice, then kill her, too, Charlton thought.

"I'll get to work," he said, and left as quickly as he could.

CHAPTER 6

Hundreds of miles south of where Will Irving paced back and forth across a flagstone terrace, his wife watched their son paddle barefoot in the shallow, lapping waters of the Helford river. While the tide was out, they'd wandered along the sandy stretch of beach beside the small harbour and scrambled over the rocks to the other side, where a longer stretch of sand awaited them. It lay at the foot of a steep bank, upon which summer homes had been built at intervals over the course of the past century or more, their fine lines and painted shutters adding a touch of charm that was reminiscent of the Côte d'Azur, in miniature. Rock stars, film producers, famous writers and artists of all description resided in the hills leading down to the waterside; they came to escape their fame, she supposed, and to enjoy a quieter pace of life where their faces were no more special than the next, where they were treated just the same by men like her grandfather, who'd lived longer than most of them and ferried them back and forth in his little boat for too many years to stand on ceremony.

Will would have hated it here, she thought suddenly.

He would have hated knowing he wasn't the richest, nor the cleverest, and the lack of pomp and ceremony would have wounded his vanity. He would never have been at home in a simple, white-painted cottage, nor enjoyed the tranquillity of a half-deserted pebble beach, where the only distractions were the sound of the water and the call of a sea bird high in the sky overhead. He would have wanted to go somewhere to see and be seen; he'd want to sail around the estuary in the largest yacht he could find, peacocking around in pristine white chinos to emulate Cary Grant on the set of *To Catch a Thief*, but without half that man's gravitas on screen nor charisma in real life.

All style and no substance, that was Will Irving.

Tears pooled in her eyes as she fought against a wave of intrusive memories, years of traumas big and small, of coercion and manipulation, of physical and mental blows. Her hands shook with anger and frustration at her own weakness, her failure to leave sooner…

That's what people would say, isn't it?

If she was to tell anyone, the first thing they'd ask is why she stayed and, thanks to her husband's wealth, would undoubtedly draw all the wrong conclusions about her character.

Gold digger, they'd whisper. *Out for what she could get.*

His was a face beloved by women of all ages—and men, too. Whenever they were out or in company, Will assumed the persona of an old-world Hollywood star, or what he imagined that to be. He held out her chair, took her arm, tipped heavily and pattered with every simpering fan who sought out his autograph or a picture. Only she knew what lurked behind the façade, and it was an ugly, festering shell of a human, one who knew nothing about what it meant to be selfless or to love another person more than himself.

That had become painfully obvious after Jamie had been born.

Following an initial wave of fatherly pride at having sired so *attractive* a child, Will had soon realised that his son would always be a younger, even more handsome version of himself. How demeaning to have this shadow taunt him daily, reminding him that with every passing hour he grew older and weaker while his son grew stronger and more vital. She'd seen the change in him immediately and had been pathetically grateful when his wrath had turned more forcefully on herself and not upon their baby son.

You could do with losing another half a stone, he'd told her, one morning three months after she'd given birth. *You don't want to start letting yourself go, like ordinary people, Kate. We're not ordinary people.*

It had been stress that had caused her to lose weight so quickly, in the end, and so many mindless people had complimented her waif-like frame, congratulating her on how quickly she'd 'bounced back'.

Then, there had been the matter of breast-feeding.

If you must do it, do it somewhere else. In fact, it would be better if you didn't bother—it'll only ruin your body.

She'd fought him on that, but stress had caused her milk to dry up, so Will had won that round, too.

You should think about Botox, Kate. You're starting to look tired…

Are you planning to wear that?

"Kate?"

She almost jumped out of her skin as Nick loomed above her, and hurriedly dashed the back of her hand across her eyes to hide the evidence of tears.

"I didn't see you there," she said, scrambling to her feet. "It's bright today, isn't it?"

Nick took off his sunglasses and offered them to her. "Here," he said softly. "These will help."

She swallowed a painful lump in her throat. "Thank you," she managed.

"I—ah—I noticed you didn't come back for the ferry," he said, turning to smile at the little boy who was trying to spell something out in the sand with one end of a stick. "Danny held the boat for you as long as he could, but he had to get home. He was worried, so I said I'd come and find you."

Kate's face fell. "Oh, my goodness, I completely lost track of the time," she muttered, running an agitated hand through her hair. "I'm so sorry to have kept Danny waiting around, and to have put you out like this. Jamie was having such a nice time and I—I was daydreaming—I just didn't think."

She looked so devastated, Nick was almost moved to give her a hug.

But it wasn't his place.

"It's no problem," he said. "You're supposed to lose track of the time, when you're on holiday. I can give you both a lift back to the creek—I've got my car parked up the hill, so we'll take the scenic route."

Kate knew that getting from one side of the estuary to the other by road was slow going and would take at least forty minutes by the time they manoeuvred the narrow, single-track lanes that were lined with acres of sprouting hedgerows and ancient forestry, which might have made the route scenic but also made it hard to see if any hare-brained drivers were rattling around the next bend.

"Are you sure you don't mind? What will you do with your boat?"

Nick looked momentarily confused, then his face cleared.

"The one I was working on today was Pete's," he told her. "The lazy good-for-nothin' doesn't know his arse from his elbow, so I said I'd give him a hand."

He flashed a smile as he thought of the man who'd been his best friend since they were knee-high to a grasshopper.

"Pete?" she exclaimed, and her face broke into a broad smile. "Is he still living around here?"

Nick told himself not to be put out about the fact she had no trouble remembering Pete Ambrose, yet could barely recollect his face at a distance of two metres.

"Yep, still causing strife to all the unsuspecting women hereabouts," he joked, though his friend's reputation had been greatly exaggerated by the man himself. "His dad owns one of the largest estate agencies in this part of the world and Pete pretends to work for him, when he's not out giving boat tours to see the dolphins."

"Pete always loved the water," Kate murmured, thinking of a pale, freckle-faced kid. "I can't imagine him in a shiny suit handing over a business card."

"He scrubs up nicely, when he has to," Nick confirmed, and then, with a weather eye on the changing skies, called out to the little boy. "Jamie? Better collect your shells, we'll be heading off in a minute!"

He seemed so natural with children, Kate wondered if he had any of his own.

"I suppose you need to get back to your own family," she said, as casually as she could. "It's getting late."

"I live alone," he told her.

"Oh," she said, and gave an awkward little laugh that grated on her own nerves. "Well, maybe you just haven't found the right girl, yet."

His smile slipped, just a fraction, then he reached out to take back his sunglasses, sliding them from her nose and back onto his own so that she could no longer read the expression in his eyes.

"Yeah," he said quietly. "That must be it."

CHAPTER 7

Ben Carew heard the arrival of Nick's Land Rover long before it emerged from the thick woodland surrounding Frenchman's Cottage, which occupied a secluded spot by the creek of the same name. It boasted its own tiny beach that had come to be known locally as 'Carew Cove', one of many small, hidden bays and shadowy, secretive places where a person could lose themselves for a few hours amongst the lush greenery surrounding the Helford estuary or, as locals called it, 'The Helford'.

The cottage was postcard-pretty, with its white-painted walls and matching clapboard boathouse that trailed with flowering creepers Ben's late wife had planted many years before, and which he continued to tend because it was what she would have wanted. It was a rare idyll; a haven from the hustle and bustle of the wider world where he could sit out on his veranda and watch the undulating water, or settle in his favourite reading chair and pick up a good book as the sun fell and the last light of day hung low in the sky. It was a good life, and the simple pleasures of air and sea had sustained him through the changing seasons.

Though he was past eighty, Ben might easily have been mistaken for a man ten years younger. His body had served him well, despite having enjoyed one too many pints of cider over the years and, he dared say, a few too many cheese and onion pasties. Although deeply lined and tanned to a warm, year-round shade of brown, his face remained mobile and his eyes just as sharp as they'd ever been—albeit, he was forced to wear reading glasses, nowadays—and he stood tall and straight-backed. For all that, he was beginning to feel his age, really *feel* it, down to his bones, which creaked and moaned like an old gate.

Still, he couldn't complain. He'd lived a full life, one he'd shared with a good woman for as long as they'd been able to, and had been blessed with a daughter...

He lifted his chin, hoping to see their faces in a celestial cloud formation far above, but there was nothing but clear blue skies.

He came back down to Earth and told himself to think of the present, and of those who remained. There were other things besides flora and fauna that he'd like to see flourish, and one of them was bounding out of Nick's car and skipping towards him with all the energy of a Labrador puppy, at that very moment.

"*Grandie!*"

Jamie's feet slapped against the wooden decking as he pattered towards him, calling out the pet name he'd given his great-grandfather, and wielding a large red plastic bucket.

"There he is!" Ben said, with a throaty chuckle. "What've you got there, lad?"

The little boy plonked himself down on the swing seat beside him, and then unceremoniously tipped the contents of his bucket into the old man's lap.

"Oh, *Jamie*—"

His mother followed at a slower pace, just in time to see river water and sand slosh all over her grandfather's unsuspecting trousers.

"Doesn't matter to me," he said, waving away her protestations. "He's just eager to show me his pirate booty, aren't you?"

Jamie broke into a toothy grin, and Ben lifted a weathered hand to ruffle his hair, pleased to see the boy smile.

"I'll be off, then," Nick said.

Kate jumped a bit, not having realised he'd joined them on the veranda, and unconsciously took a step back. Observing the action, Nick also took a discreet step away from her, leaning his long body against one of the wooden uprights.

"Stay a while and have a brew," Ben said, in a tone that was hard to refuse. "Got a nice chicken ripe for roastin', too, if you're hungry."

It was an offer Nick had accepted before, and he and Ben had enjoyed many a fine evening chewing the fat over a beer or two, talking of life, politics, philosophy, art and—his personal favourite—*music*. But, this time, Ben had his family to surround him, and they should be given space and time to reconnect without outside interference.

"Ah, that's kind, but I should be getting back," he said. "I'll be seein' you."

"I wanted a quick word about…a boat," Ben said quickly, rising from his chair with surprising agility. "I'll be back in a minute, Jamie, and you can finish showing me your shells."

Nick frowned. There wasn't a man alive who knew more than the ferryman about watercraft, and he'd never sought his opinion about a vessel before.

"Ah—sure," he said.

"I'll take Jamie inside and make a start on dinner," Kate said, and gave Nick a smile that caused something in his chest to tighten and then release again. "Thank you for the lift."

"No problem," he said. "See you, Jamie." He waved to the boy, whose hand lifted in response, before he seemed to remember himself and he turned to stomp inside the cottage, instead.

If Ben noticed, he said nothing, but let out a soft sigh and led the way down a flagstone pathway towards the boathouse he'd built on the other side of the cove. Nick followed, enjoying the sight of a heron taking flight with a fish clutched in its beak.

"In here," Ben said, and threw open the doors.

Nick stepped inside the boathouse and saw a single vessel moored there, covered in tarpaulin. It was larger than Ben's 'fleet' of two motorised passenger ferries, being a yacht of around twenty or twenty-five feet in length.

"Is she new?" he asked.

Ben didn't reply straight away, but walked across to lean his elbows on a wooden railing.

"No," he said softly. "She's old."

He didn't elaborate, and, after a moment, the penny dropped.

"I'm sorry, Ben. I should have thought—"

"You weren't to know I'd keep her," Ben interrupted him, gruffly. "Many would have turned her in for scrap, by now."

The Lady of Shalott had been a thing of beauty, in her day. Kate's father had bought it for her mother, Alice, taking the name from Tennyson's poem because an artist's representation of 'The Lady' with long red hair had reminded him of his wife and daughter. They'd sailed it around the estuary and out to sea every time they visited the area and Nick remembered being aboard with Kate and some of the other kids, wearing orange life jackets while they waved to smaller boats they passed on their way out to the sea. They'd felt like kings with the air brushing their skin, and he remembered vividly how Kate's parents had been: two smart, beautiful people with their lives before them, who'd loved that boat and the freedom she gave them.

But, for all she had given them, it was also *The Lady* who'd killed them that fateful day fifteen years before, robbing them of all their summers to come.

"Are you thinking of refurbishing her?" Nick asked, after a few minutes had passed.

Ben gave a slight shake of his head. "Couldn't face it," he said honestly. "Mind you, I can't face getting rid of her, either—but the day will come."

Nick nodded, and was about to ask which other boat required his help, when Ben took the wind out of his proverbial sails.

"It isn't a boat I need to speak to you about," he admitted, and spread his hands in mute apology for the subterfuge. "It's about Kate—and Jamie, come to that."

Nick waited.

"You and she were friends, a time ago, weren't you?"

Yeah, Nick thought. *The perennial friend, that's me.*

"We were…we still are, I think."

"That's good," Ben said, and turned to face him with serious eyes, crinkled with folds of tanned skin at the corners. "She needs a friend. My Katie needs as many friends as she can get."

"What's happened?" Nick asked, urgently.

Ben rubbed a thoughtful hand over the stubble on his chin, thinking that Debbie would have chided him for not bothering to have another shave. He supposed when there was nobody to kiss goodnight, there was little incentive.

"I'm going to tell you straight, Kate wouldn't like me talkin' to you like this, but…"

He lifted a shoulder.

"Fact is, I'm not gettin' any younger," he said. "I like to think I can hold my own—"

"Of course, you can," Nick said, without hesitation. There was nobody like Ben Carew, and not a man within a hundred miles would have thought to cross him—he commanded that kind of respect.

Ben laughed shortly. "Bless you for that, boy," he said, and Nick gave a lop-sided smile at the thought of being a 'boy' in his thirties. "But these eyes, these hands, this back…they tell a different tale."

He thought of the visit he'd paid to his GP earlier that day, and ran his tongue over dry lips. That was another tale, for another day.

"Kate's had some trouble," he said, bluntly. "More'n likely, she'll come in for some more."

"What kind of trouble?" Nick asked, and then thought of the general air of anxiety she tried, but failed, to conceal. He thought of the look in her eyes, the one he couldn't place but which spoke of things she'd seen. He thought of the boy and how he clung to her, and of the way Kate winced as he'd tried to take her hand to help her out of the Land Rover, not half an hour before. She'd made some excuse about having hurt her wrist doing yoga, but he understood now. It came to him in one great, tidal wave of understanding.

His jaw clenched hard, while his knuckles turned white on the wooden handrail.

"It's him, isn't it?" he said, very quietly. "Her husband."

Ben gave a single nod. "Has to be," he said. "She won't tell me much—not yet—but I haven't lived this long without coming to know a thing or two about human nature. I know when a person's hurtin', and she's hurtin' badly."

"Where is he?" Nick growled.

"She says he's on a film set," Ben replied, and wiped the taste of anger from his lips. "Fact is, I don't think she knows, for sure. To speak plainly, Nick, I think she's upped and left him. She and the boy came to me in the middle of the night, with barely more'n the clothes on their backs. Took two full days for her to venture out, and I can see the fear in her eyes, still. She's runnin', and I think she's ready to run again."

"Why doesn't she tell the police?" Nick whispered. "I can drive her—"

"My guess would be that she's too frightened. I'm hopin' she'll come around."

Nick swore again. "He's done a number on her."

Ben nodded. "We won't know the extent of it unless she chooses to tell us. He won't pay for any of it, unless she speaks out."

There was a short pause while both men thought of other ways to make Will Irving pay his moral debt, but neither spoke of them aloud and eventually Ben heaved long sigh.

"All these years, I thought Kate had forgotten us, forgotten what we meant to her..." he said. "I told myself she needed time away to start her new life, and then, there was her fancy husband...I thought, maybe, she needed to let the past go, to forge ahead with her future. Now, I'm beginnin' to wonder if it wasn't the other way around. What if I was so wrapped up in my own grief, my own sadness, that I didn't stop to question why my girl went quiet? Then...I think of the things I said, when she rang to tell me she was engaged...I said some things I regret."

A muscle worked in his jaw, as he remembered that conversation eight years ago, and how he'd unwittingly pushed his granddaughter further into Irving's waiting arms.

"We all have regrets," Nick averred.

"Aye, but she was all I had," Ben muttered. "She rang full of love, wantin' to tell me all about her handsome new fiancé, about how they were going to be married and would I give her away?"

He rubbed his eyes, wishing he could rub away the memory.

"I laughed at her, Nick. Told her she was nought but a silly young girl after a summer fling," he said. "I told her she was too young, too inexperienced, with her whole life ahead of her...but I didn't go softly. I was *hard* with her, because I wasn't myself—it was too soon after Alice and Rob left us, and I didn't have Debbie here to temper it. Everything, all the anger I felt, the grief, it all came pourin' out and she took the brunt."

Nick could imagine what had happened next. Kate had always been strong and independent; it would have taken some very careful handling to impart the kind of message Ben had given her, that day, or he'd have risked alienating her completely...

"She was young to be married," he said, fairly. "You cared about her."

Ben nodded.

"Aye, she was young. Barely nineteen, with her life and career ahead of her. More'n that, she was still grievin'...we all were. It was too soon to be makin' big decisions like that, and I asked myself, 'What kind of man chooses a vulnerable moment like that to prey on a girl?'" he said. "I've never met the feller, and don't care to, but she was askin' me to believe he was sunshine and moonbeams. When you're young, head over heels in love, caution's the last thing you want to hear."

True enough, Nick thought.

"Our life is our own to lead," he said softly. "We make our own decisions, but, if you ask me, there's a special place in Hell for those who prey on vulnerable people."

Ben nodded again. "Aye, he was older by almost ten years, and a lifetime's worth in experience," he said. "Kate knew nothing of men or of relationships, back then. If we hadn't lost Alice and Rob when we did, right on the cusp of her becoming a woman, maybe she would have been more clear-sighted. She'd've had her mum to talk to, for one thing, and her dad to protect her. Not an old man, like me, who didn't know how to speak to a girl..."

"You can't blame yourself," Nick said. "If that man hurt her, or hurt the boy...it's on his conscience and nobody else's."

"I know it," Ben said, wearily. "All the same, maybe it wasn't Kate who forgot us, Nick. Maybe *we* forgot *her*."

"I never forgot her," Nick replied, without thinking.

Ben smiled to himself, and knew that he'd done the right thing.

"You're a good lad," he said, and rested a hand on Nick's muscled shoulder. "She came to us for help. She'll need a village, before the end."

Nick nodded.

"I'll be there," he promised.

Shortly afterwards, as the two men made their way back up the pathway and Nick turned to bid his friend farewell, Ben decided to impart one final message.

"Remember what they say," he said.

"What's that?"

"Go softly," Ben told him.

Nick shook his head in disbelief. "Don't miss much, do you, Old Man?"

"Nope," Ben agreed. "And, less of the 'old', if it's all the same to you. Have you told her about who you are, these days?"

Nick didn't pretend to misunderstand. "It hasn't come up," he said, attempting to dodge the question.

"You'll have to tell her, sometime," Ben argued. "She'll ask me, outright, one of these days, and I won't tell her a lie."

Nick sighed. "Can't you just tell her I'm a humble fisherman, or, better yet, unemployed?"

Ben laughed. "You may as well be, for all the work you seem to do…"

Nick grinned, and the two exchanged a brief, one-armed hug.

"I'll be around," he said.

With a final glance towards the cottage, and those who lay within its sanctuary, he walked back to his car.

CHAPTER 8

"How much for a portrait?"

In her mind's eye, Kate could remember the first time she'd met Will Irving, the summer after she'd lost her parents. She'd been eighteen—and a very *young* eighteen, at that. It had been in Paris, of all places, at the Place du Tertre, in Montmartre. Historically, it was a haven for young artists and creatives, having been home to so many famous names from Picasso and Modigliani to Manet and Renoir, in its hey-day. As a young romantic, she'd longed to spend a summer walking along the same streets and working in the same light as her artistic heroes, and perhaps to discover a bit of herself in the liberal anonymity that was quintessentially Paris before starting her first term at art college in London, the following September.

Everything had been mapped out.

She remembered staying away from Helford that summer, because she couldn't stand to walk amongst the trees where her parents had walked, nor sail on the river where they'd sailed, so soon after their passing. It had always been her plan to resume her yearly visits once she was at university, and to visit her grandfather as often as she could thereafter.

Life hadn't turned out that way, and she could trace much of its misdirection to the time she spent in Paris, and one fateful day in particular.

To its credit, Paris had gone some way to patching up her grieving heart, though nothing could repair it. Her parents' death would always be a gaping wound that would never fully heal, but that elegant city had given Kate an invisible stitch that stemmed the flow of tears. It allowed her to continue to live, and not ache for them with every breath she took, nor see their reflections in every shop window. She'd walked the streets of Paris until her body screamed with exhaustion; she'd visited every museum and gallery she could find, browsed every bookshop and spent hours beneath the shade of a weeping willow on the banks of the Seine painting or merely watching the world go by, until she found herself smiling once more. She'd rented a tiny room in Pigalle, which was the cheaper end of Montmartre known more for its proximity to the Paris 'Red Light' district than its fine artistry, but it was within walking distance of the mighty Sacre-Coeur and the Place du Tertre, where would-be artists could set up an easel and do portraits for tourists in exchange for a few euros.

It had been a misty, overcast day when she'd first looked up to find Will Irving standing in front of her. Back then, he was a strikingly good-looking man in his mid-twenties, with a face she recognised from somewhere, and he possessed the kind of quiet, understated taste that was so in-keeping with the stereotypes surrounding French fashion and her childish ideal of a romantic hero.

"How much for a portrait?" he'd asked, in well-rounded English that spoke of a certain upbringing—or of expensive lessons in elocution.

She'd gawked at him, wide-eyed and awestruck, as only a teenager could be.

"Um…oh, I was just packing up…"

"That's a pity," he said, fixing her with his best smile. "Don't you have time for one last sketch?"

"It's starting to rain," she pointed out.

"Is it?" he'd said, never taking his eyes from hers, drawing her in from the very first. "I suppose it is. Why don't we sit at one of those tables beneath the canopy, over there? You could do my portrait over a glass of wine and some cheese."

He gestured towards one of the cafes lining the square, where men and women sat side by side, holding hands beneath large, striped awnings.

Lovers, she thought, and her pale skin blushed.

He'd seen all of it, she realised now, and had played her like a merry fiddle from their earliest moments. How she'd fallen for the act—hook, line and sinker—she remembered with self-loathing. How she'd believed he was everything the great poets had spoken of, and hurried to give her heart into his keeping.

What a fool she'd been.

After a couple of months' concerted love-bombing, he'd proposed to her on her nineteenth birthday, intercepting a plan to visit her grandfather with a surprise trip to New York, instead.

"We'll visit him together, soon," he'd insisted. *"We can tell him the good news together."*

"What good news?"

"*That you're going to be my wife,*" he'd said, taking her breath away. "*Will you, Kate? Will you make me the happiest man in the world?*"

He'd arranged it so they happened to be standing in Central Park, surrounded by people who cheered as he got down on one knee, his heart apparently in his eyes.

And so, she'd said '*yes*'.

Kate awoke with a sharp cry, covered in a film of clammy sweat.

She was disoriented, her eyes taking a moment to focus on her surroundings in the dim twilight of the early morning.

The creek, she remembered.

Safe, for now.

Her heart raced, adrenaline running high as her mind replayed the memories from her dream, like an old movie reel on repeat, reminding her, taunting her, shaming her about all that had gone before until she could stand no more.

Anguished and angry with herself, Kate swung her legs off the bed and reached for her grandmother's old dressing gown, which Ben had presented to her when they'd first arrived. Although the Helford could reach soaring temperatures during summer days, at night the air could be bitingly cold, and she was glad of the thick terry-towelling material to stave off the chill.

Kate checked the room next door, where her son slept soundlessly, then padded to the kitchen to pour herself a glass of water. She had it clutched between her hands when Ben found her a few minutes later, sitting on the dock looking out across the little bay.

"Thought I heard you," he said, lowering himself into one of the wooden deck chairs beside her.

"Sorry if I woke you," she said.

Ben reached for her hand and gave it a little squeeze. "I was only half asleep," he assured her. "When you get to be my age, you never sleep very deeply. If it isn't my prostrate havin' me up three times a night, it's worryin' that I've forgotten to do some damn thing or another."

She smiled at that, and he gave her a keen look.

"It's good to have you here, Kate. I've missed you. We've *all* missed you."

She closed her eyes, feeling shame all over. "I've missed you too."

He reached across to hold her hand again, cradling her fingers against his old, gnarly skin as he'd done since she was younger than Jamie.

"I always miss your grandma," he said, after a comfortable pause. "Still, there's times when I miss her even more, such as now. My Debbie always knew just the right thing to say."

Kate looked across at him, a question in her eyes, and he bit the bullet.

"I know why you stayed away," Ben said, and held onto her hand when she would have tugged it away, not yet ready to face what she needed to face.

He couldn't know about Will.

Nobody knew.

"I remember how I behaved, when you rang to tell me you were in love," he continued. "I didn't handle myself well, and the criticism put your back up—I know it did. You were young and in love, you wanted my blessing, and, when I didn't give it, you were left feeling angry and confused. I pushed you away—"

He let a long sigh hiss through his teeth, which was pure frustration at his former self.

"Didn't mean to, but I did, all the same," he said, so quietly she strained to hear. "Small wonder you haven't rushed back, eh?"

Kate remembered that long-ago conversation, and the angry words they'd shared, but she didn't blame him for any of it. She'd been wilful, with a headstrong determination not to listen to anything that might have alerted her to the truth—which was, of course, that if something looked too good to be true, it often was.

She looked out across the water and sky, which was beginning to turn from deepest mauve to a pale lilac, heralding the imminent arrival of the sun to dawn a new day.

A new day deserved a new slate.

"I was young," she said, and thought back to that girl, a lifetime ago. "Grief and anger made me stubborn, which isn't my usual nature...or, at least, no more so than the average person."

She gave him a small smile.

"Nothing wrong with havin' conviction," he said, and she had a fleeting thought that her grandfather would have made a wonderful diplomat.

"I should have listened to those around me," she admitted, thinking of her uncle and aunt who'd given her much the same cautionary advice. "I should have understood you weren't trying to ruin my happiness—you were trying to teach me *caution*.

I didn't want to listen because I was completely taken in by him."

Her lips clamped shut and she looked down at her hands, worried that she'd said too much.

"Taken in?" he asked, treading carefully.

Kate closed her eyes and a single tear escaped, blazing a trail down her pale cheek.

"How'd you hurt that arm, love?"

He was merciless in his pursuit of the truth, because the time for denials had passed.

"I—" She clutched her wrist beneath the dressing gown and turned to him with eyes that were dark pools of misery, pleading with him not to draw her out any further. "Please, I can't…I can't."

But she must, he thought. *The demon must be faced, so it could be defeated.*

"Why'd you come to me in the middle of the night, with next to nothing to call your own?" he asked. "Why're you so frightened, Katie—of everyone?"

His gentle voice was her undoing, and she wiped her sleeve across her eyes, glancing back towards the cottage to make sure Jamie hadn't woken up.

"I learned to trust no-one," she said, wretchedly. "Losing my parents taught me that nothing lasts forever, and being with Will taught me that some things last far longer than they should."

Across the cove, they watched the first rays of sunlight sweep over the creek.

"I can't stay here much longer," she said. "If I stay, he'll find us eventually and take Jamie away from me or hurt somebody else I love."

"How could he take Jamie away, or hurt you?" Ben said. "He'd have to come through me, first."

Kate shook her head, loving him fiercely in that moment.

"Will told me, many times, that he would stop at nothing to protect what he considered to be his," she said, and recognised the conditioned emotion that pricked her skin as 'disloyalty', according to Will. She wasn't supposed to speak of their relationship to anyone, yet here she was, about to do that very thing.

"He's more powerful than any of us," she whispered. "He has vast resources, a squeaky-clean reputation and he's adored by millions around the world—thanks to his most recent television show."

Much to their son's delight, Will had accepted the role of a lifetime to play Superman, the Caped Crusader, on an all-new television remake, and although the first series had barely launched, he was already being mobbed by fans on the street, which did nothing but elevate an already monstrous ego.

"They think his character matches the one he plays on screen—which is beyond reproach," she continued. "I know the reality, but nobody else does. He threatened to lie to the authorities many times—"

"What could he possibly say?"

"Anything," she muttered. "You don't know him, as I do. He'd tell so many lies, big and small, sometimes just to play with my mind. He explicitly told me that, if I ever thought of leaving him, he'd paint me as an unfit mother and gain full custody of Jamie. Then, he'd turn my son against me."

Ben took a moment to collect his thoughts, until he was sure he was in command of the anger that coursed through his body.

"Money doesn't equal power," he said. "It can help, but there are other ways to win—in my day, the truth used to be good enough."

If only it was that simple.

"I tried," Kate said. "I tried reporting him."

She told him about an incident, and her grandfather rubbed gentle circles over her hand while she spoke, to soothe the hurt.

"The police officer—who was a woman, by the way—said that she could see no physical evidence of abuse. It had been a couple of days, you see, and he was always quite careful where he…"

She swallowed.

"Anyway, I was written up as a vexatious person, a…a…time-waster, and Will suggested very strongly to the attending officer that I might be suffering from postpartum depression, which would explain my erratic behaviour. His version of events was that I'd taken to hurting myself and lashing out. He even said he was worried about my behaviour towards the baby."

She dashed away another tear.

"The next day, I had an unscheduled visit from the Health Visitor," she said. "They came every week for a month, asking me all kinds of probing questions, while fawning all over my husband, praising him for how well he was *coping*. When they left, Will told me that was only the beginning, and, if I ever went to the police again, he'd tell them I'd threatened to take my own life, or Jamie's."

"Wicked," Ben growled, and then swore colourfully. "You can still report him. I'll go with you, this time, and stay with you every step of the way."

She wanted to, Kate thought. *But...*

"If I thought they'd believe me, I would. But Will's cunning—he finds ways to *twist* things, to make you feel foolish...make it seem as though you've gone mad, or that you've misunderstood what happened. At times, he made me doubt my own sanity."

"I think they call that 'gaslighting'," Ben muttered. "I saw the old film, once."

She nodded. "It's hard to explain if you haven't experienced it," she said. "I didn't get to be this wreck... this, this...*shell* of a person overnight. He chipped away at me, piece by piece, for years. Little comments, little lies, until I couldn't trust my own judgment. When he sensed any rebellion from me, he upped the ante and used threats against Jamie, or even—"

She broke off.

"Or *me?*" Ben wondered.

She nodded, and he surprised her by letting out one of his long, rumbling laughs.

"He could try," he said, giving his nose a thoughtful scratch. "There's been many a fool who's tried to best Ben Carew o'er the years, but none've succeeded yet."

She thought of Will, of what he was capable of, and hoped it never came to pass.

Ben turned and, leaning close, cradled her face in his old, scarred hands, brushing away her tears with the pads of his thumbs.

"Now, listen to your old grandad," he said gently. "First thing's first, there'll be no more need for running. You're *home* now, and home you'll stay, for as long as you want to."

She sucked in a quivering breath, thought of how easily Will could find her here, but, looking into her grandfather's old myopic eyes, felt less fearful than she had before.

She gave a short nod.

"Good," he said, sitting back again. "Next thing is, whenever you feel ready to, we're going to go down to the station together and make a full report."

She closed her eyes, thinking of where to begin, of how to lay bare the embarrassing, humiliating, agonising details of her life for the past eight years.

"Start by writing it all down," he said, as though he'd read her mind.

"I made little notes in my diary."

He nodded. "It's a good start," he said. "The police will take things more seriously if you've got a timeline that you can show them. While you're workin' on that, I'm goin' to call a solicitor friend of mine who can help us muddle through all this."

"I don't—" She broke off, embarrassed. "I have hardly any money left. I didn't use any of my bank cards because he has access to my account and I know he'd trace me, so I stuck to cash where I could. I need to start earning some money very soon—"

"What happened to your inheritance?" Ben asked. His daughter and son-in-law had done well for themselves when they'd been alive, and Kate had been their only child.

"When we got married, Will said we should pool our resources to buy a place together," she explained. "I thought it was an investment in our future."

"Well, anybody who marries the person they love approaches things fifty-fifty," he said. "It was the same with your gran and me…she had a little bit, I had a little bit, and we both chipped in to start our life together. Most times, that's all well and good. In this case, we'll be wantin' him to give back what's rightfully yours."

She gave a tremulous smile.

"As for the here and now, don't you worry about a thing," he said, decisively. "I've got everythin' covered, and you can borrow whatever you need. That's what family's for—"

At this, she drew the line. "No," she said, firmly. "I'm grateful for the offer, and maybe I'll borrow a little bit for the next couple of weeks to tide us over, but I want to stand on my own two feet. I *need* to."

"Well, if that's how you feel about it—"

"It is."

He tried one last tack. "You know, I could always use another ferryboat captain—"

She smiled and shook her head. "I already know you have Danny for that," she reminded him. "If you really needed more hands on deck, you'd have upped his hours from part-time to full-time, already."

Ben pursed his lips because, of course, she was right—and, as it happened, he'd already offered Danny more working hours, while he paused to spend time with Kate and Jamie.

"Really, I'll be fine, just wait and see," Kate said, and realised that she meant it. "I plan to go down to the village today and see if there's anything going and, if not, I'll look further afield. Either way, I've got a strong back and a good work ethic. I'll pick something up."

Ben nodded, and there was a gleam of admiration in his eyes that seemed to say, "There she is, there's my girl."

"What about your art?" he asked. "You always had such a hand with it—"

A shadow passed over her face.

"It's been a long time since I picked up a brush," she said, flexing the fingers of her right hand. *Not since Will broke my bones, 'accidentally', four years ago.* "There are lots of other things I can do, instead."

If he sensed there was more to talk about, he decided against it. They'd covered a lot of ground already, and tomorrow was another day.

"One more thing," he did say, before they went back inside the cottage to find Jamie. "You're no shell of a person, Kate; you're strong, and always have been. You've been knocked and your heart has been hurt, among other things, which has left you with some scars. It's also left you with Jamie."

She smiled, thinking of her son.

"I know. If I could turn back the clock, I think I'd still suffer Will, so long as I knew I could still have Jamie."

They both thought of the sweet boy who would, very shortly, be waking up and demanding breakfast.

Ben forced himself to ask the obvious question.

"Did he ever—?"

"No," Kate said, in a rush. "I'd have killed him before I'd let him touch a hair on Jamie's head."

It was an unfortunate choice of words.

"As I said before, Will was very careful to make sure nobody ever witnessed anything—including Jamie," she said. "He was never warm or loving with his son other than for show, when people were around, but I tried to make up for it by showering Jamie with affection. I knew, almost as soon as he was born, that we would have to get away. I've been planning this for a long time."

She realised that she would always have her son to thank for giving her the courage she needed to plan and execute their escape. Having him to care for, even more than herself, had given her the impetus to overcome the fear of reprisals.

"Take it from one who knows," Ben said, heaving himself out of his deck chair with a wheeze.

Kate looked up at him.

"Life is long, but it's also short," he told her. "Don't let that man—or *anyone*—steal any more of it from you, whether by word or by deed. As for his threats, Will Irving might think he's Goliath when it comes to having all the money and the fame, but there's strength in numbers. We can move mountains together, sweetheart, that's a promise."

With that, he leaned down to plant a kiss on top of her head, then ambled back along the path to set some bacon fizzling.

Times like these called for a Full English.

CHAPTER 9

Later that morning, while Ben took Jamie off in his ferryboat for a 'buccaneering expedition', Kate made her way along the winding path which ran from her grandfather's cottage parallel to Frenchman's Creek until it joined the estuary, then veered south along the headland all the way to Helford village. It was a walk she'd taken countless times before, and her feet were agile as she negotiated the uneven ground through woodland heavily canopied with layers of green and heady with the scent of flowers and wild garlic. There was a quicker way to the village by road, she knew, but her heart yearned for the comfort of that mystical, well-trodden path she'd skipped along as a little girl.

The terrain rose and fell as she walked, whistling to herself with a heart much lighter than it had been the day before. For the first time in recent memory, Kate felt buoyant about the future and found herself smiling as she dodged potholes and paused to rub a hand over the bark of passing trees. She continued until the pathway reached a short section that skirted the edge of a sheer drop on one side, at the base of which was another tiny cove, accessible only at low tide. When it swept away, the tide revealed the skeletal remains of a boat shipwrecked long ago, its carcass now buried deeply in the muddy riverbed. It had been widely photographed, and she'd sketched the view herself numerous times, but the boat's remains were more than merely a plaything for children or a pretty backdrop. It was a warning that those who sailed the waters in those parts should respect Mother Nature and her fury or suffer the consequences. As a child, she'd been taught to treat both the land *and* the sea with due caution, and it was a lesson she would teach her son at the earliest opportunity.

Kate continued towards Helford, passing the occasional cottage as she drew near the outskirts of the village, until she reached the ferryboat landing on the furthermost edge overlooking Helford Passage, on the other side. She made her way down to the lookout point but found no passengers waiting nor ferryboat moored at that time, just an empty corner of the world and a perfect panorama of the estuary mid-morning. It shone sapphire blue in the sun, beckoning her to paddle in its clear waters to cool her tired feet, and she answered its siren call, slipping off her shoes to dip her toes in the shallows while she looked out at the neat rows of white-painted yachts, wayfarers and multi-coloured dinghies bobbing on the current. Her trained eye picked out a red ferryboat moored on the jetty on the other side of that narrow portion of the estuary, and, in the distance, she saw Danny help customers from the boat, as he'd done the day before.

Then, another boat caught her eye.

It was just the right size—large without being gawdy, gleaming white and sleek as they came. Without binoculars, she struggled to read the name, but could see what appeared to be the painted detail of five thin black lines around the hull, with a series of notes painted on top to resemble sheet music. She had only a rudimentary grasp of the subject, having dispensed with piano lessons at a relatively young age, so she couldn't make out which tune the notes were intended to represent.

With so many famous faces dotted in the private folds of the valley surrounding the Helford, she guessed that it belonged to one of them; probably, some well-known singer taking a holiday in the area, choosing to remain *incognito,* relatively speaking. There was no sign of anybody aboard and the dinghy was absent, so she assumed they were off somewhere enjoying themselves—which reminded her that she'd spent long enough splashing around and could no longer put off the inevitable.

She had work to do.

Kate made her way from the ferry landing along another footpath into the centre of Helford village, which was small and picturesque. Aside from the village shop, which sold the usual provisions and—most importantly—kept a ready stock of ice-cream, The Ship's Mate was another major draw for travellers seeking to assuage their hunger or thirst. It was a large, white-painted old inn perched on the edge of Helford Creek, built across three terraces from its entrance on the same level with the village centre, down to the waterside, where patrons could enjoy wood-fired pizzas and craft beers while people in dinghies or canoes passed below, at high tide. Unlike Helford Passage, the village across the water, there wasn't so much in the way of a sandy beach, but there was no shortage of fishing to make up for it.

Despite all there was to recommend it, Kate felt a certain trepidation as she passed the sea wall, beneath which a small group of children dressed in wetsuits played with their dog at low tide, their high-pitched voices carrying laughter on the air. Memories flooded in of herself at that age; of Nick, just a few years older than she and one of the 'elders' of their small childhood tribe because of it; of Pete, always smothered in sun cream to protect his pale skin; and Lucy, Joanne's daughter, always bubbly and full of fun, who'd been in the same class as Nick and Pete at their little school, nearby. They'd shared too many adventures to count; too many long, summer days to distinguish one from the next…except one.

Kate sank down onto the wall, her mind lost in the past.

She'd been sitting on that same wall, a girl only just turned eighteen, whose tanned legs swung over the edge while she held a sketchpad in one hand and pencil in the other. Nick had been sitting beside her, while Lucy had been inside The Ship's Mate finishing her shift. All three worked that summer for Lucy's mum, Joanne, whose husband, Bill, had inherited the pub from his father—and his father before him. But it was Joanne who'd grafted to make the place a success and had given them a chance to earn some money during the long holiday—knowing that, more often than not, they'd choose to re-invest their wages at the pub, usually the very same night they earned it.

Good business.

But that was before the news came.

After then, Kate hadn't returned to The Ship's Mate; it was all she could do to go through the motions of living, while all else faded to a blur.

It's your parents, Kate…

Carbon monoxide poisoning, so the coroner had said at the inquest.

The verdict was that a tiny leak must've sprung in their beautiful boat, *The Lady of Shalott*, which her father had commissioned as an anniversary gift to her mother. They'd enjoyed it all summer, believing themselves immortal; thinking of the routes they'd follow the next year and the one after that. All the while, they'd forgotten the cardinal rule they'd tried so hard to teach their daughter about life.

There were many things that were beautiful…

They could also be deadly.

The owner of the smart, musical-themed yacht she'd seen earlier must have been paying a visit to The Ship's Mate for lunch, Kate thought, because, as she thrust old memories aside and made her way towards the entrance to the inn, she caught sight of a dinghy tethered to one of the smaller jetties built along the creek. It had been designed to match its big sister, coated in white with a single double-quaver detail and, up close, she could read the name, 'TEEN SPIRIT II'.

Her lips curved into a smile.

It took all sorts...

Turning away, Kate sucked in a bolstering breath and pushed open the main door to the inn. It led straight into a smart bar area which, at first glance, didn't appear to have changed very much during the intervening years. It was scrupulously clean and tidy, and its atmosphere was cosy in that part of the building, its walls illuminated by subtle nautical-themed lights and candles not presently lit. Highly-polished wooden bistro tables were tucked here and there like miniature islands, echoing the general feel of the area, which tended towards a series of private coves and inlets. Many of them were taken up, including all the tables on the terraces outside, which were abuzz with people who'd settled down to enjoy an early lunch or a swift half as they made their way from harbour to harbour.

The walls were decorated with framed pictures of days gone by, dating back to the estuary's smuggling days, alongside a collection of more modern images taken of the staff and locals who frequented their establishment. In the centre of it all was a gilt-framed photograph of the pub landlord and landlady smiling with their daughter between them, taken about fifteen years ago, if Kate wasn't mistaken. It was an image she'd seen before, while she worked there, and she was glad it had survived the changing décor. Her eyes were drawn to the other photographs gracing the long wall of the bar area but, before she could study them, there came a loud squeal of delight.

"*Kate?*"

She froze, not yet accustomed to loud displays of exuberance, and turned to find the source of the sound.

A woman of around her own age stood at the other end of the bar, having just set down a tray of empty glasses on the end. She was curvaceous, and wore a short sundress that flattered her hourglass figure. Her hair, which had always been a pleasant mid-brown shade, was now dyed a striking shade of white-blond and curled back from her face in a style reminiscent of the 1950s. Together with the bold red lipstick she wore, Kate presumed the overall effect was inspired by the likes of Marilyn Monroe and, as it happened, the lady suited it.

"Lucy!"

They'd been inseparable friends every summer, laughing over the boys' antics and exchanging secrets during the many sleepovers they'd had, when they'd treated one another's houses as their own.

"I heard you were back in the area," Lucy said, and closed the distance between them with a little skip of delight. "It's wonderful to see you!"

Before she knew it, Kate was enveloped in a warm, perfume-infused cuddle which, after a second or two, she returned wholeheartedly. Aside from her grandfather, it had been a long time since someone had embraced her without agenda or malice, and she was reaccustoming herself to the feel of it.

"*Order up!*"

A disembodied female voice filtered through a hatch separating the kitchen and bar area, one that Kate recognised immediately.

Lucy pulled a face and began to turn.

"Let me surprise her," Kate suggested, and began making her way towards the swing door that led into the kitchen area, at the other end of the bar.

Pushing inside, she was met with a hive of activity and the mouth-watering scent of homemade fish chowder. Two sous-chefs were busy chopping and stirring, while an older teen—perhaps eighteen or nineteen—gave her a harried smile and Kate stepped aside so that he could pass through the doorway with a large circular tray full of steaming china bowls.

"Ta!" he called back.

"*Lucy!* Get your arse in 'ere!"

Kate grinned, and followed the sound beyond a gleaming central island to the far end of the kitchen, where a woman of around fifty was engrossed in the task of furiously scrubbing larger pots and stacking smaller ones into a dishwasher.

Joanne Hicks was of average height but enormous stature. Every inch of her was alive with energy, and she was the epitome of relaxed Cornish chic, with her three-quarter length jeans rolled up at the bottom and bright red t-shirt beneath a linen apron embroidered with the inn's own branded logo.

"Why don't I give you a hand?"

Her face was a comical mask of surprise when she spun around to face Kate.

"*Well!*" she declared, setting a fist on her hip. "It's about time!"

"I—"

"Bad *enough* that we don't hear a peep from you for nearly fifteen years," Joanne began, gesticulating with her hand so that errant suds of soap flew this way and that. "Then I hear from that blabbermouth Fred Lorne that Kate Ryce was back in the Helford and had I seen 'er?"

She made a sound like a *harrumph*.

"I certainly haven't, says I, because 'er ladyship hasn't seen fit to pay us a visit…"

"I'm sorry, Jo," Kate said, quietly.

Something in her voice must have sliced through Joanne's tirade, because she set down her dishcloth and stepped forward to take a good, maternal look at the woman who stood before her, who'd been a slip of a girl when she'd last seen her.

A quick inspection told her all she needed to know, and her hands came up to rest on Kate's arms, cradling her as her own mother might have done.

"You've got that look about you," she said, gently. "A sadness, just like when…"

She broke off, swallowing the words she'd been about to say.

Just like when Alice and Rob died.

Tears sprang into Kate's eyes, and she looked away. She should have remembered Joanne always had a knack for seeing things people tried so desperately to hide.

"I'll get past it," she said, firmly.

Joanne nodded. "You're a fighter," she said. "Just like your mum was."

She turned away, overcome suddenly by her own emotion as she remembered the woman who had been her friend, and whose child now stood before her, the living image of her mother.

"Well, since you're here, you can give us a hand with these dishes," she said briskly.

"Happy to," Kate said, rolling up her sleeves. "In fact, I wondered if you might have any positions going?"

Joanne was surprised all over again.

"You're *stayin'*, then?"

Kate smiled. "It looks that way," she said, and reached for a frying pan coated in grease.

"What about…well, you know, we heard you'd got married, and—"

"Where is he now?" Kate finished for her, keeping her head bent over the sink to hide her expression. "Nothing lasts forever, Jo."

Thank God.

A wealth of meaning was imbued in that simple statement and Joanne didn't press her for any more details. There would be time enough to catch up, and sometimes menial, repetitive tasks could be cathartic—she should know.

All the same, with a rich, film-star husband, why did Kate need to work as a waitress?

Had she come back for another reason?

She meant to find out.

"His loss is our gain," was all she said, and Kate gave her a smile of thanks. "As for a job—look no further, because you've come to the right place! I'm in need of a decent waitress I don't have to spend half the summer training up—that is, if you still remember the ropes?"

There was a deliberate challenge in her tone, and Kate lifted her chin.

"I'm rusty, but I should be able to pick things up again."

"All right," Joanne said, untying her apron and handing it to Kate. "Try this on for size."

It was a perfect fit.

"You'll do," she said, and was about to bustle off to her next task when Kate's quiet voice stopped her.

"Thanks, Joanne," she said. "I won't ever forget your kindness."

The other woman gave her cheek a gentle pat, as she might have done her own daughter.

"You won't be sayin' that, once you've worked here a week," she told her, with a wink.

Kate laughed. "It's coming back to me, already."

CHAPTER 10

"Careful."

Nick caught the glass in a deft hand before it toppled from the tray Kate was carrying.

"I'm still getting back into the swing of things," she said, blowing a stray hair from her sweaty brow.

"You look pretty good to me," he said, and almost slapped a palm to his own face.

Luckily—or, perhaps, *unluckily*—for him, the connotations of his remark didn't register.

"Thanks, I haven't spilled or broken anything yet," she said, with a little laugh. "Being back here at The Ship's Mate feels like I've turned back the hands of time and I'm eighteen all over again."

Nick, who, she noted irritably, looked very attractive in faded jeans and a simple white t-shirt, folded his arms across his broad chest and leaned back against the bar.

"How does that feel?" he wondered.

"*What?*" she asked, too quickly.

He looked at her as if she'd grown two heads. "What you were just talking about," he said slowly. "Being back here, and working for Joanne?"

"*Oh,*" she said, and set the tray down on the bar. "Right. Um, actually it feels…"

She paused to assess her inner state and then gave him a beautiful smile that lit up her face.

"It feels wonderful," she said, deeply. "To be productive, useful, earning my own money…I feel like I'm getting my self-respect back."

She fell silent, worrying that she'd given too much away.

"I mean, it's been a while since I was employed, what with having Jamie to look after—" she tagged on, lamely.

There was much he could have said, but Nick would rather Kate told him the truth about her marriage when she was ready, and so he said nothing of his discussion with Ben the previous day.

"It's good for the soul to have purpose," he said, enigmatically.

Kate nodded. "I should get back to work—"

"Actually, Joanne sent me here to tell you that you're due a break," he said. "Why don't you grab a drink, and I'll meet you down by the water?"

Kate opened her mouth to object, but no words came out.

"Okay," she found herself saying and, before she had time to change her mind, he flashed a blinding smile and stepped back out into the sunshine, disappearing onto the white-washed terrace beyond.

When Kate followed Nick outside a few minutes later, she couldn't see him anywhere, at first.

"Lookin' for me, beautiful?" A man who looked older than...well, *time* itself, sent her a semi-toothless grin from his perch on a nearby bar stool, and wriggled a set of preposterous bushy eyebrows.

"And make the other girls jealous?" Kate shot back. "Not likely."

He let out an appreciative laugh that soon turned into a chesty wheeze, and she gave him a couple of good pats on his back to help relieve the constriction.

"You'd be Alice Carew's girl, wouldn't you?"

All her life, Kate had known her mother by her married name of 'Alice Ryce', but, in those parts, she'd always be Ben Carew's family.

"Yes," she said, and managed a small smile.

"Nice lassie, that'n," he said. "You've got the look o' 'er."

Kate hadn't realised quite how much she'd grown to resemble her late mother but, judging by the reaction, it must have been quite a bit.

She could only take it as a compliment, since her mother had been a very beautiful woman.

"Thank you," she said.

"Fred Lorne!" Joanne's booming voice caught them both off-guard. "Leave the poor girl alone to have her break. She's got a tyrant of a new boss who's been workin' 'er fingers to the bone."

Joanne cocked her head to indicate that Kate should make a speedy getaway.

Mouthing a quick 'thank you', she gave the inimitable Fred a cheerful smile in farewell, then trotted down a series of stone steps towards the lower terrace, by the water. It was another glorious sunny day, and she spotted Nick at one of the wooden tables at the end, sitting beneath the shade of a large white parasol.

She felt a strange, nervous sensation as she made her way towards him, dodging sleeping dogs, children's sandals and other paraphernalia as she went, and put the feeling down to hunger or a lingering fear that Will would appear at any moment to spoil her happiness.

It certainly had nothing whatsoever to do with Nick.

How could it? He was just an old friend.

As if he'd heard her unspoken thought, his head whipped around as she approached.

"Hi," he said. "You look as though you could use a drink."

"A double," she agreed. "I'll settle for water, since I've got the other half of my shift to finish."

"Joanne's offered you your old job back, then?"

"This is a trial, but hopefully I passed muster."

"I'm sure you did," he said, and took a thoughtful sip from the bottle of craft beer he held in his hand. "You're thinking of sticking around then?"

She looked away, wondering how best to answer. Soon, it would become obvious to everyone that she was back for good. All the same, she was cautious to reveal too much.

As the saying went, 'loose lips sank ships'.

"I'm thinking about it," she said, vaguely. "Besides, Jamie likes it here."

Nick held back asking all the usual questions he might otherwise have asked, and instead focused on the little boy who was, even to the most casual observer, her sun, moon and stars.

"Where's Jamie today?"

"With his great-grandad," she said, relieved that the conversation had moved on. "Ben wanted to teach Jamie some of the basics of sailing, in case he should ever need to steer a boat."

"Never hurts to know how," Nick agreed. "Want any recommendations?"

"Hmm?"

He nodded towards the menu she appeared to be nursing.

"Oh," she said. "I'm just being…indecisive."

"I don't want to rush you, but some of us could eat a horse."

She chuckled, and tried to stem the anxiety that flowed merely from perusing a list of food options. Whenever she'd been out for a meal with Will, he'd often taken it upon himself to order on her behalf, as if she was too stupid to know what she wanted to eat; either that, or he'd make a barbed comment another about 'moments on the lips, lifetimes on the hips' if she showed any interest in carbohydrates.

Her eyes slid to the 'Ship's Mate Burger' and, after a brief internal fight, she decided she'd have it with all the works.

Extra fries.

Extra bacon.

Extra cheese.

And a chocolate milkshake.

Her mind made up, she set the menu down again and folded her arms on the tabletop.

"How come you're so hungry?" she asked. "Have you had a busy morning, too?"

Nick thought of how he'd woken in the early hours full of inspiration for a new song, one that would suit an up-and-coming young artist on the lookout for the right melody to launch their career. He'd spent hours working on it, taking the tune from inception to something like a first draft, until tiredness had forced him out of his studio and back to bed. Since then, he'd come out on his boat to let the sea air replenish him.

And, of course, to see if he might happen to run into Kate, again, he admitted to himself.

"You could say so," he said, raising an idle hand to return a wave from one of the locals who passed by their table.

Kate realised she had absolutely no idea what Nick did to earn his bread. Judging by his understated clothing and laid-back air of confidence, combined with strong-looking hands and what her grandfather might have called 'boat muscle', Nick Pascoe could have been anything from a shipwreck diver to an all-round handyman.

As it happened, he'd been both, on occasion.

"Do you work in Helford, then?" she prodded.

Now that the moment to tell her about himself had come around, Nick found himself tongue-tied. It wasn't that he was ashamed of being a songwriter; he was a very good one, come to that. But Ben's words replayed in his mind and the mental image of Will Irving, her husband, served to remind him that, in Kate's experience, rich, successful men had a tendency towards cruelty in its many forms. No doubt, she'd sworn herself away from them, or anyone remotely resembling the type.

Which rather put him in an awkward position.

"Oh, there's that boat again!" she exclaimed, granting him a brief reprieve.

"Which—?"

He twisted in his seat to follow her line of sight, and cursed Fate.

"I love the name—the 'TEEN SPIRIT II'," she was saying. "I suppose 'TEEN SPIRIT I' is that lovely yacht, moored on the estuary."

"You saw it?"

She nodded. "On my walk here," she said, still admiring the little white dinghy tethered to one of the smaller jetties on the creekside. "I wonder who owns it."

"Well—"

"No, no, let me guess," she said, impishly. "It has to be someone sitting at one of these tables, doesn't it?"

He said nothing, a cowardly part of himself wanting to play along with the guessing game. He wanted to gain her trust and not be consigned to the same category as her famous husband, who was the poster boy for 'Men Who Could Not Be Trusted'. How much easier it might have been if he was, 'Nick Pascoe: Boat Builder and Handyman', rather than, 'Nick Pascoe: Award-Winning Songwriter and Producer'.

"Have you seen the musical detail on the side?" she said. "I love that, it's so eccentric…"

Eccentric? he wondered about himself.

Most likely.

"It's probably one of those posers you see down at the yacht club, sometimes," she said, conspiratorially. "Lots of cable knit and chinos—you know the type?"

He thought of the cable knit jumper hanging in his wardrobe at home, and vowed to burn it at the first opportunity.

"Must be a musician," she continued, scanning the faces of those around her. "There are quite a few, living around here, aren't there?"

He took another long gulp of his drink and tried again. "Yeah. In fact—"

"It has to be him," she said, reaching across the table to tap his hand.

He looked down at her slender fingers resting on his own.

This was going to be a problem.

Kate was looking towards a man of sixty, with wild, curly grey hair and a year-round tan. He wore jean shorts, boat shoes and a black vest over which he'd slung a flamboyant Hawaiian shirt in all the shades of the rainbow. Blue-tinted sunglasses completed the 'low key' look, and Nick smiled at the sight of him, for she happened to be right. The man was indeed a famous guitarist for a band whose heyday had been during the early-eighties era of glam-rock music, and Nick considered him a friend, having jammed together several times.

Catching their eyes upon him, Jimmy Dunne raised a hand in salute, which they returned.

"See!" Kate said, triumphantly. "I can spot them, every time."

Nick's lips twitched, but he could continue the game no longer.

"Kate, I need to tell you—"

"Well, this is *cosy*."

The interruption came from Lucy, who had come to take their order. Her eyes, which had been so welcoming earlier in the day, now wore an expression of open speculation and, if Kate wasn't mistaken, a touch of something like suspicion.

She looked at Nick, who seemed unfazed, then back at Lucy.

"Ah, you're welcome to join us," she said. "There's always room for one more."

Lucy's expression softened—slightly.

"Thanks," she said, and then gave Nick her full attention. "I'm still on shift, though. Maybe I'll see you later?"

His expression was non-committal.

"I'm usually hereabouts," he said easily. "Pete'll be down later, too."

Lucy flipped her hair back, obviously irritated. "What'll it be?"

They placed their order and, after she'd left, there was a brief silence during which Kate speculated about whether Lucy and Nick had ever developed their friendship into something more serious, but she said nothing of it.

After all, that was none of her business.

"In case you're wondering, the answer is 'no'."

Her eyes flew to his face, which wore an amused expression.

"What? I wasn't wondering anything."

He laughed. "Yes, you were."

She found herself unable to look away, and she shifted on her seat, wondering why the drinks were taking so long to arrive.

"It isn't any of my business—"

"No," he agreed, polishing off his beer. "All the same, I don't mind telling you. Lucy and I are friends, and that's all we've ever been."

Kate doubted whether that's all Lucy hoped for, but she kept the thought to herself.

"Besides," Nick continued. "Pete has been in love with Lucy Hicks ever since he was old enough to know the difference between boys and girls. He's my best friend—more like a brother—and there's a code about these things."

Which made for an interesting triangle, she thought.

"He doesn't seem to have made much headway," she had to say.

"He's a slow burner," Nick said, with another of his slow smiles. "There's a lot to be said for it."

Kate thought there was a tone to his voice but, when she searched his face, she could read nothing untoward.

"Well, let's hope he doesn't take too long and miss the boat altogether."

Nick gave a short, self-deprecating laugh and ran his hands through his hair, wondering if some Higher Power was playing with his heart, purely for sport.

"I'll pass on the advice," he assured her.

CHAPTER 11

Andy Charlton had travelled through the night, unknowingly retracing many of the steps Kate and Jamie had taken on their long journey south. He'd already discovered that Kate hadn't visited her father's brother in London; her uncle, Stephen Ryce, and his family, had been away in the Lake District and weren't due to return home until the following week. One of Charlton's men had spent a few hours watching the uncle's house, just to be sure, and there had been no signs of life.

Which left the grandfather, in Helford.

Charlton had spent the long, cross-country train journey from Scotland reading the dossier on Ben Carew, including the death of his daughter and her husband and of his wife, a few years before. The old man had seen plenty of tragedy and, thanks to the machinations of his granddaughter's husband, hadn't seen Kate in a very long time, either.

Would he have welcomed her back?

Perhaps, when he realised what she'd been living with…

Andy thought of his own daughter, who had just turned sixteen, and wondered how he would have felt if she'd brought home a man like Will Irving.

It didn't bear thinking about.

He'd brushed off that unproductive line of thought and concentrated on the task in hand, making lists, marking trails on the old-fashioned map he kept in the pocket of his jacket. He congratulated himself on having dressed for the part of an outdoorsy tourist, although he was hardly a man in the habit of ambling over hill and vale at the best of times, a fact borne out by the thickening of his gut, which protruded slightly over the waistband of his canvas walking trousers.

The things he did, for the sake of his reputation.

To his surprise, it was no hardship to sit on the banks of the Helford estuary sipping a cold glass of chardonnay whilst he kept a beady eye on the red-headed beauty a few tables down. It was an easy task to raise his smartphone, affect the air of someone replying to a text or capturing the landscape, and alter the angle slightly to snap an image of Kate Irving and her good-looking male companion.

After he'd taken a sufficient number, including a nice snap of the pair of them appearing to hold hands, he slipped the phone back inside his pocket and tucked into fish and chips which he fully intended to charge as a business expense.

In his peripheral vision, he watched the woman laugh and heaved a sigh that was part resignation and part contentment.

Will Irving was not going to be pleased, when he received his report.

The next task would be to find out all there was to know about Kate's mystery man, because that would surely be her husband's first question.

After then, he would wash his hands of the whole affair…

Unless Irving made it worth his while to stay.

Kate hummed to herself as she untied her apron at the end of the shift, not minding the ache in her feet nor the one in her back. She was eager now to get home to Jamie and Ben, and her mind was preoccupied with thoughts of what she'd cook for them, when she almost barrelled straight into the solid wall of a man's chest.

"Sorry," she muttered, and her nose wrinkled at the pungent odour of stale alcohol that assailed her nostrils.

"*Alice?*"

The word was slurred, and carried with it a note of horror.

Kate stepped away, while her eyes scanned the bar area for Joanne or Lucy.

"No," she said clearly. "I'm *Kate*."

The man might have been around fifty, but looked much older. He bore the mottled look of one who had abused alcohol for too many years; the capillaries across his nose and cheeks were irrevocably broken, leaving red stains against his leathery skin. He wore the ubiquitous garb of shorts and a linen shirt, stained down the front, and he could have used a shave.

Suddenly, Kate recognised him.

"*Bill?*"

Joanne's husband had always enjoyed a drink; as a pub landlord, it was hard to avoid it. However, where the years had been kind to his wife, Kate was sorry to say the same could not be said of the man who stood before her now.

"Aye," he muttered, still a bit unnerved by the sight of her. "You're l—lil Kate. All grown up, then…"

"Yes," she said, venturing a smile. "I was just leaving."

"For the best," he muttered. "Run away, lil Katie."

"*Bill.*" Joanne's voice was long-suffering, her eyes sad as they beseeched Kate's forgiveness. "I think you should go and have a lie down," she implored him.

Bill laughed, swaying slightly on his feet. "Said the wrong thing, have I?" he mumbled, wandering around the back of the bar to help himself to another drink. "Aye, I'll go. I'll go away. Just takin' one of these for the road, my love."

"Bill, please, there are customers—"

Joanne looked acutely embarrassed, and Kate decided she'd better leave them both to it.

"I'll be going now," she said quietly. "Unless…do you need any help, Jo?"

The other woman seemed to think about it, then shook her head. "No," she said, and gave Kate a pat on the shoulder. "I'll see you tomorrow—by the way, how are you fixed for childcare?"

Kate blew out a long breath. "I need to speak to Ben," she admitted. "Jamie will be starting school in September but, until then, I'll have to think of something."

"If you're stuck, bring him along here," Joanne said, generously. "Or, I happen to know the woman who runs the summer camp, up in Mawgan," she added, referring to a village not too far away. "I could have a word and see if she has a space for him, if you like?"

"Milk of human kindness, my wife," Bill declared loudly, and raised his glass in a toast.

Joanne ignored him. "He fell off the wagon again, lately," she said, under her breath. "We're trying to help him through it."

Kate nodded, understanding what it was to feel powerless in the face of another person's demon.

"See you tomorrow, love—and welcome home."

Kate thanked her, and bade a polite farewell to the man she remembered having once been her parents' friend.

"Like seein' a ghost," she heard him say, as the door clicked shut behind her.

CHAPTER 12

"He's been sitting there for hours."

Lucy made this observation from her vantage point beside the wood-fired pizza oven, where she'd been engaged in the task of stoking the fire with logs and kindling ahead of the arrival of the dinner crowd, who would soon descend upon The Ship's Mate like a pack of ravenous wolves.

Pete twisted his neck around to get a better look at the man seated at one of the tables on the lower terrace, shifting his feet to accommodate the pile of logs he held in his arms.

"Probably just a tourist who's lost track of the time," he said. "It's easy to do."

Lucy wasn't convinced.

"Well, for someone who's got all the gear, he hasn't done much in the way of walking," she argued.

"Maybe he changed his mind," Pete said.

She scowled at him. "You've got an answer for everything, haven't you, Pete Ambrose?"

She shut the oven door with a bit more force than necessary, and began making her way up the stone steps back towards the kitchen, leaving him to follow if he wished.

Pete dumped the remaining logs in the basket beside the oven and trailed after her, as he always did.

"Obviously, I don't have an answer for some things," he muttered, darkly.

"What was that?" Lucy turned at the top of the stairs and, as a gust of wind swept in from the estuary to lift her hair back from her face while the mellow, early-evening light bathed her skin, he thought he'd never seen a more luminous sight.

"Nothing," he said. "Nothing but the ramblings of a fool."

She rolled her eyes and they carried onward to the bar, where Pete ordered himself a stiff gin and tonic.

Lucy raised an eyebrow. "Hitting the booze already?"

"It's after five," he argued, splashing a token amount of tonic into his glass. "It's a civilised hour for an aperitif."

She watched him knock back a couple of fingers and thought of her father, lying in a stupor on his bed in the apartment upstairs, but her face betrayed none of it. Lucy had learned to hide her feelings behind a bubbly mask and, when she was no longer able to laugh, she painted on the mask, instead.

"Been that kind of a day, has it?" she asked, lightly.

Pete loosened the tie that had been strangling him all afternoon.

"My dad isn't happy that I haven't shifted any expensive houses, lately."

Greg Ambrose, founder and owner of Ambrose Estates, was a successful businessman whose estate agency boasted one of the highest turnovers in Cornwall and Devon. There wasn't a prestige home he didn't know about, nor a price he couldn't put on any kind of bricks and mortar. He was a salesman, through and through, and a sharky one, at that.

His son was, much to his father's consternation, the absolute opposite.

"I just don't like buying and selling," Pete said, swilling his glass. "What's a bloke to do?"

"Why not follow your own path?" Lucy suggested. "Don't let him dictate your life. Follow your dreams."

Like Nick, she almost added.

Pete enjoyed a happy, sixty-second fantasy in which he owned and ran his own little tour boat, before reality bit.

"I need capital to strike out on my own," he complained.

"So? Go to the bank," she snapped. "Or ask Nick to loan you a bit."

She was right, he thought. *What was stopping him, really?*

His father was what charitable people might have called a 'big character'. The downside to having lived with him since birth was that, at every opportunity and in every conceivable way, he'd been reminded that Ambrose Estates was his legacy and, as his only son, Pete would be expected to carry on the dynasty.

Skivvy on a tour boat? his father had exclaimed, when he'd raised the suggestion. *If you think you're going to waste the university education I bought and paid for, you've got another thing coming. So help me, Pete, if you walk away from Ambrose Estates I expect you to pay back every single pound of tuition fees, rent, spending money and whatever else I dished out during the three years you were fannying around Exeter University—and with interest.*

Of course, his choice of university had been another bone of contention.

Exeter? Why'd you want to go there? his father had demanded. *Let me guess: Lucy Hicks is going to be there, isn't she? It's pathetic, the way you drool after her. Get yourself a proper girlfriend, son.*

Pete had taken his father's advice—or tried to. He'd dated other girls, but he'd have been lying if he said he hadn't hoped Lucy would feel a touch of jealousy when she saw them out together.

But she hadn't.

Worse still, she'd *befriended* those girls, while enjoying a stream of boyfriends he'd been forced to meet and shake hands with, in return.

Was there anything more frustrating?

Perhaps just one thing, he acknowledged. *Knowing that the girl you longed for only had eyes for your best friend.*

He couldn't blame Nick for that, more was the pity. The bloke had never looked twice at Lucy, which was probably the attraction. All their lives, the three of them had been inseparable—with Kate joining their merry band during the summers. He'd spent years listening, laughing, agreeing…waiting for one hint from Lucy that his feelings might be reciprocated, but that day had never come.

When was he going to stop banging his head against the proverbial wall?

"Penny for them," Lucy said.

Pete gulped the rest of his gin and pulled out his wallet to settle the bill.

"I was thinking it's high time for some changes around here," he said, and allowed himself to soak up the sight of her one last time before he began the process of detachment.

"You mean, you're finally going to quit Ambrose Estates?"

"It's time I looked to the future."

There was something in his voice that she couldn't quite make out, but her smile never faltered, and Lucy waved Pete off a few minutes later with her usual cheer.

Hours later, when the last of the punters had left and her mother had retreated upstairs to check on her father, leaving nothing but the quiet hum of the dishwasher and the lapping of the water somewhere outside for company in the long bar, Pete's words replayed on her mind. Lucy sat down at one of the empty tables, smoothed a hand over her pretty dress and looked around the walls of her parents' inn.

It was a fine place, she thought. A good place for the community and for people passing through. It had given her mother something to focus on, while her father retreated inwards, drinking himself towards an early grave, and provided a haven for the elderly members of the village who might have felt lonely, otherwise.

But what could she say was truly *hers,* and hers alone?

Nothing much.

Lucy had no shortage of friends to call upon for a frivolous night out, but many of those friends had begun to settle down, carving out new lives with homes, mortgages, cars and families. Their interests were different, and their priorities even more so. Conversations that once flowed easily were now stilted by her lack of interest in their chubby-faced babies, and their lack of interest in her plans to travel more widely and work as a make-up artist, or even a costume designer.

All of that was pie in the sky.

She had little savings, no partner to go home to—no home of her own, come to that.

She thought of Nick again…

Then she thought of Kate, and a small, unhappy corner of her heart wished she'd never come back to the Helford.

No sooner had the thought come than she banished it from her mind.

Jealousy is a road to nowhere, she told herself.

All the same, the heart and the mind were separate realms, and one did not always listen to the other.

CHAPTER 13

"Did you have fun on the river, today?"

"Yes!" Jamie cried, splashing his palms into his bathwater to punctuate the reply. "Grandie took me all the way to My*lurr*—"

Kate smiled as she lathered her son's hair in shampoo, knowing that he meant to say, 'Mylor', a well-known sailing village north of the estuary.

"Did you see any interesting things along the way?"

"I saw dolphins," Jamie told her, screwing up his face dramatically as she began to rinse the suds from his hair. "Ow! The soap's in my eyes! I'll go blind!"

"That would be *water*," his mother said. "I've already rinsed off the shampoo."

"Oh," he said.

"I see you've made a miraculous recovery from your temporary blindness," she drawled.

"It's because I'm so strong," he declared. "The Irvings are *always* strong."

Her hand gripped the little plastic cup she'd been using, and a chill ran through her body to hear Will's words come from the mouth of her little boy.

"It's all right to say if you feel scared or upset," she said, recovering quickly. "Strength comes in many different forms, Jamie."

"Yes, but Daddy says a man should never say 'sorry' and never back down, and he's Superman, now, isn't he? What does 'back down' mean, Mummy?"

Kate had lain awake wondering how she would ever tell her son the truth about his father, or indeed, *if* she ever would. She'd been back and forth on the issue like a yo-yo; first, her heart had screamed for justice, for some sense of the scales having been righted so that Jamie would know she hadn't abandoned his 'perfect' father for no good reason. She was angry, hurt and wanted payback in whatever form she could have it.

Then, once she cooled down, her heart invariably sang a different tune.

Temperance, it whispered. *Forbearance.*

What would it achieve to crush a child, so young? Why burden his mind with something so heavy; something he would carry for years to come, and which might affect his ability to form a stable relationship of his own, one day?

And so, she'd found a middle ground, at least until Jamie was older.

No lies, but plenty of omissions.

It was the best she could do, in the circumstances.

"Nobody is quite like Superman," she said, not answering him directly. "That's why he makes such a good hero—he always seems to do the right thing. Remember, we've talked before about the difference between things in real life and things that are pretend, Jamie? Like, when your daddy plays different pretend characters on TV?"

"Mm hmm," he said, crushing bubbles between his hands.

"Well, you see, playing so many make believe parts can sometimes make it hard for a person to remember who they *really* are," she said, although she wondered if Will Irving had ever known. "Sometimes, your daddy thinks he has to pretend to be strong, or what he thinks is being strong…"

Jamie nodded. "I know," he said. "Like when he pretended to push you on the floor in the kitchen, Mummy. He was just rehearsing an action scene, wasn't he?"

Kate couldn't speak for a full ten seconds, and she continued to pour warm water over his back while her mind dealt with wave upon wave of shock.

He'd seen.

Her son, whom she'd tried so hard to protect, had seen.

But how much?

She knew that, when he was of age, there would need to be another conversation; one that was

open and honest. But, for now, if he believed his parents had been playing parts, perhaps it was best for his young mind to continue believing that.

She drew in a quivering breath. "Is that what Daddy told you?" she asked.

Jamie nodded. "I asked him why he'd pushed you and he said he was rehearsing for a film," he said.

Kate learned something new about her husband in that moment; something that killed the final, tiny wedge of her heart that might have felt pity for the boy he'd once been, who grew up without much in the way of love or affection. At times, she might have tried to find *reasons why,* and she might have found a degree of understanding, if she really dug deep for it.

But now she knew.

There was no red mist, no 'heat of the moment' where Will lost control and was remorseful about his actions afterwards, at least for a while. There was no lack of insight into his own behaviour; he was fully aware of his actions, at all times.

His own son had called him out, and even that hadn't been enough to stop him.

In fact, he'd already thought up a believable lie to peddle to a child.

"One day," she said, "I'll talk to you about that. But, for now, I need you to know that you're *never* allowed to do what Daddy did," she said, and her tone was deadly serious. "You're *never* to hurt another person for any reason, other than self-defence. Do you understand, Jamie?"

She would not allow the cycle to continue.

She would not.

"I understand," Jamie said. "But you don't need to worry. Daddy said he'd show me some moves when I get bigger."

Kate reached down to smooth the wet hair back from his forehead, then tipped his chin up so she could look at him.

"You decide your own moves, sweetheart, and I'll help you find them. How about that?"

Jamie gave her a smile, and it was so beautiful she could have cried.

"Okay, Mummy. If I need to know any moves, I'll ask you."

"That's a deal."

Kate put Jamie to bed and found her grandfather in the living room, sitting in his favourite chair reading a novel, a cup of something hot sitting on a side table within reaching distance of a small plate of biscuits he'd placed beside it.

She was about to turn around and leave him to his book, when he let out a booming laugh.

"What're you reading?" she asked, tucking her feet up onto the sofa nearby.

"Jeeves and Wooster," he said, setting the book aside to take a swig of his tea. "Can't beat it."

She'd only ever seen the television production, but had always meant to read the stories.

"How was your first day back on the horse?" he asked.

He removed his glasses and slid them into the top pocket of his shirt, before folding his fingers across his paunch.

"It was..." She thought back, and an image of Nick sprang into her mind.

She shoved it away, firmly.

"It was good to see so many old faces again," she said. "Lucy and Joanne were kind, as always. In many ways, it felt as though I'd never been away."

"The Hicks family always had a soft spot for you," her grandfather agreed. "But then, Jo and your ma were tighter'n two peas in a pod, when they were growin' up. Might as well've been her sister she lost, that day."

They were both silent for a minute, but it was not an unhappy silence.

"I was surprised to see Bill," she said.

Ben let out a gusty sigh and tutted. "Aye, it's a pity," he said, reaching out an idle hand to snaffle a biscuit, offering one to his granddaughter. "Used to be a handsome lad, I seem to recall. Knew his parents, before they passed, and they were of good stock."

That was high praise, coming from Ben Carew.

"I wonder what went wrong?"

"There's some that just can't take the drink," he replied, swiping a hand through the air to punctuate his point. "It's a hard job, because Bill inherited the inn and he's always loved it, but, in many ways, he'd've done better to sell up and do somethin' else, where temptation wouldn't be in his path every blessed day."

Ben brushed the crumbs from his shirt, then folded his hands again.

"Joanne's a good woman for standin' by him, all these years," he continued. "Lord knows, it can't've been easy, and there was Lucy to think of."

"He wasn't ever—?" Her mind, naturally, assumed the worst.

"Not as I know of," her grandfather said, quickly. "Bill doesn't have a violent bone in his body, but he's got a self-destruct button as big as your 'ead, that's his problem."

"Joanne must really love him," Kate murmured.

Ben made a low sound in his throat.

"I remember the four of 'em—Bill and Jo, Rob and Alice—when they were your age, long before you came along," he said, nostalgically. "Your grandma was still alive then, o' course. They used to be thick as thieves."

Kate grinned at the turn of phrase, then thought of how unpredictable life could be. Which of them could have guessed that their number would be halved, and, of the two that remained, one of them was be only a shadow of his former self?

"I saw that you kept the boat," she said gently. "Why'd you keep it, Grandad?"

Ben took so long to answer, she wasn't sure he was going to. Finally, he gave a shake of his head, and looked her dead in the eye.

"I don't know, love. Somethin's always stopped me, for one thing, and, for another…"

He looked out of the window, seeing into the past.

"Feels like unfinished business," he said. "Never did sit right with me, the verdict of the inquest."

Kate's eyes widened. "*What*—?"

His old eyes were clear and uncompromising.

"I know boats, Katie," he told her. "I know *The Lady*, just like I knew her back then, when she was fresh out o' the yard. I went over every inch of her myself, before your dad bought her for your mum. There was nought wrong with 'er."

"It's been almost fifteen years," Kate said. "The police investigated everything, back then, and it was nobody's fault, Grandad. Nobody was to blame."

Her heart implored him to let sleeping dogs lie. "Maybe," he said, thoughtfully. "But, tell me how they never found the source o' the leak, Kate. They said there must've been one, for the carbon monoxide to find its way inside their locked cabin, but where was it?"

He'd gone over that boat with a fine-toothed comb, and he still hadn't found it.

"There isn't any other explanation," Kate argued, a bit desperately.

"Aye, and I know what folk'll say, and what they'll think, if I raise it all over again," Ben muttered. "They'll say, 'Ben Carew is nought but a doddery old fool who can't get over his family tragedy', that's what they'll say."

Loss was always hard to accept, Kate thought, and some people found themselves caught in the 'denial' phase of the grief cycle, perpetually unable to accept the truth. That being said, her grandfather was clear-headed in all other ways, so there was no reason to think he'd allow himself to follow a wild goose chase, if he didn't harbour a genuine suspicion that all was not what it seemed.

They sat there watching the last vestiges of day shift into night through the long glass windows overlooking Frenchman's Creek, and then the full import of her grandfather's worry hit Kate like a sledgehammer.

"If you're right, then, that means…it means…" she said, unable to finish the sentence.

Ben drained the last of his tea. "Aye," he said, heavily. "It only leaves one thing."

"You're saying it was no accident," Kate whispered. "You think they were murdered?"

Ben rose from his chair and switched off the side light, so his face was cast in shadow.

"I'm not saying they were and I'm not saying they weren't," he said. "But I've asked myself the same question for ten long years: who'd do such a thing, and *why?*"

It was a question they may never find an answer to.

CHAPTER 14

Bill Hicks longed for oblivion.

By rights, the drink should have taken him long before now, but it seemed the gods were laughing at him, keeping his body alive all these years long after his mind had already checked out, retreating somewhere deep inside where nobody could reach him. Occasionally, what he liked to think of as 'Old Bill' resurfaced, long enough to smile at a joke from a friend or to enjoy the play of light on water, before he sank again into the depths of despair, silently reliving all the mistakes and wrong turns he'd made to lead him to where he was now.

Old, and washed up.

He stopped as he reached the field gate that would lead him down into the trees, leaning heavily on the old wood until he could trust his legs to support him again.

He needed a drink.

Acid rolled in his stomach, and he felt the urge to vomit but, for once, it wasn't the booze to blame. He was on a mission, one he must complete before daybreak, but he was frightened—more frightened than he'd ever been.

He must do what he'd set out to do.

Pushing himself away from the comforting girth of the ancient oak, he continued down a dusty, pot-holed incline leading into the shadows of the forest, where the river path would take him on a winding route towards the cove where Ben and his family lived. Illuminated only by the pearly grey light of the moon, his feet tripped over the dirt and gravel and a journey that would have needed careful footwork from a sober individual became treacherous to a man like him, who struggled to remain upright and not fall prey to gravity.

"Jus' a bit further," he mumbled to himself. "Got to—to keep my nerve."

Seeing Kate Ryce had been the catalyst. When she'd been gone, it had been easy to pretend nothing had happened. He kept himself to himself and the liquor did a good job of suppressing his senses, so he could get by, most days.

So he could live with the guilt.

But, earlier, when he'd seen the girl standing there as a grown woman, he swore it might have been Alice's ghost staring back at him with those dark eyes and gleaming red hair. Hers had been an unforgettable face, and it was imprinted upon his memory for all time. To have her daughter look so much like her seemed like a message of some kind—perhaps, even, from the God he didn't really believe in.

He must atone.

Funny how people always became believers in the end.

There was no sound on the river path, aside from Bill's own feet trampling the undergrowth and the distant cry of a night-jar circling overhead. The route was slow going, and he lost his footing several times in the darkness, once so badly he twisted his ankle and cried out, his voice reverberating around the trees and sending a cacophony of birds flapping up into the inky sky.

He thought about turning back, about slinking home so that nobody would be any the wiser, but he didn't relish the prospect of making the return journey uphill on a weakened ankle and he was only five or ten minutes away from Carew Cove.

He could make it.

Mustering strength he barely knew he possessed, Bill heaved himself upward and put one careful foot in front of the other, bearing down against the pain that sang through his ankle and up his leg. He began to hum a tune in time to the beat of his slow footsteps, a military chant to keep himself going, metre by painstaking metre.

He would get there.

It didn't matter if it took him all night.

His laboured breathing was loud in the quiet forest, and served to drown out any other noise. He heard no animals scuttling in the brush, nor the gentle *swish* of the creek below, only the snap of branches buckling beneath his weight and the trail of leaves and sapling wood against his skin as he pushed through the pain.

He didn't hear the soft tread of another who followed him.

The figure kept a safe distance, at first, moving like a spectre through the darkness, watching his clumsy progress, almost laughing out loud when he turned his ankle.

Drunken fool.

They moved with extreme care, waiting patiently for a narrow stretch of pathway to appear, which curved high above a tiny cove in which the remains of an old boat lay buried.

The perfect place for an accident.

Up ahead, Bill stopped again to catch his breath, feeling light-headed now from exhaustion and alcohol withdrawal. His fingers shook and he clutched the bark of a tree, and his head swam as he realised how close he stood to the edge of the verge leading down to the little cove where he'd played as a boy, many years before.

For a moment, he fancied he heard the echo of his own joyful laughter as he and Joanne, Alice and Rob had splashed about in the shallows.

Tears leaked from his eyes, and he rubbed a weary hand over his face, preparing to push away from the tree and complete his final journey.

He never made it that far.

"Bill."

He turned too quickly, almost losing his balance, and, before he could right himself, there came a single, hard shove against the wall of his chest that stole the breath from his body.

Suddenly, he was falling, eyes wide, mouth gaping, while his fingers clutched at nothing but air.

Moments later, there came the sickening *crunch* of his body meeting the rock and shingle below and, while the breath rasped in and out of his punctured lungs, the last thing Bill saw was a familiar face looming above him, resolute and resigned.

Then, a cloud passed over the moon, and there was nothing but endless night.

CHAPTER 15

"I realise this may not be the news you were hoping for."

Will Irving gave himself time before speaking, to be sure he remained in control of the rage that pumped through his body.

"What's his name?" he asked, when he could trust his own voice.

"Nicholas Pascoe," Charlton replied, reaching for the notepad where he'd scrawled extensive notes about the man. "Aged thirty-four, resident of the area his whole life, aside from a spell at the Royal Academy of Music between the ages of eighteen and twenty-one and a couple of years spent in London, afterwards, presumably learning his trade."

He paused, unsure how much his client would want to know.

"Go on," Irving rasped. "What else? What does this musical prodigy do, nowadays, aside from busk on the waterways?"

Charlton pulled a face. "Ah, *well*, I'm sorry to tell you that Nick Pascoe is something of a star on the music scene," he told him, a bit nervously. "He's an award-winning songwriter; he writes for all the big artists." He rattled off some names. "They call him 'Rainmaker' because he has a knack of writing just the right song to launch a new artist's career. There was a write-up about him in *Rolling Stone*."

Will's head began to throb, demanding that he hit something…*break* something.

"I've never heard of him," he spat.

"He keeps an extremely low profile," Charlton said. "He could probably have been a very successful musician himself, but he seems to prefer being the one behind the scenes."

Irving couldn't imagine it.

"He has money, then." He stated the obvious. "What kind of ballpark are we talking about? I need to know what level of clout this man has."

Charlton wasn't surprised at all by Irving's assumption that money equated to power; it was how he lived his life. He took a moment to do a quick calculation in his head from the information he'd been able to find, which included royalty shares and named credits on some of the biggest hits of the past five years.

"Probably somewhere in the multi-millions," he admitted. "Not that you'd know it, from the look of him—although, he has a nice yacht on the estuary, and I checked out his house, earlier today. I'd say it must be worth a few million, alone."

Irving demanded the address, and immediately did a quick search on his desktop computer, so he could picture the nest where this man and *his* wife had evidently made a mockery of him.

The house turned out to be in an unusual setting, from its position on the map.

"Accessible mostly by water," Charlton agreed. "The surrounding woodland it is so thick, there's no road—just a footpath. The house has been built on its own peninsula, a short boat ride from Helford village—"

"So, her friend has means," Irving snapped. "I suppose Kate must be congratulated for being able to pick 'em."

Charlton said nothing, but might have remarked that, when his wife met him, Will Irving hadn't been quite so well heeled, and he happened to know she'd stumped up most of the money for a down payment on their first house, neither of which were the actions of an avaricious personality.

"I want his picture, and any more details you can find," Irving continued. "I'd like to see for myself where my doting wife has been spending her nights."

"Ah, well, I don't actually have any reason to believe—"

"She's a treacherous *bitch!*" Irving roared. "If you haven't managed to catch her, it's because she's given you the slip, but I know her...I know her better than anyone."

He spoke the last words almost to himself, like a prayer.

"What about the grandfather?" he asked.

"Ben Carew still operates his ferryboat business between Helford village and Helford Passage, although nowadays he has a young man by the name of 'Danny' who helps him," Charlton said. "Over the years, he's accumulated land around his cottage at Carew Cove—"

"He has his own *cove?*"

"Well," Charlton laughed, "that's not its formal name, but the folk in this area have taken to calling it that, given how long the family have occupied that particular spot, right on Frenchman's Creek."

"Like parasites," Irving said. "Just like his granddaughter. He's hoovered up the land around *his* cove. So, what?"

"In days gone by, it can't have been worth very much, but now, there's a huge premium on land on the waterside and he's probably sitting on a gold mine."

"Which will all go to Kate, eventually," Irving said, thoughtfully.

All that I have, I give to thee...

"How's the old man's health?"

Charlton told himself not to second guess the questions he was asked by his clients.

"Strong as an ox, by the looks of him," he replied. "No obvious ailments, which isn't bad for a man of eighty-one."

He'd probably be one of the old duffers they'd have to put down, eventually, Irving thought—just like his mother, who refused to die in the nursing home where he'd deposited her several years ago.

He asked a few more pertinent questions about his wife, demanding a blow-by-blow account of her movements.

"She's got herself a little job, now," he sneered. "Which means she must have decided to stay put, at least for now. I'm surprised she needs to work, given what you've told me about the new man in her life."

Charlton had seen a young, attractive woman with an air of fragility that was only just discernible, but a tough backbone. He'd seen her work tirelessly, with a smile that never faltered, and knew that Will Irving could never understand that he'd married a woman who was more than just flesh and bone; more than a pretty plaything to add to his collection, or a doll he could try to break. Some people enjoyed hard graft, and the dignity it brought.

He wasn't one of them, of course, but he understood the type.

"When did she meet him—this, *Nick Pascoe?*"

"It seems they've been friends since childhood," Charlton replied, and listed a couple of other names from the circle of friends she'd known in her former life. "I haven't been able to ascertain whether they've been in regular contact prior to her arrival in Helford, sir, but I can continue to look into that, if you'd like."

Irving thought of his wife—his *property*—being in the hands of another man, and a muscle began to tick in his jaw. He calculated how quickly he could travel to Cornwall, factoring in the various appearances and work commitments he had lined up.

"How would you like me to proceed?" Charlton asked him.

"Stay where you are," Irving told him. "Keep a close eye on her, and let me know if anything changes."

"Yes, sir. I should tell you, my expenses—"

"Will be covered."

Charlton smiled like a cat. "It'll be my pleasure, Mr Irving."

CHAPTER 16

The following day dawned brightly, without a cloud in the sky.

Nick watched the sun rise from his terrace overlooking the water, one hand nursing a cup of decent Italian coffee while the other hand patted the furry head of a golden retriever by the name of 'Madge', whom he happened to be dog-sitting that weekend.

"Not a bad view, is it, Blondie?"

The dog gave him a look of haughty disapproval, unaccustomed as she was to being objectified just because her fur happened to be a rather lovely shade of caramel blonde.

"Merely a figure of speech," he tagged on, holding both palms out in open apology.

Forgiven, at least for the present, the dog ambled back through the patio doors and, to his amazement and delight, came back a moment later with a lead clutched in her jaw.

He could have sworn he put that in a drawer.

"Where did you find this?" he muttered, reaching down to pick up the lead.

The dog waited, even lifting her chin to facilitate access to her collar.

Nick gave a little shake of his head.

"I get the feeling you're trying to tell me something," he joked, and knocked back the rest of his coffee in three big gulps. "All right—you win. Let's go for a W-A-L-K."

This time, he was sure the dog rolled her big brown eyes, as if to say, "I can spell."

"Where shall we go this time?"

Nick had enjoyed the pleasure of Madge's company on several occasions, mostly when her owners sought his help looking after her while they took a well-deserved break somewhere exotic. Luke and Gabrielle were good friends of his, the former being the owner of a string of high-end art galleries in the South-West and in London, amongst various other things, while his wife was a respected local bookseller who'd turned Carnance Books from a cosy affair into something of an institution, with people travelling for miles around to visit or to attend one of the many literary events she hosted. Madge was their beloved pooch, not dissimilar in temperament to 'Nana' from the Peter Pan stories, and it was a mark of their friendship that Nick was entrusted to look after her.

"C'mon then," he said, clipping on the dog's lead. "Let's go exploring."

The man and his borrowed dog hopped into the little motorboat Nick kept for short journeys, and he grinned at the sight of Madge's upturned face as she relished the feel of the wind through her fur, tongue lolling with pleasure at the sheer delight of skipping across the crystal-clear water.

He found a quiet spot on the outskirts of Helford, tethered the boat on a friend's jetty for ease, and then led Madge along a narrow footpath that connected with the river route running from the village towards Frenchman's Creek.

When they joined the main footpath and it became clear which way they were headed, the dog treated him to a meaningful glance, apparently being possessed of a sixth sense which allowed her to know the true reason for his choice of walking route.

"I know," he muttered. "But I *did* promise Ben that I'd stop by, from time to time, so I've got a perfectly legitimate reason to be here."

The dog made a sound like a raspberry.

"All right," he exclaimed, throwing his hands up. "I want to see her, okay? I admit it."

Now, he was sure the dog smiled.

"There's no need to look so bloody smug," he said, sticking his hands in the pockets of his shorts. "I'm just 'good old reliable Nick, the perennial friend'—and masochist, it seems."

Madge ignored him and scampered off ahead, following her nose.

"See?" he said to the trees. "Might as well be talking to myself, for all these women listen."

Maybe you haven't found the right one, yet.

Kate's words replayed in his mind, and his chest lifted and fell in one agitated motion.

"Maybe I'm a glutton for punishment who should be in his studio working, not wasting half the morning chasing a girl I used to know," he mumbled to himself.

Just then, there came a couple of loud barks from the dog, who had never once emitted a bark in all the time he'd known her.

He began to run.

For once, Kate slept remarkably well.

After years of disturbance and, more recently, being plagued by nightmares and memories best forgotten, she wakened without any shortness of breath or palpitations in her chest; only a sense of having been well rested and, more than that, having a renewed joy at simply being alive.

Her mood lasted throughout breakfast, where she chatted happily with her son and grandfather, before he took Jamie off to see the seals at a nearby sanctuary in the village of Gweek. Ben indulged Jamie with infinite patience and, though she queried whether it was becoming too much for him—after all, Jamie was a bundle of restless energy—Ben waved away her concerns and told her to spend some time 'getting to know herself again' while he bonded with his only great-grandson.

So, she had.

Before she was due to begin her next shift at The Ship's Mate, Kate tidied and cleaned, laundered and ironed and, when there was no more drudgery to be done, decided to take her grandfather's advice and head off into the village early to enjoy the sunshine.

Her fingers itched to take a sketchbook so she could spend some time capturing the early-morning waterways, but she didn't own one.

Not anymore.

Instead, Kate took plenty of photographs as she wandered through the glades, once again choosing to follow the longer route along Frenchman's Creek towards Helford. She smiled as the trees enfolded her, every now and then stopping to close her eyes, allowing the dappled light of the sun to caress her skin while the stillness of the forest permeated her mind. It was a novelty to be able to trust another person again, and she was overcome by the luxury of freedom, however brief.

Locals said that the trees had power and she'd laughed it off as absurd superstition. But perhaps they were right, after all. There was something about the power of sunlight and sleep, of fresh air and the earthy scent of life renewing that was powerfully cleansing to a bruised soul. Whether you wanted to call it 'magic', 'power' or happenstance, she didn't much care. All she knew for certain was that she was profoundly grateful for it.

Kate walked happily for several minutes until she reached the usual stretch of pathway spanning the cove and its shipwrecked vessel, and she looked down into the chasm as she passed by. The first thing she noticed was that the tide was out, leaving the boat's carcass bare to the morning sunshine. The second thing she noticed was what, at first glance, appeared to be a jumble of old clothing.

Frowning, her footsteps slowed, and she moved closer to the edge of the pathway to peer down.

Terrible, that anybody should want to fly-tip, she thought…

Then, she saw clearly.

It was not old clothing, nor any other detritus washed up from the river.

It was a body.

CHAPTER 17

Kate's first thought was to try to help whichever poor soul had taken a fall down the bank.

"Hello!" she called out. "Hello! Can you hear me?"

From her position, it was impossible to see a face, or even to tell if the person was still conscious, but she hurried towards an opening in the undergrowth that had been used for years as a cut down the steep bank, giving access to the cove below. It must have rained lightly the previous evening, she thought, or perhaps it was the remainder of the morning dew, but the ground was slippery underfoot and she threw out a hand to grasp low-hanging branches to steady herself as she made her way carefully towards the bottom.

When her feet hit the soggy mud-flat, it was a struggle to remain upright, and she stuck to the edges where the ground comprised of a thin line of shingle beach, gripping the edge of the mossy bank for balance. She kept up a stream of friendly, inane chatter for the benefit of the man—for, she could see it was a man lying with his back to her, a little further away—in case he was injured but could still hear.

"Sorry it took so long to get down here," she said, a little out of breath by the time she drew near. "Are you—*you*—"

She let out a strangled gasp.

In the seconds it took her to survey the full scene, she saw that the man was Bill Hicks, and he was beyond any kind of help—that much was obvious. Up close, his body was horribly twisted; his right leg swept over the left, which was broken badly and lay at an uncomfortable right-angle to the rest of his spine. His skin was a deathly shade of grey that was almost translucent, and his blood had succumbed to gravity, pooling on the underside of his body. His eyes, wide and staring, were covered with a film of white, and had already fallen prey to the birds.

There was a long, open gash on the underside of his skull, which lay against the jagged edge of a rock that was stained dark red.

Kate heard the buzz of flies, or it might have been the sound of her own blood rushing in her ears, and began stumbling backwards, needing to put distance between herself and the shell of what had once been a person. She bore down against rising nausea, breathing hard through her teeth as she tasted bile and black dots began swimming in front of her eyes.

"Help," she whispered, and tried to put one leg in front of the other. "Oh, God. *Help!*"

Just then, a dog's bark broke through the haze, and she lifted desperate eyes to seek out the source.

"Here!" she called out. "Down here!"

Nick thought he heard a woman's voice—Kate's voice—carrying on the wind, and picked up his pace, running full pelt through the trees until he was reunited with the dog, who stood to attention and continued to bark urgently.

"What is it, girl?" he asked. "What—?"

"*Help!*"

"Kate," he whispered.

Much later, he would recall the sensation of his stomach falling and his heart slamming against the wall of his chest, as he'd imagined the worst.

As it was, the 'worst' might not have been what he'd imagined, but it was bad enough.

"Kate! Stay there, I'm on my way!"

He began picking his way down to the cove the same way she had done, minutes before, and told the dog to stay put. Madge might not have liked it, but her arse hit the floor, and he made a mental note to shower the animal with treats for stellar obedience, later.

"Beat that, Lassie," he muttered to himself, as he half-slid down the bank. "Kate! Are you hurt?"

"No—no, it's not me—"

Suddenly, she was there, bedraggled and pale but unharmed, and Nick forgot himself; he forgot what might have been right or wrong, and all the reasons why he should keep his distance. He did what felt most natural, what they both needed, and threw his arms around her to hold her shaken body against him, never so glad to see her alive and well.

Kate froze, expecting to feel repelled, but she felt only relief and a deep sense of homecoming. Her body unfurled itself, relaxing against him, and she allowed herself to be comforted.

"I thought you were hurt," he muttered, somewhere above her head. "I heard the dog barking and I panicked. It's a steep bank, here, and I thought you'd fallen—"

"Not me," she said, brokenly, her voice muffled against him. "Bill. He must've fallen sometime last night."

Nick lifted his head from where it had been happily resting on top of hers, and looked down into her frightened face, then across to where the man's body lay.

"Oh, God," he said, pulling away. "Is he injured?"

"He's dead," she said, in an odd, faraway sort of voice. "He's gone, Nick."

He looked again at the body and, this time, he saw the true damage. To his embarrassment, he felt his stomach react, and looked away swiftly, working hard to remain in control of his body which desperately sought to reject what his mind had seen.

"We...have to..."

Kate sounded light-headed, he thought, and, when he grasped her shoulders in his hands, he saw that her pupils were hugely dilated.

Shock, he realised. *She's going into shock.*

"Hey," he said, curving a supportive arm around her waist. "Stay with me, now, Kate. Look this way, that's right."

"Can't breathe," she whispered, barely audibly. "Nick, I can't—can't—"

Without a word, he swung her up into his arms and strode quickly towards the other end of the cove, remaining upright by sheer force of will. He laid her down gently on a patch of shingle beach, supporting her head with one strong hand while the other elevated her feet to improve blood flow.

"Breathe in through your nose, slowly," he told her, and counted the breath with her. "Then, out through your mouth…one…two…three…that's right. Same again."

He waited until her colour had improved, then set her legs down, remaining beside her as she came back around.

"Sorry," was the first thing she said. "I feel so weak—"

"Stop apologising for everything," he suggested. "Anyone would have had a shock, finding Bill like that. In fact, I almost took a funny turn, myself."

"You're already funny," she pointed out.

"True," he said, and flashed a grin so that his eyes twinkled aquamarine against his tanned face. "Feeling better now?"

She nodded, but carried on looking at him, a fact he put down to her still not feeling one hundred per cent.

"We should call the police," he told her. "It seems you were the first one to discover Bill's body, and Joanne must be worried sick."

They both thought of how much worse it was going to get for the woman they both loved like a favourite aunt, and then of their friend Lucy, who'd lost her father that day and didn't yet know about it.

Though, perhaps she'd already lost him, long ago.

Nick began to reach for his mobile phone, but, of course, there was no reception to be had.

"We'll have to call from Frenchman's Cottage," he said. "Is Jamie at home? I wouldn't want him to overhear anything he shouldn't, and be upset about it."

Later, Kate would count that as one of the moments she realised she loved Nick Pascoe, for, even in the depths of shock and confusion, he thought of her young son and his welfare.

Mutely, she shook her head, blinking away sudden tears.

"Come on," he said, misreading her tears as a product of nervous exhaustion. "Let's get you back home."

They rose to their feet and, with a final glance towards the man they'd both played with as a child and looked up to in their youth, began to climb the bank, at the summit of which a dog awaited them with a motherly look in her eye.

CHAPTER 18

"I can't be the one to report this."

Nick paused in the act of picking up Ben's telephone and looked across to where Kate sat perched on the extreme edge of the sofa, with the dog lying across her feet protectively.

"What do you mean?"

She reached down to stroke the dog.

"I—I didn't want to have to tell you this just yet," she began, and wished fervently for water to ease her mouth, which had run bone dry. "I *would* have told you, but not like this..."

"Told me what?"

Kate looked at him and tried to remember the boy she'd once known, but could see only the man—strong, capable, and probably unable to understand why others couldn't be the same. Her stomach quivered at the thought of losing his friendship a second time, so soon after it had been rekindled, but she'd grown used to managing on her own and trusting very few people, so she would survive whatever fall-out might ensue.

She had to survive.

"You've probably guessed that my marriage has failed," she said simply, and nodded when he chose not to deny it. "I'm planning to begin divorce proceedings because my husband has been domestically abusive, in some form or another, almost from the very beginning."

She didn't look up from her therapeutic ruffling of the dog's hair, and so she missed the quick flash of sympathy that crossed his face. By the time she risked a glance, she caught only the residual anger he felt towards a man he'd never met and misunderstood its cause; Kate assumed he was frustrated by her weakness—as she was with herself—and ducked her head, almost too ashamed to continue.

"Jamie and I came here for sanctuary, because it's the one place Will has never been," she said softly. "He knows I have a grandfather, but they've never met and Cornwall's a long way away for him to come looking for us, on the off chance it's where I'd choose to run to."

She lifted a hand, then let it fall away in resignation.

"I know he'll find us, one day, because it's in his nature to…to *hunt*," she said, bleakly. "But we're safe here, for now, and I'm not ready for him to know where we are, Nick. I need time to protect Jamie and to get a legal team in place. If I make the report, it'll get back to Will, especially if it makes the news."

Nick wanted to talk to her properly, to treat what she'd confided in him with the attention it deserved, but there was a man lying dead out there, and the tide would be coming in within the next two hours.

There was little time for sentiment.

"I'm so sorry to hear that, Kate, truly I am," he said, with quiet sincerity. "But we don't really have a choice. You were the first to find the body—"

She nodded, then raised shaking fingers to her brow, which she began to knead.

"I—yes, you're right. I know you're right," she whispered. "But, Nick, on the walk back here, I was thinking… what if Will is down here *already*? What if he came across Bill and mistook him for my grandfather? You don't understand how low he will stoop to hurt me, Nick, because it isn't who you are.

It wouldn't occur to you to think of these things, but I *have* to think of them because it's been my life for almost fifteen years. I've been conditioned to think of all the possibilities, of what I stand to lose, and I know it's possible that Will could have pushed someone…"

Her voice had risen, and with it came a rising sense of panic which the dog obviously heard too, for Madge's head raised and she glanced across at Nick with a questioning look in her eye.

"Hey," he said, moving across to take Kate's hands in his own while he patted the dog's head to reassure her that all would be well. "Listen to me: Bill *fell*—it's obvious that he did, Kate. There isn't any reason to think it was more than that."

He sighed, thinking of the man who'd poured him his first pint.

"Bill was…well, he had issues with alcohol," he said. "He'd suffered with it for years, and we've all been as understanding as we can be but, the fact is, this wouldn't be the first time he'd wandered off in the middle of the night, half-cut. It's dangerous ground, even without ten pints of cider and a bottle of whiskey to help you along."

Kate looked away, her mind still racing.

"Sometimes, you have to stay and fight," he said, and watched her head whip back around. "You could speak to the police about what happened with your husband, and explain why you'd like your name kept out of it—"

She laughed—not at him, but at the idea of the police understanding her situation. She'd been burned before and told him as much.

"They're not all like that," he persisted. "I happen to know the local bobby, and she's decent."

Kate searched his face, and wondered if there was some history there.

Not that she was interested, of course.

"We can't delay any longer," he added, with an eye for the time. "We got back here as quickly as we could, but let's not push it."

"Okay," she said, gripping her hands tightly together. "Make the call, Nick."

He nodded, and, as the number for the local police station began to ring, he looked back across to the woman, thought of her child, too, and hoped he'd done the right thing.

They heard the squad car arrive twenty minutes later.

"It'll be all right," Nick told Kate. "Just tell them what happened, that's all you need to do."

She'd tried that once before, Kate thought, *and had been branded a liar.*

She heard him opening the front door, and then an attractive, dark-haired woman of around her own age entered the living room with a younger man in his mid-twenties. Whilst she was in civvies, consisting of well-fitting jeans, boots and a linen shirt, her partner was in police uniform—but the authority was all with the former.

"Mrs Irving? I'm Detective Sergeant Sophie Keane," she said, holding out her hand, which Kate briefly shook. "This is my colleague, Police Constable Alex Turner."

"Please, call me Kate," she said, and invited them both to sit down.

"Thank you," Sophie said, and made an idle note of the way Nick settled himself beside her on the sofa, a little closer than would have been usual between friends. "Before we get started, I want to reassure you that the scene is now in hand, and I've dispatched a team of forensics and police staff to make sure Mr Hicks' body is properly taken care of, with all the dignity it deserves."

"Thank you," Nick told her. "It's awful to think of him lying out there, in the elements."

Sophie nodded, but she was watching the woman by his side, who appeared excessively nervous. Then again, it wasn't every day that you discovered a dead body, and perhaps she'd grown too cynical after having seen so many herself.

"I understand you were the first to find Mr Hicks' body. Would you mind talking us through what happened, please?"

Kate nodded.

"Yes..." She tried to think clearly. "I left the house here at about quarter past nine. We're early risers, so I'd been up and about before then doing odd jobs around the house. I thought I'd take a walk into the village before work—"

"Where do you work?"

"At The Ship's Mate," she said. "I started yesterday."

If Sophie was surprised to learn that she happened to work for the dead man, her face betrayed nothing of it.

"All right," she said. "What time were you due to start work?"

"Um, the shift was due to start...around now, actually," Kate muttered, eyeing the time and thinking of Joanne. "At eleven. We work odd shifts, so the place is always staffed."

Sophie nodded.

"Have you—has anybody told Joanne yet?" Kate worried. "She must already be wondering what's happened to Bill, and then, when I don't turn up for work…"

"You don't need to worry. I'll be paying Mrs Hicks a visit as soon as we've finished here."

Kate's heart broke for her, all over again.

"You were telling me that you'd decided to take a walk into the village," Sophie said, bringing the conversation back around to the facts. "Can I ask why you decided to take the river path, rather than the road? It's much quicker, that way."

Kate told herself these were all reasonable questions; it didn't mean they doubted her.

"I prefer the river route," she said. "I love the trees and it reminds me of when I was younger."

"I understand you're staying with your grandfather, Ben Carew," Sophie said. "I take it, you're referring to visits you made when you were a child?"

Kate nodded, and thought she heard a note of surprise in the other woman's voice.

"Yes, we came every summer."

"That's how we know one another," Nick put in, for the sake of completeness.

Sophie nodded, and made a note.

"All right, so you left here at around quarter past nine," she said. "Did you see anyone on your journey?"

Kate shook her head.

"Nobody—that is, until Nick came along."

"All right. How did you come across Mr Hicks' body?"

Kate tried hard not to think of the man's dead, staring eyes, and clasped her fingers together. As if he'd read the turmoil in her mind, Nick placed a warm hand over hers, and gave her fingers a squeeze.

Sophie noted that, too.

"Um, well, I'd walked as far as Pirate Bay," Kate said.

"Pirate Bay?" Sophie queried.

"Sorry," Kate muttered. "I mean the little cove with the shipwreck, down on the creek. When I was growing up, I called it Pirate Bay."

"I see. What time did you arrive at…ah, Pirate Bay?"

Kate hadn't checked the time, so she had to give her best guess.

"I suppose I'd been walking for twenty or twenty-five minutes at a normal pace," she said. "Although I stopped here and there, so perhaps it might have been half an hour, all told."

"So, if we estimate that you reached the cove at around nine-forty-five, that would be realistic?"

Kate nodded.

"All right. How did you happen to see Mr Hicks from the top of the pathway?"

"I think, purely by chance," Kate said honestly. "I always look down as I pass by and, this time, I spotted what I thought was a jumble of clothes or rubbish. I'm sorry, that sounds terrible—"

Sophie shook her head.

"Not at all. What made you question your first assumption?"

Kate swallowed, thinking back to that first flicker of understanding.

"It was a combination of things," she said. "People don't tend to dump their rubbish around here, for starters, so I thought that was highly unusual. Then, when I looked again, the shape and size seemed... well, *human*."

Sophie looked up from her pad and fixed Kate with a stare.

"Why didn't you report it, then?"

Kate was taken aback.

"I thought somebody had fallen," she explained. "I didn't think they were—that they'd be *dead*—I thought they might be in need of help."

"What did you do, then?"

"I called out, I think, asking if they needed any help, but there was no response, so I made my way down there, to check."

Sophie thought of the trace evidence that could have been trampled, and sighed inwardly. It wouldn't be the first time, nor the last, and people always had the best of intentions.

Or, rather, *most* people did.

"Did you see anyone else down there, aside from Mr Hicks?"

Kate shook her head, feeling suddenly cold.

"No, there was nobody but…but Bill and me."

She thought of the sense of loneliness and isolation she'd experienced, the shocking reminder of her own mortality as she'd been faced with the loss of another's, and felt nausea rise up once again.

"I was only down there for a minute or two before I heard the bark," she said.

"The bark? Oh—" Sophie spied a regal-looking Labrador retriever sitting quietly across the room. "Is that your dog, Mrs Irving?"

"I'm looking after her," Nick explained, and rattled off his friend's details. "I was out walking Madge when we came across Kate, down by the cove."

"I'll come onto that," Sophie said. "What brought you so far from home? Your house is on the other side of the village."

While Kate was left to speculate on how this attractive female detective happened to know where Nick lived, the man himself was momentarily lost for words because, of course, Sophie was right. He'd travelled away from home to be near Kate, perhaps even hoping he could have walked with her to work.

"I like the walk along Frenchman's Creek," he said, a bit defensively.

"That makes two of you," Sophie remarked.

"And many other tourists, every year," he shot back, and she inclined her head to acknowledge the point.

"So, you found your paths crossed," she continued, while her silent colleague made scrupulous notes. "Around what time, would you say?"

She looked between the pair of them.

"It must've been just before ten," Nick said. "I didn't check the time, but that'd be my guess."

Kate nodded.

"I heard Madge barking and, a couple of minutes later, Nick came down to see what had happened."

Another one trampling the scene, Sophie thought.

Nick explained what he found, when he arrived at the cove, then described their movements up until that point, whereupon he paused meaningfully to allow Kate to step in and discuss what was, to him, one of the most important elements of their exchange.

Her safety.

"Detective, there's something else I need to tell you," she began, and her voice shook with repressed emotion. "I need to make a separate report, at a time that's convenient to you, regarding my husband, Will Irving."

Sophie Keane raised a single eyebrow, thinking of a man she'd often enjoyed watching on the small screen, and wondered what his wife could possibly have to discuss.

"Of course," she said, falling back on procedure and process to mask her surprise. "We can do that as early as tomorrow morning. Can I ask what relevance this may have to the current incident?"

"Hopefully, not much," Kate replied. "But I need to know that my name won't appear anywhere in the local press."

It took her a moment, then Sophie thought she understood.

"I'll do my best to ensure that doesn't happen," she said. "I can't make any promises, Kate. We have more leaks than a drippy tap, in these parts."

"It's important," Nick said quietly.

Sophie didn't reply directly, and turned back to Kate.

"Can I ask what your relationship was to the deceased?" she asked.

"I—Bill was like a second father, growing up," she said. "He and my dad were always good friends, just like Joanne and my mum."

"I understand your parents are deceased?"

Everyone remembered that particular tragedy, even Sophie, who'd been twenty at the time and just out of the academy.

"Yes," Kate said, dully. "They passed away fifteen years ago."

"My condolences," Sophie murmured. "So, you'd describe your relationship with Bill Hicks as… friendly?"

Nick frowned, not liking the turn the conversation seemed to be taking.

"Yes," Kate said, not quite understanding. "I hadn't seen him in years, of course, until I ran into him briefly yesterday."

"When was that, Mrs Irving?"

Kate wished she'd stop calling her that, and felt a headache begin to brew.

"It was yesterday afternoon, at the end of my shift," she said. "I ran into him—quite literally—and he mistook me for my mother, Alice. We exchanged a couple of words, then I came away."

"Did he seem out of sorts to you?"

"Ah—" Kate wondered how much to say of the late Bill Hicks' penchant for alcoholic beverages. "Well, he...I suppose I'd have to say he was drunk. He was swaying and slurring, and seemed unhappy about something."

"Did he say what that something was?"

Kate shook her head.

"And, until then, that was the first time you'd laid eyes on Bill Hicks for fifteen years?"

"Yes," Kate said. "Why do you ask?"

Sophie chose not to answer. "In which case, do either of you know why Bill Hicks would have been out walking in the direction of this cottage late into the night?"

"I have no idea," Kate said. "Unless he wanted to speak to me or my grandfather about something, I suppose. Even then, why wouldn't he just wait until he saw me on my shift, this morning? He could have taken me aside at any time."

"Does it matter?" Nick wondered. "Bill often went walkabout, so there might not have been any rhyme or reason as to why he picked that spot to fall down."

"You assume he fell?" Sophie said.

"Well, didn't he?" Kate said.

"Maybe," Sophie replied, but thought of the body she'd inspected less than half an hour ago, and had questions that needed answering. "Thank you both for your time—I may have some follow-up questions, so if you'd kindly remain in the area for the time being, I'd be grateful."

This last was directed particularly towards Kate.

"What happens now?" Nick asked, as they rose to their feet.

Sophie looked at the man she'd once shared a few good dinners with, and a couple of even better nights, then at the woman with the red hair.

"Process and procedure," she said simply. "I'll be in touch."

"What d'you make of 'er?"

DS Keane looked across at her constable inside the comparative privacy of their squad car, then back out of the windshield at the sweeping view of Carew Cove.

"Kate Irving—née Ryce—has been home less than a week and, suddenly, she's finding bodies," Sophie said. "Not just anyone, either, but Bill Hicks, a man she'd known since childhood and whose wife had only just employed her. Both Kate and Nick seem to think he fell, or that's what they want us to think, which could mean they didn't notice the tracks on the ground down at the cove and beside the vic's head."

There had been *three* sets of indistinct footprints in the mud, not just two. Given the tide timings, it was highly unlikely someone else had found Bill's body prior to Kate's discovery, that morning, and chosen not to call it in. That only left four possibilities, in Sophie's mind:

One, that Bill Hicks' death was no accident, and the third set of prints belong to his killer, then Kate and Nick that morning.

Two, Bill Hicks' killer was Kate, and her set of footprints was doubled up, after she returned to the scene that morning, with the third set belonging to Nick, who happened to interrupt her visit.

Three, Bill Hicks' killer was Nick, and his footprints were doubled up, after returning to the scene that morning. Kate's footprints provided the third set, and her discovery beat him to it, which must have been frustrating.

Four, Bill Hicks' killer was person or persons unknown, whose footprints have yet to be identified and may never be.

She laid all this this out, for PC Turner's benefit.

"Surely, it couldn't have been either Kate Irving or Nick Pascoe who made the first set of prints," her constable remarked.

"Why not?" Sophie wondered, and started the car's engine. "The prints were average size, which could mean a larger female footprint or a smaller male print. Either way, one or both of them could have been returning to the scene, rather than discovering it for the first time."

Turner nodded, picturing that.

"But why would she...or *he* want to do Hicks harm?"

Sophie shook her head. "I don't know, Alex, but these are the questions we need to ask ourselves, and more. For starters, I want to know why Hicks was on the pathway to Frenchman's Cottage in the early hours of the morning—because, if I'm any judge, he died somewhere around that time. Who was he on his way to meet?"

"How do you know he wasn't just wandering around, like Nick suggested?"

She gave a small, mirthless smile.

"Because, young Padawan, there was something interesting in the dead man's pocket that requires an explanation."

"What?"

She drew out a plastic evidence bag from a large box briefcase on the back seat, and handed it to him.

"What do you make of that?" she asked him.

PC Turner, who had high hopes of progressing to detective one day, took this as an opportunity to apply himself.

"It's an old newspaper clipping," he said, and Keane rolled her eyes.

"An astonishing deduction."

"Yeah, yeah," he muttered. "It's dated...*oh*."

"Yeah," she agreed, snatching back the clipping once he'd finished reading its contents. "Fifteen years ago, and the article is all about the death of Kate Irving's parents. Now, tell me this, Watson: why the hell would Bill Hicks be carrying this around with him, all these years later?"

Turner shook his head, thoroughly confused.

"Exactly," she muttered, and fired up the engine.

CHAPTER 19

They found Joanne Hicks halfway up a ladder, changing a lightbulb in the main bar.

"Hello there, Sophie! How's your mum keepin'?"

DS Keane gave her a tight smile, and cursed this part of her job, which was always the very worst.

"She's well, thank you, Joanne. Do you have a minute, please?"

Joanne looked back over her shoulder and pulled a face, then began descending the stepladder.

"Oh, gosh, it's Bill again, isn't it?" she asked. "What's he gone and done, this time, and who do I need to apologise to?"

Keane and Turner neither confirmed nor denied, both officers being more than aware of prying ears in the long bar.

"Can we go somewhere private?"

Joanne sighed, and gestured towards a tiny room she used as the manager's office, though it was barely larger than a broom cupboard.

"This way," she muttered.

Once the three of them squeezed themselves inside, she shut the door.

"Please, just say it quick," Joanne begged them. "Honestly, Bill was doing so well, until lately, I really thought we'd turned a corner…where is he, anyway?"

"Mrs Hicks…Joanne," Keane amended. "I very much regret to inform you that your husband was found dead, earlier this morning. You have our deepest condolences."

Joanne stared at her for a long moment, while tears pricked her eyes.

"Don't be ridiculous," she declared eventually, and gave a funny little laugh. "Bill isn't *dead*. He can't be. You've made some sort of mistake."

Sophie Keane had heard every sort of denial, every kind of grief manifested, in her time, and it never became any easier.

"I'm sorry, there's no mistake," she said. "Your husband's identity was confirmed by two material witnesses, as well as myself."

And that had been a sight she wouldn't forget in a hurry.

Joanne felt her legs begin to buckle, and lowered herself carefully down into the desk chair she'd bought recently in a garage sale.

"What happened?" she whispered.

"We don't know yet," Keane told her. "But we'll do our best to find out."

"Where…where did you find him?"

"Your husband was found near the old shipwreck, on Frenchman's Creek."

Joanne propped her head on one hand, resting an elbow on the edge of her bureau.

"I—I'm sorry, I can't…I don't understand. What was Bill doing all the way out there?"

Keane and Turner said nothing, because they couldn't tell her the answer to that.

Not yet.

Joanne's eyes filled with tears, and she swiped them away with the back of her hand.

"I should have known this day would come," she said, almost inaudibly. "I've tried for so many years to keep him level, to stop him from hurting himself, but I always knew the drink would kill him in the end…"

She broke off, her voice hitching on a sob.

"I've failed him," she cried, brokenly.

Keane wasn't without a heart, and hers went out to a woman who had done nothing except love someone too much.

"Turner? Can you fetch Mrs Hicks some tissues, please?"

Her colleague excused himself, leaving the two women alone.

"What happened?" Joanne asked, wretchedly. "I woke up this morning and couldn't find him anywhere, so I knew he'd gone off, again. The last time, he turned up in Carol Riley's garden, passed out on her lawn and, God forgive me, I thought, 'Please, just let it be anywhere else. Please, don't embarrass me like that, again.' "

Joanne scrubbed the tears from her eyes.

"But he always finds his way back, or I get a call from someone in your team…or someone in the village, and I tell him, 'This is the last time, Bill', while I call him all the names under the sun. Last night was the same; I sat in bed cursing him for humiliating me, again. If I'd only known what happened…I would never have thought such a wicked thing, I swear—"

"It isn't wicked to hope for better," Sophie told her, and decided to risk asking a few pertinent questions.

"If you're up to it, can you tell me when you last saw Bill?"

Joanne blew out a shaky breath, visibly struggling. "Ah…that would've been just after eleven, last night. I went upstairs to check on him, because he was in a bad way, earlier in the day. He was passed out cold, on his bed."

She didn't say 'their' bed, because they hadn't shared a bedroom in too many years to count.

"You didn't see him again, or hear him leave?"

Joanne shook her head. "It had been a long day," she said. "Just like every other. I was tired and, as soon as my head hit the pillow, I went out like a light. I'm afraid I didn't hear a thing."

Sophie nodded, and made a note.

"Did Bill seem different to you, or discuss anything that was upsetting him?"

Joanne rubbed an absent hand over her forehead, then shook it.

"Not really," she said. "He always rambles when he's drunk…he never said anything important."

She looked up at the young woman.

"Why are you asking me all this?" she asked. "I thought…I assumed Bill had fallen somehow, or had an accident?"

Sophie Keane opened her mouth to reply, but then the door burst open behind her to admit Joanne's daughter, who saw her mother's distress and aimed a look at the only other person in the room.

"What's going on here?" she demanded.

"Lucy, it's…it's your dad," Joanne said softly. "He's passed away."

Lucy's world came to a standstill, the air contracting in time with her heart, so heavy and stifling she could hardly breathe.

"What do you mean?"

"He was found up at Frenchman's Creek," Joanne told her. "He'd—"

She paused, turning back to the police officer.

"You never told me how he died," she realised. "Or, who discovered him."

"We believe he suffered a fatal injury to the head," Sophie said, careful to avoid discussing how that injury might have come about. "As to your other question, he was discovered by an employee of yours, Kate Irving, who was on her way into the village and happened to find him."

"Poor girl," Joanne muttered. "That's all she needs, just now."

"What do you mean, Mrs Hicks?"

Sophie was all ears, when it came to finding out all she could about the stranger in their midst.

"Oh—nothing, I'm sorry, I don't know what I'm saying. My head is all over the place."

"Another question then," Sophie said. "After that, I'm going to have to ask you to accompany me to the hospital to make a formal identification."

Joanne closed her eyes, not sure if she could do what needed to be done.

"Do you know of any reason why your husband would have gone to Frenchman's Creek at that time of night?"

Joanne glanced across to where her daughter stood, pale and pretty, in a cotton summer dress. She was a woman in her thirties, but Lucy would always be 'her little girl' and she had her best interests at heart, always. That being the case, she didn't want to say anything that might upset her.

"Lucy, love? I wonder if you would mind getting me a cup of tea?" she asked. "I could really use one."

Bolstered by the simple task, needing a distraction from her own shock, Lucy nodded and left the room to make for the kitchen.

Soon after, PC Turner arrived bearing tissues, which he passed to Joanne.

"Thank you," she murmured, and blew her nose. "I—I didn't want to say this in front of Lucy. Despite everything, she loved her father and thought the world of him, so I don't want to jeopardise that."

Sophie nodded. "We understand, Mrs Hicks."

Joanne drew in a tremulous breath. "Bill had been talking about...about ending it all," she whispered. "He kept talking about his life being a waste, and that he couldn't live with himself, any longer..."

She shook her head, remembering. "He said it periodically, usually when he was due to pass out," she said. "To be honest, Sophie, he said it so many times, I stopped believing that he'd ever do anything silly. But, now..."

She was unable to continue.

"Do you know why Mr Hicks threatened suicide?" Sophie had to ask.

"I assumed it was because of the alcohol, and knowing he wasn't much of a husband to me, or a father to Lucy," Joanne said. "But, there was another thing..."

She put a hand to her mouth, torn.

"If there's anything at all you think we should know, now's the time to tell us," Sophie said.

Joanne nodded. "It may be nothing, but...when Bill saw Kate, yesterday, he came over all strange. He said it was like seeing a ghost, and he seemed really unsettled. I think he might have frightened Kate, a little bit," she confessed. "Anyway, he started rambling about the past, particularly about Alice and Rob—that's Kate's parents, who died in a boating accident."

"I remember," Sophie said, and exchanged a meaningful glance with her constable. "What did he have to say about that, Mrs Hicks?"

Joanne frowned, trying to remember snippets. "Ah... he said he couldn't live with himself any longer, and that he was sorry. It was as though he blamed himself for something...I wish I'd pressed him for answers, especially now. I could have talked him around."

"You believe Mr Hicks could have committed suicide?"

Joanne lifted a hand in mute agreement. "I don't know what else to think," she said. "If you found him at the bottom of the incline, he might have thrown himself down there."

"He might have done," Sophie said. "But I must tell you from the outset, Mrs Hicks: we're treating your husband's death as 'suspicious'."

Joanne stared at her, lost for words. "Who...who would want to—?"

"That's what we're going to find out."

CHAPTER 20

When he'd been in the Police Force, Andrew Charlton had always known who'd make a good informant, or who he could tap up for hush money. Reading people was a skill he'd developed as a child growing up with a conman for a father, who'd taught him all about how to play people; how to manipulate and cheat and lie and steal and not have anyone realise you'd done it, until it was too late.

Some fathers passed on pocket watches...

He'd built a lucrative business on the back of his father's early teachings, and one of his greatest lessons had been how to don a cloak of invisibility and move around unnoticed, unseen, never drawing attention to himself.

Such as when he'd witnessed Bill Hicks' murder, the previous evening.

Andrew shivered, just thinking of it.

He hadn't expected to see what he'd seen. In fact, he'd stumbled across the pair of them by chance, on his way back from snooping around Ben Carew's boathouse, under cover of darkness. There'd been nothing of interest, there—nothing he could lay his hands upon easily, in any event, and he'd concluded that anything of value or importance must be within the cottage.

So, he'd picked his way back towards the village where he'd parked his car, hurrying for cover when he heard Hicks' heavy footsteps approaching further along the pathway. He'd watched the man weaving and stumbling, and wondered what had brought him that way, so far from home. Drunkenness was the obvious answer, of course, but Charlton had learned early doors that the most obvious answer wasn't necessarily the *right* answer.

What did Bill Hicks want with Kate and her family?

It was an interesting question, one he'd ruminated on as he'd waited for the man to continue along the pathway, and one he'd still been thinking about when he spotted another movement in the trees, seconds before a figure emerged like some terrible apparition.

He'd watched in mute horror as the newcomer shoved Bill off a precipice, without a second thought. No long goodbyes, no explanations or apologies.

He'd waited with his heart in his throat for endless minutes, expecting them to move on, to retreat the way they'd come, but things hadn't worked out that way.

Bill hadn't died, straight away, you see.

They'd sworn violently, cursing the man who lay somewhere far below hovering between life and death, before making their way down into the cove where he'd fallen, presumably to finish the job.

Andy hadn't stuck around to see, and had taken the chance to scuttle away, running full pelt through the trees towards the road, avoiding the route the killer had taken.

Safety, first.

It occurred to him that he should probably have made an anonymous call to the police, or ambulance service.

Ah, well.

The man didn't have much to live for, anyhow, and besides, thanks to Bill Hicks, Andy had another fish to hook, now. Somebody out there didn't want anybody else to know what he knew, and they'd pay to keep his mouth shut.

THE CREEK

There was nothing quite so satisfying as a double payday.

Joanne closed The Ship's Mate early and, by the time all the punters cleared out, it resembled the *Mary Celeste;* eerily quiet, without any of the usual sounds of industry they'd grown used to. While her mother lay down to recover from the unenviable task of having to identify her father's battered body, Lucy took her little motorboat and made her way across to the north shore of the estuary, to an inlet she'd always loved and where she could let her tears flow freely without much chance of being disturbed.

She couldn't face the pity of the town, just yet.

That was where Pete found her, building an enormous sandcastle. As soon as Nick called him with the news, he'd cancelled his plans to have dinner with an attractive veterinarian he'd met earlier in the day and motored to the place he knew Lucy would be.

New resolutions, be damned.

"Need some help with that?"

She looked up from her task to find him suited and booted, looking older and more in command of himself than she could ever recall. For reasons yet unknown, she found herself ridiculously glad to see him.

"Pete," she said. "I'm so pleased to see you."

He made his way across to where she knelt in the sand and, uncaring of his suit trousers, knelt beside her.

"I heard what happened to your dad," he said, rolling up his sleeves to begin scooping out a moat for her castle. "I'm so sorry, Lucy."

"People are going to say he was so drunk that he fell and hit his head," she said, not looking up from her furious moulding of miniature people in the sand. "Or maybe they'll say he did it deliberately."

"Do you care what people say?"

She blinked away a fresh bout of tears. "Everybody cares what people say," she muttered. "Even people who say they don't."

Pete smiled, despite the circumstances, because one of the things he loved about the woman sitting in the sand beside him was her brutal honesty—even when, at times, it could be hard to hear.

"The police don't think it was an accident, and neither do I," she continued.

"What d'you mean?"

"I mean, they think it was suspicious," Lucy said, rubbing the back of her arm across her eyes, to stem the flow of tears. "They won't even tell us all the details yet, but all I know is they're treating it as a suspicious death. That could mean *murder*, Pete."

The word hung on the air, polluting it.

"That can't be right," he said. "Nobody would want to hurt your dad. He was a good man."

"Good men are killed every day," she argued. "It would explain why he was out in the middle of the night—"

Pete drew in a breath, not knowing quite what to say. It was a fact universally acknowledged that Bill Hicks hadn't kept to ordinary schedules, mostly because he never knew what time of day it was, but he could hardly say that to the man's daughter.

"Was he in any kind of trouble?" he asked, taking a different tack. "Is there anybody who would have wanted to hurt him?"

Lucy's hands fell limply to her sides. "I—I've been asking myself those questions all day," she whispered, and raised eyes that were raw from crying. "He wasn't in any trouble that I know of. The inn is in great shape, mostly thanks to mum's management, and does a roaring trade. He didn't have any enemies."

She turned to look out across the water, and thought of her father…

"How did you hear about what happened?" she asked suddenly, taking in his smart attire. "Where've you been?"

He shrugged. "Nick rang me," he said. "He knew I'd want to know, so I could come and find you. I had a meeting with the bank manager."

"Why..." Lucy blinked, as though seeing him for the first time. "Why did you want to come and find me, Pete?"

He gave her a patient smile. "You know why, Lucy. I think you've known for a long time."

She stared into his eyes and wondered why she hadn't noticed before how green they were, and how *kind*. She wondered why she hadn't seen the cut of his jaw, nor the lithe strength of his arms sheathed in the dark blue suit he wore.

She saw it all, then, in one blinding moment.

"You—"

"I love you, Lucy." He nodded. "I've *always* loved you, ever since we were kids, but it's all right—you don't have to worry. I know you don't feel the same, and that's okay. I'm working on being a good friend to you, and being content with that."

"Why would you want to settle?"

He frowned at her. "What do you mean?"

"Why wouldn't you want me, if you had a chance?"

His mouth ran dry. "Are you saying I've got a chance?"

"Do I need to spell it out, Pete Ambrose?"

"You're grieving...you're vulnerable," he said, stoically, and held up his hands. "This isn't the time..."

"I'll be the judge of that," she said, shuffling a little closer. "I'm looking at a new man, one who took my advice and went off to the bank, one who wants to do his own thing—isn't that right?"

He nodded. Only that day, he'd endured a blazing row with his father, and had moved into the cabin of his little boat until he found a cottage of his own.

"That's what I thought," she said softly. "Now, for the final test of compatibility."

"What test?" he asked, not daring to believe...

She took his face in her sandy hands and tugged it closer.

"Think of England," she whispered, and planted a kiss on his upturned mouth.

CHAPTER 21

"How're you holding up?"

Ben stood beside his granddaughter at the sink, washing the dinner dishes while she dried. In the living room, they could hear Nick laughing with Jamie as they set up the new 'Hot Wheels' set he'd acquired that day from the gift shop across the water and Kate reflected that, only a week ago, he was a boy who'd possessed everything material he could ever wish for, who wore designer clothing his father insisted upon, and hardly laughed at all. Now, Jamie wore scruffy board shorts, a t-shirt with a crab on the front and his hair stuck out at all angles from a day spent on the water—and he'd never been happier.

"You're too good to us," she said to her grandfather. "I'm so grateful for all you've done."

"Agh," he said, and dunked another plate in the water. "It's only a few plastic cars. He's no trouble, that lad."

Kate smiled, and half-wished that he *was*. She hoped Jamie came home covered in mud, one day, eyes bright with mischief.

There was time for that.

"Terrible for you to have to find Bill, that way," Ben said, keeping his voice low as he revisited the topic that was uppermost in their minds. "Did the police say what happened to him? I s'pose he must've lost his footing, or some such."

Before she could answer, Nick came back into the kitchen looking every inch the big kid, himself.

"Jamie's happily occupied," he said, heading over to the kettle to set it to boil. "Madge is presiding over things."

Kate smiled.

"I just had a call from Pete," he continued, reaching for the teabags. "He was talking to Lucy—"

"Oh, how's she doing?" Kate asked. "I wasn't sure whether to get in touch with her, or leave her and Joanne to grieve in private...."

"I think Pete was the perfect person to lean on," Nick said, with a wink. "But she did say that the police are treating Bill's death as *suspicious*."

Kate and Ben turned to look at him with twin expressions of surprise.

"Suspicious?" Ben repeated. "How d'you mean?"

Nick shrugged. "Lucy doesn't know any more than that," he said. "All she knows is that they have reason to believe her father's death may not have been an accident."

Ben turned back to the dishes, and continued soaping them while he mulled it over.

"Does anybody know why Bill was out this way, last night?"

Nick made a small sound in the negative.

"Pete says Lucy and Joanne are as much in the dark as anyone," he replied. "Nobody seems to know why he'd make his way out here. Most people are saying he wandered around the pathways and fell, and it's a miracle it hasn't happened before now."

"That's what it looked like," Kate said, doubtfully. "But the police must have reason to think otherwise."

Nick began pouring water into three cups.

"I don't remember seeing anything unusual, at the time," he said. "But then, I wasn't really looking for anything. I was focused on getting down there to help you, if you needed me."

Ben smiled to himself, and dipped another plate in the water.

"Did you notice anything?" Nick asked her.

Kate sighed, rubbing a tea towel over one of the wet plates in thoughtful circles, while she cast her mind back.

"I—" She frowned a little. "Well, actually, it was to do with the rock."

"What rock?"

"The rock where Bill hit his head," she said, and grimaced. "It was covered in blood, and his head was sort of slumped against the edge of it, where there was a big gash."

Nick remembered.

"It's just that…the rock was too far away."

Both men waited for her to explain.

"I mean to say…if he fell down the incline, he'd have landed at the bottom of the ridge," she reasoned. "On the shingle part of the cove. Instead, he was a bit further along, in the silt left over from the tide the previous day, and I suppose it seemed a bit weird that he'd have landed so far away from the edge. The trajectory seems off."

Ben hadn't seen the body himself, but he could imagine the scene from her description.

"He might have rolled a bit further," he said. "But he wouldn't have had the impact against that rock, certainly not enough to crack his head—that's what you're saying?"

She nodded, feeling cold.

Noticing it, Nick handed her a cup of tea and decided to change the subject.

"That's enough for one day," he declared. "Besides, I have something I've been meaning to give you. Wait there."

He wandered off into the hallway, where he'd left his backpack containing dog treats and various other things, and came back a minute later with a parcel wrapped in brown paper, embossed with the logo of a quality art shop in Truro.

"Just a little 'welcome back to the neighbourhood' present," he said, feeling awkward.

Kate rubbed her hands over the back of her jeans, looked towards her grandfather, who whistled beneath his breath, then back at Nick.

"You don't need to buy me presents," she said. "I—I don't have anything for you…"

"I don't give in order to receive," he said softly. "Now, just take the damn thing, will you?"

She laughed, and took the parcel in her hands, weighing it, trying to guess what it could be.

"Oh, my God," he said, in a pained voice. "You're one of *those*. Just rip it open, for the love of Blackbeard's Ghost, before we all die of old age."

"Me, especially," Ben chimed in, to make them laugh.

"Okay, okay," she said, and took it across to the kitchen table to unwrap.

When she'd unfolded the layers of paper and bubble wrap, Kate sat holding a beautiful antique painting set in her hands, consisting of a polished walnut box complete with brushes and watercolours, charcoals, erasers and even a miniature water bottle for painting 'on the go'. A set of sketchbooks of different paper weights was included in the package, so she could start using it straight away.

"Nick…"

"It might not be right," he said quickly, surprised to find he was a jumble of nerves. "I happened to see it in a window the other day, and I thought of you."

Ben smiled again, thinking that the world was made up of small kindnesses such as these.

"It's beautiful," she managed, while trying to keep tears at bay. "I'm sorry, I can't use it."

She placed the art set back on the table, with infinite care.

"It's so kind of you to think of this," she said. "But I—"

Kate looked at her fingers, which moved slowly and painfully, especially when they were cold.

"I'm not the same as I was."

She stood up quickly and left the room, before she could embarrass herself any further.

Nick watched her go in bemusement, then turned to Ben, who hung the discarded tea towel on the Aga, to dry it.

"I don't understand," he said. "I thought she would love it."

"She does love it," Ben said. "It's a wonderful thing you tried to do, but it's her *fingers*. He broke 'em, four years ago."

Something dark and dangerous flashed in Nick's eyes. "He broke her fingers, knowing she was a gifted painter," he snarled.

Ben nodded. "I think, when Will Irving did that, he broke something more than bones. He took a bit of her spirit, and she hasn't quite recovered it, yet."

Most men would have left it at that, but Nick was not 'most men'.

"Bugger that, and bugger *him*," he declared, and snatched up the paint set before heading off in search of her.

"This'll be interesting," Ben said to himself, and went off to play cars with his great-grandson.

CHAPTER 22

"So, you're just going to let him win?"

Kate looked up with a startled expression from her position on the veranda, outside.

"I don't know what you mean."

"You know exactly what I mean," Nick argued, plonking himself beside her and setting the paint set between them, like a battleground.

Then, he reached for one of her hands, before she could object.

"Hey—" she started to protest.

"Just a moment," he said, holding her fingers gently. "How does that feel?"

He prodded her skin here and there, finding various pressure points to gauge where she suffered with the most residual damage.

"Have you had a scan?"

"Not lately," she admitted. "At the time of the... the..."

"Attack," Nick supplied, and she bobbed her head in agreement.

"Yes," she said, and didn't pull her fingers away, but allowed him to continue holding her hand as they sat together with the sun setting across the water. "When Will broke my fingers, I went to the hospital...well, he took me, and said I'd had an accident with the fridge door. Three of my fingers were in cast, but they've never healed the same and they're often stiff. I found I couldn't sketch in the same way, or even hold a pencil with the same dexterity."

His hand tightened carefully around hers, as a gesture of support, and she edged a little closer to him, seeking...she didn't know what.

"Things could improve, with a little physio," he said, focusing on the future rather than on the past. "I know a little bit about looking after hands—they're my tools, too."

She thought of all the work he did on boats, carrying and lifting, and nodded her understanding. It would be very inconvenient for him to lose the use of his hands, for they provided the tools for his trade... even if he was a jack of all trades.

"The GP gave me some exercises, at the time," she said. "I tried to follow them but, when I didn't see much progress, I'm afraid I grew too disheartened to continue."

Nick thought of the specialist he knew in London, one who'd helped him with a bad case of carpal tunnel syndrome that had almost prevented him from finishing some important songs, a couple of years back. It would be an easy matter for him to take Kate to see him, and get an expert view, but she could be as stubborn as a mule when it came to accepting help. No doubt, it was because she'd managed for so long without support that she struggled to accept help when it was offered, but he hoped to change that, one day.

"I have some resistance balls—"

He caught the look in her eye, and realised how that sounded.

"You have...resistance balls?" she queried.

He took a deep breath. "I *meant*, I have a hand exerciser you can borrow," he said, with as much dignity as he could muster. "You use them whenever you remember to during the day, a little bit here and there, and, over time, you should see improvement. I have the name of a good specialist, too."

She smiled at him, but her eyes held a touch of sadness.

"This is all very kind of you—" she started to say.

"You'd better not be about to tell me to shove my well-intentioned kindness where the sun doesn't shine," he said. "Because, if you think I'm about to let you walk away from a God-given talent, you've got another thing coming."

She raised her eyebrows. "I'd say that was my decision."

"Sure, it is," he agreed. "But can you honestly tell me that your 'decision' hasn't been influenced by the actions of that arsehole you married? Can you tell me, if he hadn't tried to break your confidence, you wouldn't have kept going, or kept trying?"

No, she couldn't tell him that.

"You don't understand," she said, testily, and rose to her feet to pace away from him. "I remember how things *used* to be, what I *used* to be able to do. It's upsetting when I find that I can't produce the same outcomes with a brush or a pencil. It makes me feel like a failure."

Which is exactly what Irving wanted, Nick thought, and hated the man all over again.

"So, you adopt a slightly different style than before," he said, and stood up to face her. "Artists through the ages have done it, why can't you?"

"How would you know?" she demanded. "You're not an artist—are you?"

He remained silent, and knew it was past time to tell her about his own little side hustle.

"How would you know how it feels to have the *one* thing you love taken from you?" she continued, on a roll now, unable to prevent the frustration she'd felt for years come pouring out.

"More than you might think," he said, very softly.

"What if I'm no good?" she said, admitting the truth of the matter. "Painting and drawing was my joy, my solace…better to have the memory of it, than the pain of being unable to translate the things I see on paper, anymore."

"You could take the coward's route," he said, and waited for her eyes to light up again, which they did.

"I'm no coward," she said, flatly.

"What else would you call it?"

"Self-preservation," she argued.

"Same difference." He shrugged, and folded his arms across his chest.

She was distracted by the action, which pulled the material of his shirt tight across his arms, and was angry at herself all over again.

"Look, there's no shame in working at The Ship's Mate your whole life," he said. "Or doing any other kind of gainful employment. But, Kate, there are people out there who'd give their left leg to have a tenth of your talent. It's a betrayal to them, and to *yourself*, to let it go to waste. Besides, you're letting the bastard win, and I never thought you were a quitter."

He bent down, picked up the paint box again and shoved it into her arms.

"Think about it," he suggested, and stalked back into the house.

CHAPTER 23

Joanne gave up on sleep, somewhere between the hours of two and four.

Her fitful dreams had been full of memories of her late husband—the first time they'd met, as children in the playground; the first time they'd held hands; the first time they'd kissed…then, years later, his face as they'd welcomed Lucy into the world, so full of joy and hope. Bill had been so much a part of her life, present at so many 'firsts' that it was hard to imagine he wouldn't be there to witness any of her 'lasts'. They would not grow old together, nor sit side by side when—*if*—Lucy was ever married, or bounce a grandchild on their knees. Joanne would be the one to do that, but without anyone to share the experience with.

It was funny, she thought, how the world continued to turn. Somehow, she'd expected the Earth to stop spinning on its axis; for people to stop laughing and talking and going about their daily business, simply because they should have known of his passing.

Instead, life went on.

"Mum?"

Lucy came downstairs dressed in plain leggings and a t-shirt and, for once, her face was bare of any make-up to conceal the ravages of a lack of sleep and a surplus of tears, which had plagued her throughout the night.

"What are you doing up so early?"

"Couldn't sleep," Joanne said, and went back to scrubbing the long bar until it shone. "I've cleaned the kitchen, organised my accounts, re-filled the napkins and straws, wiped down the menus, scraped out the grate in the pizza oven…"

She paused, sure there was more.

"Oh, and I've checked the barrels," she said. "Your dad normally does that, but…"

Joanne fell silent.

"You don't have to do any of this," Lucy said, coming over to rub a hand over her mother's back. "You're allowed to cry—scream and shout, if you need to."

"Thanks, love, but busy-work is what I need," she said. "It keeps my mind occupied."

"Surely, you're not thinking of opening the pub today?"

Joanne supposed it was a bit soon. "I just thought it would keep me busy," she explained. "I can't stay in my room for weeks on end, Lucy. It isn't in my nature."

Joanne had never been idle.

"Can I do anything?" Lucy asked. "Get you anything?"

"No, love," Joanne said, patting her cheek. "Really, there's nothing you can do, it'll just take a bit of time to get used to not having your dad around anymore, that's all."

"I still don't understand what happened," Lucy said.

At that moment, there came a tap on the outer door.

"Oh, goodness—tell them I'm not quite ready, will you?" Joanne said. "We'll open up at eleven, ahead of the lunch sitting. That'll give me time to get in touch with Kate and the other staff, to see if they're ready to come back in."

Lucy made her way to the old front door, which looked almost as old as the inn, and loosened the bolts before swinging open the door, a polite rebuff ready to go.

But it died on her tongue when the door opened to reveal DS Keane and PC Turner, looking disgustingly bright-eyed and bushy-tailed.

"Sophie," she said, remembering the woman who'd once attended the same children's ballet classes at Mawgan Village Hall. "Come in."

Joanne looked up at the sound of footsteps on the wooden floor.

"Mrs Hicks, I'm sorry to bother you again, so early," Keane began.

"No need to be sorry," Joanne averred. "Do you have any more news for us?"

Lucy walked across to stand beside her mother, united.

"We were hoping to ask you a couple of questions about the death of Mr and Mrs Ryce," Sophie said, taking them both by surprise.

"*Alice and Rob?*" Lucy exclaimed. "They died fifteen years ago! What do they have to do with my dad…or anything?"

Sophie gave her a level look.

"That's what we'd like to know," she said, and turned back to Joanne, who looked pale around the gills. She was sorry for causing the woman any further distress, at what was an already distressing time, but needs must.

"We found several newspaper clippings on your husband's person," she said. "We'd like to know why he had them with him, when he died."

She turned to PC Turner, who, after a second, got the message and reached inside a brown paper envelope to retrieve a series of small newspaper cuttings that were yellowed with age, and coated in protective plastic.

"This is what we found," Sophie said, and placed the plastic sheath on one of the smaller bistro tables for the women to examine.

The first one read:

POPULAR COUPLE FOUND DEAD ON LUXURY GHOST YACHT

Robert and Alice Ryce, daughter of local man Benjamin Carew and his late wife, Deborah, of Frenchman's Creek, were found dead this morning in the cabin of their yacht, 'The Lady of Shalott', which was moored in Carew Cove whilst they were visiting in the area. They are survived by an eighteen-year-old daughter, Kate, who was staying with local friends, the Hicks family, at their home—local drinking hole, 'The Ship's Mate'. An inquest is due to be held in the coming weeks...

Another clipping read:

INQUEST RULES ACCIDENTAL DEATH

An inquest into the deaths of Robert and Alice Ryce (née Carew), who were found dead on their yacht a week ago, was held today at County Hall in Truro. Evidence was provided by boat building experts Fullman & Sons of Falmouth, as well as expert forensics and police reports following extensive examination of the vessel, 'The Lady of Shalott', which was commissioned by the late Mr Ryce for his wife as an anniversary gift and built by Fullman's. The Police Pathologist gave evidence that the cause of death in both victims was acute carbon monoxide (CO) poisoning. CO is an odourless, tasteless and colourless gas with a higher-than-average accidental death rate amongst boat operatives in the South-West. Owing to the toxicity levels found in both victims and no other evidence suggestive of third-party interference, the Coroner entered a verdict of 'Accidental Death' and agreed with the experts, who suggested that a tiny leak was likely to have formed in the internal pipework of the locked cabin, causing the space to fill with carbon monoxide over the course of many hours, such that when the victims entered their cabin to sleep later that night, they were exposed to and inhaled toxic levels of carbon monoxide that proved fatal. Local Councillor for Truro and well-known businessman, Greg Ambrose, said today that the Coroner's verdict was a salutary lesson for all boat users to remain vigilant at all times in checking their vessels, and that lessons would be learned...

A final clipping read:

LOCAL MAN MOUNTS APPEAL AGAINST CORONER'S VERDICT

Respected local ferryman, Benjamin Carew, who lost his daughter and son-in-law lately to carbon monoxide poisoning in the biggest tragedy reported on the Helford in many years, has today mounted an appeal against the decision of the Coroner that their deaths were 'accidental'. Carew, who also lost his wife, Deborah, in recent years, has been vocal in his belief that 'The Lady of Shalott' had somehow been tampered with, prior to their deaths, and has pointed to a lack of physical evidence showing any leak site on the vessel. Many in the area have sided with Carew and a JustGiving page has already swelled to over eight thousand pounds made up of donations from around the area, to assist in his legal fees and quest for the truth. Conspiracy theorists say that local boat-builders, Fullman & Sons should not have been called upon to give expert evidence at the original inquest two months ago, and demand an independent enquiry and assessment. Carew has declined to comment at this stage, other than to remark that it was only after much argument that the police returned 'The Lady of Shalott' to him following completion of their investigation, and that he was only just in time to save her from being destroyed for scrap, thereby removing any remaining evidence that could have been missed...

Joanne sat back, and rubbed a tired hand over her eyes.

"I remember all this, at the time," she said softly. "Alice and Rob were our friends, and Kate had been staying over with Lucy, here, the night they died. It was a miracle she wasn't taken, too."

"As I understand it, the Ryce's preferred to stay on their boat?" Sophie said.

"I couldn't tell you," Joanne said, and shook her head. "I'd have thought they'd stay overnight at

Frenchman's Cottage, with Ben. Perhaps it was bad luck that they decided to go onboard when they did."

"But, if the carbon monoxide was filling up for hours, it was really just a matter of time before they inhaled some of it," Lucy said, sadly.

"But, it's a question of volume, isn't it?" Sophie pointed out. "Whether Rob and Alice Ryce inhaled a small amount of carbon monoxide, or enough to *kill* them, really depended on when they went into the cabin and when the leak began."

And whether anybody happened to know about either of those things, ahead of time...

"You may be right," Lucy said. "I still don't understand what any of this has to do with my dad."

Joanne was staring down at the clippings, and had turned very pale, which was a red flag.

"I think your mum could use a drink," Sophie said. "Could you get her something? Maybe tea with plenty of sugar?"

Lucy made a small sound of concern, reached down to kiss her mother's head, and then hurried off to the kitchen.

"Well, Joanne?" Sophie said, quietly. "We've got a minute or two of privacy, if you want to use it."

Joanne put her head in her hands.

"Oh, God," she said, and wondered where to begin. "I—I never thought this would be relevant. I haven't spoken of it in...well, in over fifteen years."

"Go on," Sophie urged.

"If I could turn back the hands of time, I would."

Turner's eyes goggled, and Keane gave him a warning glance, eyeing his notepad meaningfully so that he'd take the hint and start making some notes.

"We're listening, Mrs Hicks."

"I'll just come out and say it," Joanne said, half to herself. "The summer before Rob and Alice died, I had an affair with Rob. It had been ongoing, off-and-on, for a number of years, but nobody knew about it until the summer that Rob and Alice died. Even then, it was only Bill who... who..."

She drew in a shaking breath and put a hand to her mouth.

"It was only Bill who found out," she whispered. "I told him...I couldn't live with the guilt, so I ended things with Rob, and I told him."

PC Turner opened his mouth as if to say something, but one look from Sophie had him snapping it shut again.

"Let's go back a bit, Mrs Hicks," she said. "You're telling me you'd been conducting a romantic affair with the late Robert Ryce? May I ask, for how long?"

Joanne hugged herself, hating to remember that time in her life.

"We'd known one another for years and, of course, Alice was a lifelong friend...which only makes it so much worse on my part, I know," she added, miserably. "As I said, I deeply regret this—"

"We're not here to pass judgment, Mrs Hicks," Sophie told her, but kept a sharp eye on the kitchen door for Lucy's imminent return. "How did things begin between you and Mr Ryce?"

Joanne made a small sound that could have been confusion.

"I hardly remember," she sighed. "I suppose we were both lonely, in our own ways. Alice was a wonderful friend but could be distant and was very much tied to her work, which didn't leave much room for time with Rob. For my part, Bill's alcoholism was really starting to take hold, back then, and he wasn't himself. It was embarrassing, at times, and did nothing to stir up any romance, that's for sure."

"So, you grew close."

"Yes, I suppose we did," Joanne said. "We were friends for years, as I say."

"Did Alice ever find out?" Turner couldn't help but ask.

"I—I really don't know," Joanne confessed. "She never said anything about it, and always acted just the same with me, so I assume Rob never told her and I know that I certainly didn't."

"You said that you could no longer live with the guilt," Sophie said. "What changed?"

Joanne's lips twisted.

"Alice spoke to me about how she was beginning to worry that Rob had been distant…it rang an alarm bell. Then, I thought of our children…of Kate and Lucy…" She shook her head. "It wasn't right, and I told Rob it needed to stop."

"How did he take it?"

"Rob?" Joanne gave a little shrug. "He was devastated, of course. He relied on our meetings, I think, and…I don't know for sure, but I started to suspect his feelings ran a bit deeper than mine, whereas, underneath it all, I still loved Bill. I just wished he was the man I'd married."

There was a short pause while they allowed that to settle in.

"You say you told your husband about the affair," Sophie said, after a minute. "When was this, Mrs Hicks?"

Joanne raised frightened eyes. "It was...oh, God, it was a couple of days before they died."

Turner and Keane said nothing, but the cogs began to turn. Joanne looked back down at the clippings Bill had kept all those years, and then back into their unreadable faces.

"The—the Coroner returned a verdict of accidental death," she said, hoarsely. "It was an *accident*. Bill would never...you can't think he'd have done anything. He couldn't have."

"Couldn't have what?" Lucy asked, coming back into the room.

"Couldn't have hurt anyone," Joanne finished, but her eyes strayed back to the clippings while her mind wandered back into the past and thought about where he'd been, during the hours when a leak might have sprung on *The Lady of Shalott*.

CHAPTER 24

Kate took her time getting ready that morning, applying make-up and blow-drying her hair as she used to do every day to meet her husband's expectations but, this time, it was to give herself a sense of false confidence in order to find the courage to delve into the sordid details of her former life and make a formal report to the police. Sleep had been elusive the previous evening, not only because of what had happened to Bill Hicks, but because of the altercation she'd had with Nick, if you could even call it that. To her annoyance, his words had burrowed beneath her skin, planting seeds that had sprung into life sometime during the twilight hours and refused to stop growing.

After some considerable soul-searching, she'd come to the only logical, if infuriating, conclusion.

He was right.

It had been easier to avoid painting, all these years, and to turn her back on the talent she'd once possessed and which, it turned out, she might still harbour. Easier to succumb to Will's conditioning and believe that she was no good; that she had no means of making her own living and way in the world.

He was wrong.

Once, she'd had the opportunity to study at one of the finest art schools in the world, and she'd made the mistake of turning down that chance, instead placing all her hopes on a happy future with the man she'd loved. Years had passed since then, and she'd never be eighteen again, but there was still time yet.

She looked across at the little painting she'd completed that very morning, which she'd laid on the windowsill to dry. It might not have been her finest work, for she knew that was yet to come, but it was a damn good effort and something that she was proud of.

Hopefully, it would suffice as an apology.

Tucking it into her bag, she made her way downstairs and, with a peck on the cheek for her grandad and another, longer squeeze for Jamie, she prepared to make her way to the local police station.

"Sure you don't want me to come with you?" Ben asked her.

"I'd rather you looked after Jamie," she murmured, with a smile for her son who was engrossed in morning cartoons. "I'll be back soon."

Just then, they heard the rumble of a car's engine on the track leading down to the cottage, and they peered out of the window to see Nick's Land Rover approach.

"Did you ask him to come?" she asked.

Ben shook his head. "Didn't have to," he said.

Just another thing to be grateful for, she realised, and watched Nick stride from the car towards them with Madge at his heels, looking sickeningly awake and ready for the day.

"He's a morning person," she muttered. "Who'd have guessed that?"

"What's that, love?"

"Nothing."

In another masterstroke of consideration, Nick offered to babysit Jamie, thereby allowing Ben to accompany his granddaughter to the police station. As much as he might have wanted to be the one to hold Kate's hand, and as much as a part of him was morbidly curious to know about her past so that he could know her better, he knew, instinctively, that he would rather Kate told him in her own time, once she grew to know and trust him better.

As she and Ben drove off in the man's ancient Toyota, Nick sank onto the sofa beside Jamie and watched a cartoon featuring some sort of talking blob, before deciding that life was too short.

"Hey, ever wanted to learn an instrument?"

Jamie gave him a suspicious look. "What *kind* of instrument?"

Nick almost laughed, and thought that the kid looked like the image of his mother, when he pulled a face like that.

"Well, how about guitar?"

"I don't have one," Jamie said.

"I do," Nick replied, and disappeared back to his car, where he tended to keep one of his acoustic guitars in the boot for…well, musical emergencies, he supposed.

"Cool!" Jamie declared, and sat up a bit straighter on the sofa. "Can I try?"

"Sure, you can," Nick told him. "But, let me show you how to hold it, first, and then I'll show you a few chords."

"What's a chord?"

Nick smiled, and thought it was like rediscovering his favourite thing, all over again, through the eyes of a child.

"It's when you play three different musical notes, or pitches, at the same time, to create a harmony," he said. "Like this."

With a strum of his fingers, he created a smooth 'C'.

"Here, you try."

They carried on that way for a few minutes, with Jamie's small fingers copying Nick's larger ones, plucking and strumming until they had the bones of a melody.

"What do you want to call it?"

"Mummy's Song?" Jamie said, and Nick ruffled his head, deeply moved by the child's love for his mother.

"She'll love it," he said, and was inspired to write something himself.

"Hey, Nick?"

"Mm hmm?"

"Do you like my mummy? It seems like you smile a lot when you're together. Daddy never smiles."

Nick didn't know what to say, then the answer came so easily.

"I love her," he said. "But I'm just her friend. I'd like to be your friend, too, if you'll let me."

The child looked up at him, seeming to search his soul, until he nodded.

"You can be my friend," he said. "I don't have a lot of friends."

Nick gave him a playful nudge.

"You will. Just wait and see."

On which note, he decided to make a few phone calls, to help things along.

"Sorry to keep you, Kate."

DS Keane entered her office and shut the door behind her, nodding towards Ben who was seated in the other visitor's chair beside his granddaughter.

"It's no problem," Kate said, although the added wait hadn't helped her anxiety over-much. "Thank you for making time to see me."

"I was actually planning to ask you a couple of follow-up questions, so we can kill two birds with one stone. Would you like a drink?"

Kate shook her head.

"I drank pints of water before coming here, but it doesn't seem to have done much for my dry throat," she said. "I think it's a by-product of knowing that what I have to say will be difficult."

"I appreciate that," Sophie said. "I want you to take your time, and I've cleared the rest of the morning to allow us to go through whatever you need to discuss. All right?"

Kate wasn't used to such a professional response, and felt better immediately.

"Thank you," she said. "Do you mind my grandfather being with me?"

"I'd say he's the best person to have by your side." Sophie smiled.

Kate fidgeted a bit on her chair. "How far back should I go?"

"All the way to the beginning," Sophie said, and clicked her rollerball pen in preparation to begin. "Any dates and times you have would also be very useful."

At that point, Kate produced a diary, heavily annotated.

"Everything I remember from the past eighteen months is in here," she said. "Before that, I'll be relying on memory."

Sophie took the diary, flipped through the first few pages of tear-stained content, and nodded.

"Go ahead," she said quietly. "I'm all ears."

By the time it was done, and there were no more tears to be shed, Kate felt exhausted. It had taken an hour and a half to go through the basic timeline, but it seemed far longer, and her body cried out for sleep.

However, they were not finished, yet.

"Thank you again, Kate. I know that can't have been easy," DS Keane said. "You've demonstrated great strength of character in making your report, which I've noted and will file on our systems here. A lot of the content is historic and, unfortunately, corresponding medical reports weren't always made at the time—"

"How could she, if she was being threatened?" Ben asked.

"I understand that," Sophie said, holding up a hand. "I'm merely setting out the pitfalls of any civil or criminal action mounted on the back of these allegations. Our system isn't perfect, but it's supposed to presume innocence, until somebody is proven guilty. For that reason, we need as much hard evidence as possible."

She ran through some ideas on that score.

"How would you like to proceed?" she asked Kate, at the end of the discussion.

"We have a solicitor who can help with divorce proceedings and anything to do with Jamie," Kate said, with a smile for her grandfather. "I'll be seeking full custody."

Sophie thought of all the means at her husband's disposal, the kind of fight somebody like that would put up, simply to punish her, and didn't envy the woman her task nor the road ahead.

"Good luck," she said, and meant it. "From our side, you should let us know if there are any further incidents—"

"I will."

"As for these historic allegations, would you like to press charges?"

Kate looked to her grandfather again, and drew in a deep breath.

"Yes," she said. "I would."

Sophie nodded. "All right then," she said. "I must warn you, this will probably attract a lot of publicity."

Kate had assumed that would be the case, and was used to it, after fifteen years of living with a man who courted the press like the narcissist he was.

"I can handle it, and I'll do my best to keep Jamie out of it."

"We'll all help," Ben said.

"It is possible that, being down here, you can shield your son from the worst of it," Sophie agreed. "There are several celebrities who manage to keep a low profile, most of the time—take Nick, for starters."

This last remark was thrown out so casually, Kate almost missed it.

"I'm sorry—do you mean Nick Pascoe?"

Sophie looked surprised. "Of course," she said and, glancing at Ben's pained expression, realised that she'd managed to put her foot in it, somehow. "Ah—that is—I mean to say, he isn't a movie star, or anything…"

"What is he then?" Kate asked, turning to fix her grandfather with an accusatory stare. "It seems I'm the last to know."

Ben cleared his throat and tried to look old and fragile, in the hope it would inspire some sympathy.

It didn't.

"Don't try that with me, y' wily old fox," Kate snapped. "What don't I know about the man who's babysitting my son, at this very moment?"

"Nothing bad!" Ben said, quickly. "Nick's done very well for 'imself, that's all. He's, ah, you might say he's a songwriter."

"That doesn't sound too bad," Kate said.

"He writes songs for some of the biggest musical acts in the business today," Sophie put in, drily. "He also produces."

Kate might not have worked in that industry herself, but she could imagine.

"Ah," she said, eloquently. "I see."

"He was going to tell you, I'm sure of it," Ben said, not liking the murderous look in her eye. "He was concerned that you'd think differently of him, or associate him with someone like…"

"Like Will?" Kate supplied.

"On the plus side, he has no criminal record," Sophie said, to try to lighten the mood. "No pops for indecent exposure, that I'm aware of."

Just a propensity to keep secrets, Kate thought, and felt her heart sink.

"You said you had some more questions for us, detective?" she said, filing the rest away for later. "I should really get back to my son."

Sophie sighed, and made a note to send Nick a word of apology. She hadn't meant to tread on any toes, and was sorry if she'd been the unintentional cause of discord in whatever relationship was forming between the pair of them.

"Right, yes. It's a sensitive topic, but I need to ask both of you about the nature of your parents' relationship, before they died," she said.

Kate was lost for words. "Why do you need to know about that?" she asked. "What does it have to do with anything, now?"

"If you could just answer the question, I'll go into that in a moment."

Kate spread her hands. "I lived with them, so I was the closest observer of their life together," she said. "They were two people who were madly in love, and perfectly suited, as far as I could see. They demonstrated a relationship I aspired to…"

That she still aspired to, one day.

Sophie folded her hands on top of her desk, wondering how to ask indelicate questions delicately.

"There was never any discord?" she asked. "No hint that either party was unhappy in the marriage?"

"What're you drivin' at, Sophie?" Ben Carew had known her since she was a toddler catching the ferryboat with her parents, so DS Keane forgave the lack of formality.

"Mr Hicks was found in possession of three old newspaper clippings, when he died," she said. "They all concerned your parents' death, the inquest and its aftermath—especially your appeal, Mr Carew. We're trying to understand why these clippings were with him when he died, and why they were important to him, fifteen years after the event. Certain information has been relayed to us that might suggest a motive for Mr Hicks having possibly…" She ran a tongue over her lips, treading carefully now. "Having possibly played a hand in your parents' death. That puts a new complexion on his death, too."

Kate and Ben looked at one another, then back at her.

"I don't think I'm followin'," Ben said. "You're tellin' me, I could've been right, all those years ago, when I said Rob and Alice didn't die accidentally? You're thinkin' Bill could've been a part of that?"

Sophie neither confirmed nor denied.

"We're exploring lots of different possibilities, Mr Carew," she said. "At this stage, I need to know whether you had any reason to suspect Mr Hicks' involvement in their death, or any reason to think Rob and Alice's marriage was under threat."

"Absolutely not," Ben said firmly. "First of all, Bill Hicks was a peace-lovin' feller, for all that he enjoyed a drink. Never lifted a finger to anyone, in all the years I knew him. Secondly, Rob an' Alice were a happy, lovin' couple…soul mates, you might say. There wasn't ever any whiff of ought amiss."

Kate nodded her agreement. "They hardly rowed," she said softly. "When they did, it was only ever about silly things; never anything big or important."

She leaned forward. "Detective, if I'm reading this correctly, are you suggesting that Bill was having an affair with my mother…or, I suppose, that Joanne was having an affair with my father?" she asked. "I can't imagine either one of those scenarios."

And yet, Sophie thought.

There would be some difficult conversations to come between Kate and Joanne, if she was any judge.

"People can surprise you," she said. "But, for present purposes, it may be enough that Bill believed your father to have been having an affair with his wife. In those circumstances, people can act out of character."

"It wasn't true," Kate said. "It can't have been."

"We all want to believe those we've loved were perfect people," Sophie said, sympathetically. "But, sometimes, life is more complicated."

Kate knew that to be true for some people, but she felt sure she would have *known*…

"You think Bill did something and was on his way out to see us, the other night, perhaps to confess?"

"It's a possibility," Sophie said.

"If he was, then he never made it that far," Ben replied.

Sophie Keane looked into Ben's sharp, bird-like eyes, and wondered…

What would a man do, to protect his family?

Almost anything.

After the pair of them left, PC Turner rapped a knuckle on Keane's office door and entered bearing tea and biscuits.

"Thought you might be in need," he said, waggling the digestives.

Sophie pointed a finger at him.

"I want you to know, Alex, that sucking up to the boss with cups of tea and packets of biscuits won't get you anywhere in the police hierarchy," she said, before crooking the same finger to grasp the proffered mug and take a long swig of builder's brew. "On the other hand, it can't hurt, either. Pull up a seat, Turner."

He grinned, and plonked himself into one of the visitor's chairs that had been recently vacated.

"How'd it go, with Kate Irving and her grandfather?" he asked.

Sophie Keane wasn't about to spill the confidential details of their discussion about Will Irving, but she gave him the headlines and moved onto more interesting facts relating to their present investigation.

"On the one hand, we've got Joanne Hicks confessing to an affair with Rob Ryce, before he died," she began. "An affair that was kept very hush-hush, to protect everyone around them, until Joanne cracked and spilled the beans to her husband in a fit of conscience—"

Turner slurped his tea loudly, and she sent him a look of mild disgust.

"As I was *saying*," she continued. "She confessed to it just a couple of days before Rob and Alice were killed, in what looks now to have been circumstances that were less accidental than was thought at the time."

Sophie paused to sip her tea, warming her hands around the edge of the mug.

"On the other hand, I've just had Kate Irving in here, telling me that her parents had the perfect marriage, that she saw nothing untoward or even a hint that her father was having an affair," she said.

"Mind you, eighteen-year-old kids with lives of their own don't tend to be the most observant."

"How about Ben Carew?" Turner asked. "Did he know anything about it?"

Sophie shook her head. "He says not," she replied. "But, just play along with me here, while I consider a hypothetical scenario…"

Turner nodded eagerly, and she made a mental note to ask him to be less…well, *eager*.

"Let's say that Bill Hicks was overcome by jealousy, when he heard that his wife had been having an affair with one of his best mates—not just briefly, either, but on-and-off every summer, for years," she said. "Let's say a red mist descended, and he decided to wipe the guy out, in such a way that it looked accidental. Maybe he tampered with the boat, knowing when Rob and Alice would be back on the vessel, after spending a day on land visiting friends in St Ives. He could have arranged a hose, fed it into the cabin area, and filled it with carbon monoxide during the day when they'd be away—Kate was with his daughter Lucy, back in the village, and Ben Carew was operating his ferryboat business for the summer crowd."

"There'd've been no witnesses," Turner agreed. "He could've popped onto the *Lady of Shalott* without having to worry anyone would see him."

Sophie nodded. "Bill was the type of character to come and go, without always letting people know his movements, so nobody would necessarily think anything of it," she said. "He could've snuck back later in the day, removed the hose and left the cabin nice and ready for their return."

"Why would he want to harm Alice? On this analysis, she was as much a victim as he was," Turner pointed out.

"Yeah, but she's collateral damage," Sophie said. "He's not thinking straight, remember?"

Turner nodded.

"Bill gets away with it, but struggles to live with himself," she continued. "He drinks more and more, retreating into his own little world. Joanne never suspects a thing, and she thinks he's forgiven her for her transgression. Instead, he's taken the ultimate revenge, and deprived a daughter of her parents."

She bit into a digestive, imagining the psychology.

"It's bearable, since Kate goes away to live in London with her father's brother and his family," she mused. "Bill never has to see her, and be reminded of what he took from her—until, one day, she walks back into his pub looking for work, and she's the spitting image of her mother."

"She really is," Turner agreed. "I had a look at the old file, and it's uncanny."

Sophie nodded. "Must've come as a shock to him," she said. "Seeing Kate standing there, looking like her mother's ghost. Maybe it broke him, and he decided to head out to Frenchman's Creek the other night to make his confession."

"But he fell on the way?" Turner offered.

Sophie shook her head.

"You've seen how the body was found," she reminded him. "You've seen the rock he was supposed to have fallen on. It doesn't ring true, and forensics agree with us. The man was moved, and finished off on the edge of that rock. He didn't land on it, initially."

Turner managed to join the dots.

"You're thinking maybe…Bill Hicks made it to the cottage, told them what he had to say, then turned around and was making his way *home,* when he fell… or, was attacked?"

Sophie nodded.

"We assumed, at first, that he was on his way somewhere," she said. "But what if he was on his way *back?*"

Turner shuffled in his seat. "It could have been Kate," he said. "She's the younger of the two."

"Possible," Sophie agreed. "She's young and fit, and, in this scenario, had been confronted with her parents' killer. It would have been easy to prey on an infirm, drunk old man, to take her revenge. When Nick Pascoe came across her, the other day, she could have been returning to the scene to check his body for anything incriminating, which she didn't get a chance to do, after all."

"It's plausible," Turner agreed. "Mind you, Ben Carew is still a force to be reckoned with. I wouldn't want to cross him."

Sophie agreed. For a mild-mannered old man, Carew possessed a thread of steel that could be intimidating to lesser mortals.

"It's equally possible Ben Carew took revenge for his daughter and her husband," she said. "He was very vocal about never believing their death was an accident, and it was clear at the time he took it hard. That kind of obsession with finding the truth can eat away at a person, over time, make them bitter… perhaps even a little unhinged."

Turner thought of the man he knew, who'd operated the ferry back and forth for years, as a quiet, no-nonsense sort of person who could always be relied upon. But, as he was beginning to learn, still waters could run deep.

"I guess it could have been neither of them," he had to say. "Some third party, for some unknown reason."

"It's possible," Sophie agreed. "Nick Pascoe has certainly cultivated a fast friendship with the lovely Kate Irving. People do foolish things for those they admire."

"What about her husband—Will Irving?" Turner asked. "Might he have had something to do with this?"

"That's an interesting question," she said. "Especially as I took the trouble to run a thorough check on our domestic abuse survivor, to see the extent of the life she'd led with this dreadful man—or, so she's told us. D'you know what I found, Turner?"

He waited.

"Diddly-squat," she said, roundly. "No long history of abuse, no police reports—except one, where the attending officer noted that the report was vexatious, and likely a product of postpartum depression, following the birth of a child. The officer contacted the local Health Visitation Team, so they could keep a close eye on mother and baby."

"And?" Turner asked. "Did they find anything?"

"No," Sophie said. "They found nothing against Kate Irving to suggest she was unfit...but they found nothing against Will Irving, either. That's the point."

Sophie ran her hands through her hair and stood up to walk around a bit, stretching out the muscles in her back while she thought.

"I've seen plenty of cases where women didn't make reports, or mistakes were made on the police side," she admitted, after a minute or two. "I wouldn't want to be responsible for perpetuating the same errors because, on the face of it, we've got a woman who's sustained fifteen years of emotional and physical abuse, and who's finally had the courage to tell her story. Set against that, we've got a suspicious death and a woman without a paper trail to support her allegations against a man with no criminal record and a squeaky-clean image."

"She doesn't strike me as a victim," Turner said. "She seems...pretty *strong*."

"She is," Sophie said. "But victims don't always wear badges that say, 'I need help', Alex. Remember that."

CHAPTER 25

"I've got a bone to pick with you."

Nick looked at Ben, who held up both hands in mute surrender, and promptly abandoned him in favour of playing with his great-grandson and the dog, who was enjoying splashing about in the shallow waters of Carew Cove.

"Sorry, lad, but, at my time of life, I've got to think of my blood pressure. I'm an old timer, and can't afford to take risks."

"I thought you didn't want to be called 'old'!" Nick threw after him.

He turned back to face the angry-looking redhead standing before him, and tried to look serious when his abiding thought was that she looked nothing short of magnificent when she was riled up.

"Ah, what's the trouble?"

She gave him a tight smile. "This," she said, slapping the morning gazette down onto the kitchen table.

He craned his neck to see the headline. "Local man found dead," he read aloud.

"Not *that* part," she said, snatching it back up again. "It says here, '*The grisly discovery was made yesterday by local celebrity, Nick Pascoe, and a female companion...*'"

She looked up, her eyes spitting fire. "*Celebrity*, Nick? You kept that one quiet, didn't you?"

He sucked in a long breath. "Let's go out on the water," he suggested.

"I'm not going anywhere with you," she blustered. "I want to know why you kept this from me!"

"Isn't it *obvious?*" he threw back. "You happen to have had a bad experience with male celebrity figures, in the past. I wanted you to get to know the real me, so that we could be friends again, before the rest of it muddied the waters. I didn't want anything to put you off."

"Put me off?"

"Well, you know..." He raked nervous hands through his hair, while her eyes followed the action. "I didn't expect to do so well with my music. Nobody does, really. Half the time, I forget that people know my name, because my kind of 'celebrity' isn't the red-carpet kind, and I certainly don't do anything to court any favours."

She eyed his jeans and faded t-shirt, and had to smile.

"You've had a bad experience," he continued. "The last thing I wanted was for you to associate me, in any way, with that kind of life, or with the life you've had with *him*."

"Why?" she asked softly. "Are you just being a good friend again, Nick?"

They looked at one another across the table, and there was a crackling silence.

"You need time to recover," he said. "You need to find yourself again, without any romantic entanglements to throw you off-course."

And he couldn't stand to be anybody's rebound.

"I haven't had any romance in my life for a very long time," she said, while outside they heard the happy laughter of her son and the occasional contented *yap* of a dog. "I'm not sure I'd recognise it, even if it was standing right in front of me."

"Wouldn't you?"

She met his eyes, and felt something quiver, deep inside. "Well, for instance, when a man I've known since we were kids brings me a beautiful, intricate painting box that must have cost a lot of money, should I consider that a thoughtful gift from a friend, or something more?"

She didn't wait for him to answer before continuing.

"When that same man talks to me as nobody has dared talk to me since I came home—because they've been frightened that I'm too fragile or too weak to stomach the message—and tells me that I need to strap on my Big Girl Pants and get back to the business of *living,* which includes picking up my paintbrushes again, should I consider that a friendly message or something more meaningful?"

She watched him, trying to see behind his eyes and into his heart, before realising they were one and the same.

"When I've felt repulsed by men for too many years to count, and never expected to want to be held by any man *ever* again, how do you think I should feel when a simple hug yesterday from you was enough to have me rethink everything?"

His heart quickened, and something soared inside him. "What are you saying?"

"I have something for you," she said, and walked across to her bag, where she'd stored the first small painting she'd completed in almost five years.

She held it out to him.

"For me?"

She nodded, and clasped her hands together to stop their nervous flapping while he drew the sheet of watercolour paper from the brown envelope where she'd stored it.

On it was a beautiful image of a man and dog beside the water, with the sunset at their backs.

"This is me and Madge?"

Kate nodded. "I painted it from memory, after seeing you both down by the waterside yesterday," she said. "It's both a 'thank you' and an apology, Nick. I'm sorry I wasn't more gracious, yesterday, but I was frightened. I want to thank you for knowing exactly what I needed, *and* what I needed to hear. I hope you like it."

"I'll treasure it," he said, holding it carefully in his hands.

She watched the way he set it down, as if it were made of precious diamonds, and thought of how much care he'd shown in the past few days. More than that, she remembered all the years before, when he'd laughed with her, cried with her, held her and, yes, she realised...

He'd loved her.

"I'm sorry it took me so long," she said.

"Really? I think you whipped this painting up pretty quick..."

She shook her head, and walked around the table towards him.

"I don't mean the painting. I mean, I'm sorry I didn't see you properly, as I should have done from the beginning."

"I wrote you letters," he said, needing to know why she hadn't replied. "I probably made a fool of myself."

Her face fell. "What letters? I never heard from you, after I left."

This time, he shook his head, and moved a step closer.

"I sent you more than a dozen letters," he said. "To your uncle's house, in London."

"I never got them," she said. "I'm sorry, Nick."

Perhaps it was their way of shielding me from the past, she thought, and made a note to call her uncle at the first opportunity.

"What did they say?" she asked.

He lifted a shoulder, looking at her face, her hair...

"They said 'I love you', in a thousand ways," he said, and raised a hand to run a fingertip down the smooth skin of her cheek. "Every love song I've ever written has the echo of you, Kate. I didn't realise, at the time, but I know it, now."

"Even *Boom-Tickety-Boom?*" she asked, referring to one of his less illustrious efforts.

"Even that one," he laughed. "And, as it happens, the proceeds from that little number helped buy my house."

"In that case, you're welcome."

They smiled at one another, and linked hands.

"What now?" he wondered.

"Let's see where the wind takes us, shall we?"

Neither of them was aware of the long-range camera capturing their kiss from the far edge of the trees; they saw only each other, as if for the very first time.

CHAPTER 26

In the end, Kate and Nick did go out on the water, and took Jamie and Madge along for the ride.

Borrowing her grandfather's boat, they motored from Carew Cove along Frenchman's Creek to the estuary, where they turned south towards the sea, passing Helford Creek as they went, waving to friends and neighbours along the way until they reached another secluded inlet.

"That's my place," he said, and pointed towards a white-painted house sitting high on its own headland, with a large terrace wrapped around three sides to take advantage of the views from every angle. A boathouse and jetty had been built at the water level, and behind it all was acres of lush green forest and not much else.

"It's beautiful," Kate said. "I don't remember the house being here, before?"

"I built it," he explained. "Not with my own bare hands, although I did chip in with the decorating. I bought the land first, and waited until I could build something on it. I've always admired that spot."

Jamie pointed up ahead. "You can see the sea!"

Nick grinned at him. "There are seals who come to visit me," he told the boy. "And deer, in the woodland. A pheasant by the name of Dudley is an occasional visitor."

Jamie giggled.

"Is this the only way to get to it?" Kate asked.

Nick slowed the boat as they approached the jetty, and came alongside.

"I suppose I could cut down some trees and have a proper access road put in, but it would be a long one," he said, and she could see what he meant. It would have to wind right through the trees to the headland from the main highway, three miles back. "I happen to like that it's a bit cut off from the world. I can work in peace, and I don't get anyone bothering me with junk mail or canvassing for the local elections."

She smiled. "How d'you get your post?"

"I pick it up from the village store, in Helford," he said. "Sometimes, Henry drops it off for me, if he happens to be out on the water. Most people send e-mails, these days, anyhow."

It was a singular way of life, she thought, but he was such a sociable man that it obviously hadn't affected him.

"There's a path through the woods and around the headland, so you can walk to the main road, if you want," he said, and jumped off the boat to tether the line. "Often, the people whose work I produce like to come here to record because it's away from everywhere, completely without distractions."

Jamie took his hand and jumped onto the jetty with Madge at his heels and, after a moment spent thinking that her son seemed very comfortable in Nick's company, Kate followed.

"Ready for some lunch?" he asked them.

"I'm staaaaaarving," Jamie said.

"Your mum not been feedin' you, eh?" Nick sympathised, and, without another word, swung the little boy up onto his shoulders as they began ambling up the pathway to the house. "That's terrible."

Jamie laughed, and ran his fingers through the leaves of a weeping willow tree as they made their way through a sub-tropical garden, filled with palm trees and giant ferns of all description.

"This is something else," Kate said. "It's like the Glendurgan Gardens, on a smaller scale."

The gardens were a local attraction across the water, maintained by the National Trust for everyone to enjoy, but here, Nick had his own version in miniature.

"My mother had a hand in helping to design it," he said, and Kate asked after his parents, who were both away in Tenerife at a time-share they owned over there.

"Can't see why anyone would want to leave here," Nick said. "But it's each to their own."

Presently, they emerged onto a large terrace and Nick deposited Jamie back onto his feet so he could fish out his keys.

"Don't know why I bother locking up," he said. "It's hardly as if the place is vulnerable to intruders, and I have a pretty good security system installed, even if they did decide to pay me a visit."

He pointed at a set of discreet cameras she never would have noticed, and some heavy-duty floodlights.

"The lighting has been wired in a radius through the trees and down the garden to the jetty," he said.

"The cameras are dotted all around, too, so I know who's arrived before they've even set foot on the property."

It felt as safe as Fort Knox, Kate thought, and it was a good feeling.

"Welcome," he said, and held open the door so they could precede him. "To Casa del Nick."

Nick's home was beautiful inside and out.

He had a warm, open personality and this was reflected in his décor, which spoke of a man well-travelled, with an appreciation of fine art mingled with trinkets and mementos that held meaning for him. Much like at The Ship's Mate, one wall had been reserved for framed photographs and, to her delight, she found several that included herself as a younger woman, dressed in summer clothes with an arm slung around his waist and, in another one, she and Lucy were seated on the beach with Pete lying between them half-buried in sand, made to look like a mermaid.

Kate laughed. "I remember that day," she said. "I'm so glad you captured these moments, Nick."

"You can have copies, if you like?"

She nodded, still looking at the different memories.

"Mummy, Nick, look at this!"

Jamie skipped towards an acoustic guitar on a stand beside a large, u-shaped sofa, not far from a grand piano that stood in the window so Nick could look out at the water while he tinkled with melodies.

"Oh, now, be careful with that," Kate said.

"It's okay," Nick told her, and rubbed a hand on her arm, almost without thinking. It was a fleeting touch, no more, but it seemed to burn her skin, and, to her surprise, she realised she wanted to know what it might feel like if he touched her more thoroughly.

"Here you go," Nick was saying, as he helped Jamie to sit comfortably with the guitar. It was an adult's size, but he managed to manoeuvre himself so that he could play a tune.

"This is Mummy's Song," he declared, and began plucking a series of notes interspersed with a few chords which, together, made a sweet melody of his own making.

At the end, Kate was choked up.

"That was beautiful," she managed, and reached down to pull the little boy into her arms. "Thank you, sweetheart."

Then, she looked up at the man who was no longer her friend, but so much more.

"You helped him to learn this?"

Nick nodded.

"It was no challenge," he said, with a wink for Jamie. "Next, we move onto Nirvana."

She continued to smile at him, a world of hope in her eyes.

"Come on," he said, taking her hand. "Let me show you the rest."

CHAPTER 27

Much later, when the sun had slipped off the edge of the world and nocturnal animals left their burrows to forage in the undergrowth surrounding the riverbanks, Andy Charlton made his way back from the designated meeting point with a spring in his step.

He'd just *known* everything would go to plan.

Some people knew when to fight, others knew when they were beaten, and the fish he'd hooked understood from the get-go which category they fell into. He felt sorry for them, in some ways; if he hadn't happened to witness their little brouhaha the other night, they might have continued onward through life without a care in the world, while the close-knit community of Helford continued to look up to them as one of its finest members.

But he *had* seen, and that changed everything.

Now, they'd have to pay for the privilege of respectability, and they'd keep paying for many years to come. Small price for getting away with murder, some might say.

Naturally, they'd put up a token denial. He'd heard plenty of 'you're mistaken' and 'I don't know what you're talking about' but, the fact remained that, if that were *true,* they wouldn't have been willing to meet him in the dead of night to discuss the matter. Instead, they'd have done what an innocent person would have done, which is contact the police.

Of course, they'd done no such thing.

They needed a couple of days to pull the money together, they'd told him, which was fair enough. People didn't generally keep that kind of cash just lying around the house, and they'd need to withdraw it without attracting too much attention.

He was a reasonable man.

While he waited, he planned to accumulate some more very interesting images for his other client, and would collect on those, too.

Different fish, different methods of reeling them in, same tasty supper at the end.

Charlton whistled an old Frank Sinatra tune, something about strangers in the night, and made his way back through the silent streets of Helford, across the little pedestrian bridge spanning the creek and along the road on the southern side, passing the car park at the top of the hill and continuing upward to the passing place, where he'd left his rental. The roads were narrow and winding and, as he neared the edge of the village, the houses fell away so that the tarmac was lined by high banks of hedgerows and trees that might have been hundreds of years old. There were no streetlamps, just the glow from houses he passed by and, the further he walked, the further away they became.

"Bloody country lanes," he muttered to himself, as he wheezed up the hill.

Soon, he was alone in the countryside, or so it felt, and he could no longer see any of the houses or the comforting light shining from their little cottage windows. Although he was not a man given to flights of fancy, nor was he afraid of the dark, Andrew Charlton experienced a ripple of fear.

"Ridiculous," he told himself. "Get a grip."

Still, when he saw the headlights of a car approaching somewhere further up the hill, their yellow glow illuminating the surrounding darkness, he was oddly relieved to know that other people were around and obviously making their way into the village. It was not Brigadoon, after all; despite its rural setting, Helford was a popular place for tourists and a local yachting hub, so it was foolish to feel isolated.

The headlights grew brighter as the car hurtled down the winding hillside and Andy could only marvel at their confidence travelling at so great a speed, on roads such as those.

"Must be local," he mumbled to himself, and prepared to step aside to allow them to pass.

There was nowhere safely to stand off-road, so he plastered himself against the high bank at one side, which should have left enough room for the car to pass by.

But its driver had other plans.

Rounding the corner at speed, the car came to an emergency stop, swerving in the road as its driver caught sight of him.

Andy raised a hand to shield his eyes against the glare of the headlights, unable to make out the driver or much else about the make or model.

He swung his arm to indicate there was enough room for them to pass by.

"Go on," he called out. "There's nothing coming the other way!"

The engine revved, and the car began to roll towards him, slowly at first, but then with clear intent.

In that moment, Andy knew.

"Oh, God," he muttered to himself, as the car picked up speed. "Look, let's forget about it! I didn't see anything, after all!"

There was no way of getting to his own car, which was parked further up the road, so he did the only thing he could.

He ran.

Breath came in and out of his body in panting bursts as he struggled back down the hill, shouting for help into the silent night, but there was nobody to hear.

Behind him, the car surged forward and connected with his body, rolling over him with a heavy crunch of bone and muscle. The driver stopped, put the car in reverse for good measure, and Charlton was no more.

CHAPTER 28

Kate awakened the next morning to the sound of sirens.

"Mummy!"

A moment later, Jamie came running into her bedroom dressed in his Marvel pyjamas, jumping excitedly and pointing towards the window.

"There's three police cars outside! Come and look!"

Still groggy from sleep, Kate swung her legs off the bed and was about to do that very thing, when there came a series of loud bangs at the front door.

"I'll get it!" her grandfather called out, already dressed for the day in shorts and a blue t-shirt bearing a slogan which read, 'Sunday, Monday, Happy Days!'.

Kate hurried to dress herself while barely managing to hold Jamie back from charging outside to look at the squad cars, and, when she eventually emerged into the cottage with her son in hand, it was to find DS Keane and PC Turner talking to her grandfather in hushed tones.

"What's all the ruckus about?" she asked them, noting the time was barely eight o'clock.

"We apologise for the disturbance, Mrs Irving, but we have a warrant to search these premises and to impound your grandfather's vehicle."

Kate looked towards Ben, who stood tall and proud, his face a mask of barely-concealed anger.

"Why on Earth would you need a warrant?" she demanded. "We'd have shown you anything—"

"There are processes to follow," Keane told her. "We'll be as swift as we can, but I might suggest you and your little boy vacate the premises while our officers conduct their search."

"Can I help?" Jamie asked. "I'd like to be a policeman when I get big."

Sophie Keane looked down at the little boy and felt all manner of emotions, chiefly a melting sensation in the region of her heart.

"Thank you," she said, as seriously as she could. "But we'll manage on our own, this time. What I would like you to do is go and get your clothes on and brush your teeth, so that you can go for a nice outing with your mummy. Okay?"

Jamie took her request as a direct order from a superior officer, and hurried off to do her bidding.

"This job has its perks," she said, and excused herself to go and speak to the forensics staff who were unloading their kit, outside.

Kate smiled and thought that, in other circumstances, they might have been friends.

"Are you all right, Grandad?" she asked of Ben, who looked visibly shaken by the intrusion.

"Fine," he said. "They're just doin' their jobs, aren't they?"

"Why do they want your vehicle?" Kate whispered. "What's happened, now?"

"There was a hit and run, late last night," he said, and wondered how it had all come to this. "Apparently, they've got reason to think one of us might've been involved."

"*What?*" Kate raised her hands to her face, unable to take it in. "That's crazy—"

"Apparently, the bloke was a private investigator," he explained. "They think Will hired him to keep tabs on you, love."

Kate felt her stomach sink, but it was only what she'd expected of her husband.

"That's no surprise," she said. "I knew he'd find me, and I suppose he had to rely on the services of some private snoop."

"Well, he's a dead snoop, now," Ben remarked. "Somebody ploughed into him and, since we're the only ones with any reason to want him out of the way, they're pointin' the finger at us."

Kate was dumbfounded. "They seriously think either you or I could've snuck out in the middle of the night and run over this person?" she whispered. "On top of what happened to Bill?"

He gave a nod, and watched through the kitchen window as a forensics team dressed in polypropylene suits examined his Toyota.

"Your Gran used to drive that," he murmured. "Prefer boats, myself."

Kate put her arm around his waist and rested her head on his shoulder.

"There's nothing to find," she said firmly. "I'll take Jamie for a walk into the village and, by the time we come home, it'll be over, you'll see. This is all some horrible mistake, and they'll probably find it was a drunken tourist who wasn't watching where they were going."

"I hope you're right," Ben said, and thought of what might happen now that Will Irving's dog had been put down.

Maybe the man would come down and do the dirty work himself.

Kate took Jamie into Helford Village, which elicited a stream of complaints from the little boy who would much rather have stayed to watch the police in action, but he was appeased by the promise of an ice lolly and time spent on the beach. Before then, they had a house call to make, one she could put off no longer.

They made their way to The Ship's Mate just before nine, to find it still closed for business. However, knowing Joanne and Lucy would be up and about preparing the inn for the day's influx of customers, Kate rang the bell on the outer door and waited.

A couple of minutes later, Joanne opened it.

"Kate," she said, warmly. "And this must be Jamie?"

He gave her his best, toothy smile.

"Come in, come in," she told them, and made her way through to the dining area. "How about a milkshake to kickstart the day, young man?"

Jamie's eyes lit up, and Kate nudged him.

"Yes, please," he said, very politely.

"Why don't you run and collect some shells, while I make it?" Joanne suggested, and, with a nod from his mum, Jamie raced down to the shingle beach to begin hunting for the pick of the crop.

Joanne chuckled, and began chopping bananas and strawberries to mix in with ice cream and milk to make one of her famous 'Super-Duper Shakes'.

"He's a cutie," she said. "You'll have your hands full, in a few years' time."

Kate smiled, and knew it was true.

"I'm sorry I haven't come around before now," she said. "I wasn't sure whether you'd want to see me, at such a difficult time, especially as I was the one to find Bill the other day."

"You're like family to us, love. Never feel that you wouldn't be welcome."

Kate reached across the bar to give the woman's hand a supportive squeeze. "I'm so sorry about what happened…and, even more so to have been the one to find him."

Joanne nodded. "I am too, love. Nobody would have wanted this for Bill, least of all me, and I wouldn't wished that for you, either."

She put the fruit in a blender and flipped the switch. "You'll always be welcome here," she added, once the cycle had finished. "There's no cause to stay away from us, just because of what a few silly bodies are sayin'."

Kate's heart sank. "What are they saying?"

Joanne sighed, and shook her head. "You know what it can be like around these parts," she said. "Folk have far too much time on their hands, for one thing. The police've been askin' around about Bill's death, so people've got wind it's bein' investigated as suspicious. That's more'n enough to set tongues waggin'."

She paused to retrieve a tub of vanilla ice cream from a freezer in the kitchen, and returned a moment later.

"If that weren't enough, there's all the talk about your parents, rakin' everythin' up after so many years," she said, and wondered if she should tell Kate what she'd told the police, or leave it to come out, eventually.

Maybe it didn't ever need to come out, Joanne thought.

"O' course, then there's that man bein' found dead, up at the top of the hill," she said. "Fred Lorne discovered him, first thing, and rang for the police.

You can bet your boat that most of the estuary'll know about it by now, if he's got ought to do with it."

Kate thought of the whole village and surrounding countryside wittering about the events of recent days, about the police arriving at Frenchman's Cottage that morning, and put two and two together.

"They think we're involved," she said. "People think I…or my grandfather…had something to do with it all, don't they?"

"Don't pay any attention to gossip," Joanne advised her. "D'you think I believe any of that nonsense?"

She shook her head. "I hope not," Kate said. "Joanne, I swear, we know nothing about it—"

Joanne smiled. "I *know* neither you nor Ben would ever have hurt Bill, or that feller last night," she said. "Lucy knows it, too."

"Where's Lucy?"

"Spent the night with Pete Ambrose—on his boat, no less," Joanne said, with a meaningful look. "Nice lad, all told, and he dotes on my Lucy."

Kate nodded, but thought of how her grandfather would feel when he learned what the village was thinking, and what they were saying.

It would crush him.

"What can I do?" she wondered aloud.

"Nothing you can do, love," Joanne said kindly. "Just ride the storm out, that's all any of us can do. Come back to work, hold your head high, and carry on as normal, that's my advice."

With that, she wandered outside to let Jamie know his milkshake was ready.

CHAPTER 29

By the time Kate and Jamie returned, the police had finished their search, and Carew Cove was once again a peaceful haven of birdsong and lapping water. Ben's Toyota was missing but, aside from that, it was as if the morning's intrusion had never occurred.

After a brief search, Kate found her grandfather in his garden, weeding and tending the flower beds his wife had planted.

"Debbie would've been ashamed to see the state these were in," he muttered. "The moment you start letting things slide, everything else goes with it."

In truth, the garden was in fine shape, but they both knew the real reason for his sudden impetus for physical exertion.

"Jamie? Why don't you set up the Junior Monopoly, or Scrabble?" she said. "I'll come and play with you, in a minute."

Her son gave a *whoop* and raced indoors.

"Are you alright?" she asked, now that little ears were out of range.

Ben's lips pressed together. "I'll bet it's the talk of the county, by now," he said. "Ben Carew's house raided by police, and his car impounded. I don't know how I'll hold my head up."

"But you will," she said softly. "You're in the right, and you know what you always taught me."

"*Right is might*," he said. "Aye, I know. Easier sayin' it than livin' it, sometimes."

Kate smiled.

"After the police left, I looked out the old files from the police investigation into your mum and dad's death," he said, and her smile vanished. "I know you don't want to go over it all, love, but we've got to face facts. Bill Hicks wanted to tell us somethin' about what happened, and it must be in that file. There must be *somethin'*, Kate, some little thing we've missed, all these years…"

"What if there isn't?" she asked him. "What if we'll never know how they died, and why Bill Hicks wanted to speak to us about it? They're *gone,* Grandad, and nothing we do now will bring them back."

"No," he agreed, sombrely. "But it'll set things right, and stop the folk around here comin' up with wild tales about us havin' clubbed Bill to death, or mowed down that private investigator."

"They can't really believe any of that," she said.

"You'd be surprised what people will believe," he muttered. "Just look at our government, and it'll tell you how credulous folk can be."

She laughed shortly. "You have a point there," she said. "The police were asking a lot of questions about whether mum and dad had a happy marriage. I don't remember there being any problems, but I wonder if I'd have noticed, if there were. Can you shed any light on that?"

Ben stood upright and stretched his neck to ease the kinks. "It's like I told the police," he said. "I never saw a couple more in love than your mum and dad—unless you count me and my Debbie."

There was no higher praise than that, Kate knew.

"You should know somethin' else, though," he continued, looking uncomfortable. "There's a bit more tattle goin' round the village about your Dad havin' had an affair—"

"Who?" she asked. "Who are they saying he had an affair with?"

Ben said it as quickly as he could. "To tell you the truth, they're sayin' it was Joanne."

Kate said nothing at first, then she shook her head. "Absolutely not," she said. "I don't believe it."

It was the response Ben would have expected, and he happened to agree with her. "Seems unlikely," he said. "But that's what folk are sayin'."

"Whether it's true or not, if Bill happened to believe it, that could have been a motive for him doing something to punish my father," Kate thought aloud. "I guess that's what the police are wondering about—and now they're wondering if one of us paid Bill back for whatever he may or may not have done."

"Aye, maybe they think we've had our revenge."

"There's just one problem with that, aside from the obvious point that neither you nor I could have killed anyone," Kate said.

"What's that, love?"

"Neither could Bill," she said flatly. "He wasn't built that way."

"Tell that to the town," Ben said.

"I will—" She paused, watching her grandfather's face contort with pain. "Grandad? *Grandad!* What's the matter?"

He clutched his left arm, while his legs gave way, and she rushed forward to break his fall, cradling him in her arms.

"Can't...can't breathe..."

"Jamie!"

The little boy came rushing outside.

"Pick up the telephone in the kitchen and dial 999," Kate told him. "Ask for an ambulance and tell them to come to Frenchman's Cottage as quickly as they can. Do it now, Jamie."

He nodded vigorously and rushed back inside to do his mother's bidding.

"Stay with me," she whispered to Ben. "Stay with me, now."

They were lucky.

An ambulance had been on its return journey from a scheduled call-out in the area, and was therefore less than five minutes from Frenchman's Creek, arriving in time to administer life-saving defibrillation and immediate oxygen.

Once stabilised, Kate and Jamie accompanied him in the back of the ambulance for the forty-minute journey to Truro Hospital, the latter keeping up a happy stream of questions about the various bleeping machinery that served as a useful distraction to all of them.

Nick found them in the waiting room, soon after Ben's admission.

"I came as quickly as I could," he said, leaning down to bestow a kiss on Kate's cheek, and a ruffle of the boy's hair.

Reaching inside his jacket pocket, he produced a KitKat, which he handed to Jamie with a wink.

"Thought you might be starving," he said.

"I was!"

"I must be psychic," Nick told him, and tapped the side of his temple.

Kate smiled, and mouthed 'thank you'.

"How's Ben doing?"

"He's stable," she said, using the word the consultant had used when he'd described her grandfather's condition. "He had a heart-attack, but apparently not as serious as it could have been. The paramedics got to him in time."

Her eyes filled with tears, and she looked away, unwilling to cry in front of Jamie.

"It's okay to feel upset," Nick murmured. "Isn't it, Jamie? You've had a big shock, I'll bet?"

"Yeah," he agreed, smearing chocolate around his mouth. "I rang for the ambulance, Nick, and remembered the right address."

"That's brilliant," Nick told him. "I'll bet you helped save your Grandie's life today, Jamie."

"Really? I did?"

Nick nodded, then looked across at Kate. "What's the prognosis?"

"Apparently, the heart attack was caused because he has an arrhythmia in his heart and, it turns out, he'd been referred for a scan that was due to happen next week," she said.

"What's a—a—?"

"It means his heart races a bit too fast," she told Jamie. "The doctors need to reset it."

"How? Is it like a computer?"

Kate smiled and leaned down to kiss the top of Jamie's head.

"I suppose it sort of is," she said. "But, in this case, Grandie will go to sleep for a couple of hours and, while he's sleeping, the doctors will give his heart a kind of…shock, which will hopefully force it to beat at a normal pace again."

"When do they plan to do it?" Nick asked.

"Straight away," she said. "They're taking him in tomorrow morning, all being well. For other people it would normally be a day-case, but he'll stay for a few nights because of his age and the added risks involved."

She didn't need to elaborate; Nick could readily imagine the risk factors for a man of eighty-one.

"He wants to go through with it?"

Kate nodded. "He's adamant."

"That's Ben," he said, with a smile. "Knows his own mind—and heart."

CHAPTER 30

"Come home with me, Kate."

Hours later, when they could do no more except leave Ben to sleep, Nick held a tired Jamie in his arms and knew it was time to go.

"I can't leave him here in hospital alone," she said. "What if something happens? He'd have nobody."

Nick sighed, trying to think of what Ben would want.

"He certainly wouldn't want to see you both tired and hungry," he argued. "You need to keep your strength up, if you're going to be any use to Ben when he comes through this."

Kate glanced at Jamie, who gave a huge yawn and leaned back against Nick's chest.

"The doctor said he'd be out for hours, probably until the morning," Nick reminded her. "And they'll call you, if anything changes. I'll drive you back here, myself."

"You shouldn't have to run around after us," she murmured. "I'll bet you've got no work done, in the time we've been here."

Nick thought of the late nights and early mornings he'd spent writing new songs—mostly love songs, it had to be said—and knew that his unstoppable wave of creative inspiration could only be thanks to the woman sitting in front of him.

"Oh, I do a bit here and there," he said. "Besides, I'm happy to help."

Kate tried to imagine how Will would have behaved in the same situation, and couldn't, simply because he wouldn't have been sitting there cradling their son in his arms, nor offering her any kind of support.

"You're probably right," she said. "It doesn't help to sit here in the waiting room, or crowd around his bed, when he doesn't even know we're there. I'll check in with the hospital later this evening, just in case, but, all being well, I'll come back first thing in the morning, if you wouldn't mind giving me a lift…"

"My pleasure, Kate."

Nick looked down to find Jamie had fallen asleep against him, enjoying the soothing rise and fall of his chest and the solid beat of his heart.

"C'mon little guy," he said, and lifted the boy up into his arms, resting his sleeping head against the solid muscle of his broad shoulder. "Time to get you tucked in, I reckon."

She might have been tired and overwrought from the events of the day, but she could still see clearly, and Kate saw everything she'd ever wanted in that one, simple gesture.

"It could be a good idea for you both to stay with me for a couple of days," Nick reiterated, as they made their way down the rubber-coated hallway towards the exit. "I don't like the thought of you and Jamie being alone at Frenchman's Cottage, especially since Irving knows where you are, now."

There could be no doubting it, especially now they knew he'd hired someone to seek her out.

"That man probably took photos of us," she realised, shivering slightly as they stepped out into the early evening air. "If he did, and Will saw them... Nick, he's insanely jealous. Even when there was no cause to be, he'd fly into a rage if he felt a man was being over-familiar. Please, be careful."

Nick wasn't a fool, nor was he in the habit of proclaiming any false bravado. In his line of work he had, from time to time, needed to deal with overzealous fans or individuals with obsessive tendencies. He knew how difficult they could be, and how persistent, so he didn't pretend otherwise. If Kate was telling him her husband had a similarly obsessive nature and, moreover, was physically violent, then he would listen—after all, he might be a physical match, but even the strongest person could be taken unawares.

"I'll be careful, I promise," he said. "So long as you will be, too."

She nodded. "I've got an appointment with a solicitor early next week," she said. "We managed to get an emergency injunction which says he's not allowed to come anywhere within the Helford estuary—that's something, and he's not a fool, Nick. He knows he has a reputation to protect, so, if he flouts that injunction, he risks being arrested. No amount of PR management can prevent that being reported, and it wouldn't sit well with his fan base at all."

Nick settled Jamie on the back seat of his car where, she noted, he'd purchased a small booster seat.

Always thinking of them.

"What about the criminal and civil cases against him?" Nick said, once they were on the road. "Does Irving know about those, yet?"

She swallowed, thinking of how angry her husband would be, when he found out. "Not yet," she said. "The solicitor said he's due to be served first thing tomorrow."

Nick nodded slowly. "We'll be ready."

They made a pitstop at Frenchman's Cottage to collect a change of clothes and, at the last moment, Kate scooped up the old cardboard file Ben had kept, which contained all the old paperwork he'd been able to compile relating to her parents' death. After that, they drove down to the village, where they left Nick's car and transferred to his motorboat so they could complete the short journey to his home by water.

Madge was waiting for them at the door, her brown eyes full of concern, and Kate spent several minutes stroking her fur to calm them both.

"It's alright, girl, we're back now," she said. "Everything's going to be okay."

Madge laid her head on Kate's lap.

"Jamie's out for the count," Nick said, coming back into the living room a moment later. "I put him in the spare room, next to yours."

Kate didn't look up from where she continued to stroke the dog's head.

"And where do you sleep?"

Nick ordered his body not to react to what was, he was sure, a purely innocent question.

"I'm in the master bedroom, next floor up," he said, conversationally. "It's a bit like a look-out tower. You get the best views of the estuary from up there…"

"Maybe you could show me," she said softly.

"N—now?"

Kate raised her eyes, and nodded. "Unless you're too tired to give me a…thorough tour."

Nick shook his head slowly. "Never too tired," he promised, and held out a hand, which she took.

They checked on Jamie one last time as they passed his room, where he was sleeping soundly.

"How about that view?" Kate said.

Nick gestured for her to go ahead. "I've got a whole new perspective I can show you," he said, and flashed a smile.

Kate paused on the first step and turned back so their faces were inches apart.

"It's been a long time since I've made love," she said quietly. "I'm not sure I ever have. Can you show me?"

He had no words, so he leaned forward to bestow the gentlest of kisses.

"I'll show you for the rest of my life, if you'll let me, Kate."

CHAPTER 31

"How's the view?"

Kate turned over and gave Nick what could only be described as an extremely self-satisfied smile.

"Not bad," she said. "Not bad, at all."

"Is that the best you've got?" he teased, curving an arm around her waist to pull her closer. "I'll have to try harder, next time."

Kate shook her head, not having all the words at that moment to tell him how transformative those long, beautiful hours of the night had been for her; how much he'd made her feel alive again, as a desirable woman in her own right.

"We should get up," she said instead, leaning forward to press a kiss to his lips. "I know a little boy who'll be waking up, soon, and we need to tread gently with him. He doesn't understand about his father, yet."

Nick nodded. "There's no rush," he said. "It's no hardship to love Jamie, but only when he's ready. I won't force anything, Kate."

She put a hand on his heart, in silent thanks. "It may take some time for him to come around to understanding his world has changed," she said. "Can you be patient?"

He laughed. "I've waited more than fifteen years already, when you think about it," he said. "What's another couple, in the grand scheme, if there's the promise of a lifetime's happiness on the other side?"

Kate could hardly believe it.

"Are you sure I'm—*we're*—what you want?" she asked him. "Some men wouldn't like the idea of bringing up somebody else's child."

"Some men are assholes."

She rolled her eyes. "I'm serious," she said. "Divorcing Will won't be a bed of roses. He's going to make it as difficult for me as possible, and he'll play dirty, I know it. He might drag you into the fight, and I wouldn't want to see anything happen to you or your career, because of me."

"Are you kidding? My PR team have been begging me to strum up a bit of drama," he joked. "I'm far too boring for the music industry. I should have a beard and a few tattoos, for starters."

"I prefer you without either," she said, shyly.

"I always wanted to be a Kurt Cobain character but, to be honest, I'm more of a James Blunt, and I'm absolutely fine with that."

She laughed. "I don't think you're like either," she said. "You're special."

"It's been said many times," he laughed.

She threw a pillow at him, and then rolled out of bed, preparing to make her way downstairs to greet her son when he awoke.

"Kate?"

She turned back, a smile still on her lips.

"I mean it, you know. However long it takes, I'll wait for both of you."

"I love you, Nick Pascoe."

"That's because I'm special."

She laughed again, and made her way downstairs.

While Nick took Jamie out with Pete for a tour of the deeper waters, to watch dolphins frolic and sea birds call to the wild, Kate borrowed Nick's Land Rover and drove back to the hospital in Truro, where she sat in the waiting room leafing through Ben's old file while he underwent his defibrillation procedure, under general anaesthetic.

Minutes, then hours, ticked by as Kate turned the pages. She read over the statements given by all those who'd known Rob and Alice Ryce, especially their inner circle of family and friends. She read the pathology report and, oddly, being within the hospital setting helped her to get through it with a clinical eye, managing to detach herself from the thought of her parents laid out on cold metal slabs to look at the pathologist's conclusions objectively.

No matter how many times she read and re-read, there was nothing new that stood out; no vital clue that changed everything. The story remained the same as it had been, fifteen years ago…

Rob and Alice Ryce had taken a trip to see friends in St Ives on Thursday 7th August, a fact corroborated by those friends, and by others who were in attendance. They hadn't returned until late, after midnight, choosing to sleep in their cabin on the boat rather than disturb Alice's father, Ben. Unbeknownst to them, a tiny leak must have sprung in the pipe feeding the stove in the cabin of *The Lady of Shalott,* slowly feeding carbon monoxide into the confined area over the course of several hours. Nobody had been seen entering or leaving the yacht during their absence—but then, Kate had been away from Carew Cove visiting her friends in the village, while Ben had been operating his ferryboat between Helford and Helford Passage throughout the day, stopping in for a couple of pints of cider with his friends at The Ship's Mate, later in the evening.

Therefore, nobody had been around to witness a third party's arrival, even if somebody had accessed the yacht during that time.

That night, while Ben slept in his cottage and Kate laughed with her friend Lucy while they watched *Scream* on her bedroom television at The Ship's Mate, Rob and Alice Ryce had returned from St Ives by taxi, motored the short distance from the wooden pier at the end of Ben Carew's garden onto their yacht, which was moored on the creek, and had subsequently died, collapsing to the floor of their cabin following asphyxiation by carbon monoxide poisoning.

They never saw it coming.

Nobody had.

"Mrs Irving?"

Kate looked up to find the consultant standing beside her, and she hurriedly closed the file, dragging herself back to the present.

"It's 'Ryce'," she said quietly. "Kate Ryce."

"My apologies," he said, easily. "Ms Ryce, I thought you'd want to know that your grandfather has come through his procedure with flying colours. We're very optimistic for a positive outcome, and a full recovery, if things continue as they are."

The relief was overwhelming.

"I can't thank you enough," she said. "He means so much to me…to many people."

The consultant nodded and talked her through the stages of Ben's recovery then, a short while after, headed off to help the next person.

When he came around, the first thing he saw was Kate's face.

"Who're you?" he asked, feigning confusion.

Her face was a picture, and he let out a peal of husky laughter. "Sorry, love, couldn't resist," he said.

Kate swore softly, and leaned over to kiss his cantankerous old cheek.

"You had me going, for a second," she said. "How are you feeling?"

"Like I've been dragged through a hedge, backwards, then trampled by an elephant," he wheezed. "But, I'm still alive, so it could be worse."

Kate propped her head on her hand, wondering how he could find the energy to be funny, at a time like that.

"You scared us all," she murmured. "I wish you'd told me about the arrhythmia."

"The GP only picked up on it the other day," he said. "I didn't want to worry anyone, when it might have come to nothing."

Kate reached across to take his hand, feeling how fragile his skin was, how papery beneath the tan.

"From now on, you should tell me anything that's worrying you," she said. "I know I've had a few things on my mind, but your health is *always* more important to me. Is that clear?"

He smiled. "Just then, you reminded me of your mum," he said, and laid his hand over hers.

Kate thought of her mother and grandmother, and again of the file she'd read. Then, she glanced around the room and noted all the cards, the bouquets of flowers and messages of goodwill that had filtered through overnight, and knew they would mean a lot to the man lying pale and weak on the bed beside her.

"They're keeping you in here for a couple of nights, for observation," she said, rubbing his fingers to warm them. "I'll come back during visiting hours, every day, until you're ready to come home."

She nodded towards the cards and flowers.

"See? Nobody has forgotten about you, Grandad. It takes more than a few rumours to outweigh sixty years of community service."

"Takes many good deeds to earn a good reputation," he said softly. "Just one bad deed to lose it."

They wondered who amongst the names written on the cards had forgotten that maxim, and who would commit the ultimate sin to keep their reputation intact.

"Somebody knows more'n they're sayin'," Ben said weakly, before his eyelids drooped again and he fell into an exhausted sleep.

Kate watched him for long minutes before pressing another kiss to his forehead.

"I'll find them," she said. "I promise."

CHAPTER 32

As morning became afternoon and the sky softened to a mellow amber, Kate made her way back to Frenchman's Cottage to collect another change of clothes for herself and Jamie. The cove was quiet when she arrived and, before hurrying back to Nick's house, she paused to look out at the creek, remembering when her mother's yacht had anchored there every summer. The past was a powerful driver, and Kate found herself wandering down to the boathouse to pull the heavy tarpaulin away from *The Lady of Shalott,* revealing her aged lines and butchered interior that was the product of so many hands having pulled her apart, searching for answers. The sight of her was enough to bring tears to Kate's eyes, an outpouring of emotion so strong it clogged her throat and blurred her vision.

She remembered the yacht as it had been, back then.

She could picture her mother, tall and slim, with red hair held back in a long plait or a ponytail, and her father, blond and bronzed like Robert Redford, laughing as the wind caught her sails.

Kate sank to the floor and rested her head back against the edge of the wooden wall, closing her eyes while images played in her mind's eye.

She pictured the boathouse back then, and remembered sitting on the farthermost edge with her sketchbook, trying to capture the elusive shades of mauve and lilac on the still water of the creek, as the light hovered somewhere between day and night.

"I know it's awkward—"

She heard her mother's voice entering the boathouse somewhere behind her, obscured by the motorboat her grandfather kept in there.

"All I'm asking is for you to be patient, a little bit longer," Alice said. *"She's going through a hard time, a phase, and it'll pass. We're leaving in a couple of weeks, anyway."*

Her father muttered something rude.

"It's getting out of control," he said. *"I won't put up with it much longer, and neither will—"*

They'd left the boathouse again, their conversation receding into the sands of time, and Kate reached out in her sleep, trying to capture the threads of a story half-told.

"Kate," her mother said. "Wake up, Kate."

Her eyes flew open, as if somebody had tapped her shoulder.

Rather than heading directly to Nick's house, Kate parked his car and made another pitstop, this time at The Ship's Mate. As usual, it was teeming with customers, but they were short-staffed and, after checking that Jamie and Nick could make do without her, Kate offered up her services to help.

It didn't hurt for the neighbourhood to see her face, either.

"Hello, stranger," Lucy greeted her, when Kate entered the bar. "Wasn't sure when I'd see you, again."

"I called in to see your mum, yesterday, but you were out," Kate explained. "I'm so sorry about your dad—I wanted to give you both some time to yourselves."

Lucy had heard the rumours but, like Joanne, she chose not to believe a word of them.

"We're keeping busy, as you can see," she said. "I guess you know what people have been sayin'."

Kate's face became shuttered.

"About my dad," Lucy added. "They're sayin' he killed your parents, and that's why you and Ben decided to push him down into Pirate Bay."

Kate's face betrayed no emotion, which was a trick she'd learned during her time with Will Irving. "What do *you* think?" she asked.

Lucy paused in the act of wiping down the bar, pushed a tray of drinks towards one of the serving staff who came to collect it, and turned back to her friend.

"It's obviously a load of old hogwash," she said, succinctly. "For starters, my dad couldn't have harmed a fly, and that's a fact."

Kate released the air she'd been holding in her lungs, and reached for an apron.

"Much as it was a terrible tragedy—and you know how much I thought of your mum and dad—these things do happen," Lucy continued. "It doesn't mean anything nefarious happened, or that anybody set out to hurt them. Accidents can happen, can't they?"

Kate supposed that was true, but she had her doubts, in this case.

"It's forced me to think back to those last few days," she confessed, keeping her voice low for the benefit of any idle ears. "I remember we'd spent most of the day together, hanging out with Pete and Nick, then we came back here to do the afternoon shift, then I stayed over and we watched *Scream*—"

Lucy smiled at the bittersweet memory. "We had popcorn and scared ourselves silly," she recalled. "It was great—until the morning came."

Kate nodded. "The coroner thinks my parents died shortly after entering their cabin, which was some time after midnight. They'd been away in St. Ives for most of the day, visiting friends over there."

Lucy nodded. "I remember. Your grandad popped in here for his supper and a couple of pints, then went home around nine or thereabouts."

Kate had helped to clear away last orders, that evening, so she remembered waving her grandfather off.

"He took himself off to bed," she said. "He was still operating the ferryboat full-time, back then."

"I remember that night for another reason," Lucy said, and rested her forearms on the bar. "It was one of the first times my dad got himself blind drunk—you know, so drunk that he had to be put to bed. I helped him upstairs, with mum, and she had to sit with him for hours to make sure he wasn't sick on himself."

Kate made a small sound of sympathy.

"Hello, Kate," Joanne said, entering the bar area with her hands full of empties. "How's your grandad doing?"

"He's much better, thank you," she said, automatically. "Thank you for the card and flowers."

"No trouble," Joanne murmured. "Anything we can do to help?"

"You've got enough on your plate," Kate said. "But I appreciate the offer."

Conversation paused as business picked up, and the three women fell into a pattern of work for the next few hours, with Kate making a particular show of talking to many of the locals who stared openly and whispered as she cleared plates.

"Yes, as you can see, Fred, nobody's slapped any handcuffs on me, yet—unless you think you're up to the task?"

That had caused an eruption of laughter from the old man's fishing cronies, and put paid to any more whispered remarks for the time-being.

"You handled yourself well tonight," Lucy said, when their shift was drawing to a close. "It isn't easy to keep a game face on, when part of you wants to just crawl away and hide."

"If you can do it, so can I," Kate remarked.

Lucy looked up in surprise. "I didn't realise it was that obvious," she said, with a little laugh.

"It isn't," Kate said. "But I've known you for too many years not to notice when you're playing a part."

When the last punter had left, at around eleven-fifteen, Joanne joined them in the long bar and slid onto one of the stools with a grateful sigh.

"My feet," she muttered. "I think I'll treat myself to a nice, hot bath this evening."

"I'm off to Pete's in a minute," Lucy said. "But, I can stay to lock up, if you like."

"I don't mind doing it," Kate said. "If you want to head off?"

"Would you?" Lucy said. "That'd be great." She took off her apron.

"Lucy, about what we were saying before," Kate said, before she could rush off.

"Which part?"

"When you were telling me about Bill, the night before my parents died."

Lucy nodded, wishing she could forget. "Mum was there, too, weren't you?"

Joanne looked up from where she'd been massaging her right foot. "What's that, love?"

"The night before Rob and Alice died, dad had a big blackout," Lucy said. "You and I had to help him up the stairs and you sat with him all through the night, you were that worried."

Joanne shook her head. "You're thinking of a different night, lovie."

Lucy frowned, thought about it, and then shook her head. "No, it was definitely that night, because I remember hoping he didn't disturb our movie," she said, smiling sadly at Kate. "I was still embarrassed by it, back then."

"It happened so often, it's easy to get the days mixed up," Joanne said. "Your dad might have had a few, but he was still conscious."

Lucy remembered a man who could barely put one foot in front of the other, but didn't bother to argue.

"Well, I'm sure you're right," she said, and left it at that. "Thanks again for locking up, Kate, and give my best to your grandad, from me."

"Thanks," Kate murmured, while her mind tried to capture something elusive that hovered around the outskirts, tantalisingly close but just out of reach.

"Well, I'll be off," Joanne said. "Another long day tomorrow. Thanks for comin' in to give us a hand, love."

Kate gave her a distracted smile.

"Sure—anytime. Enjoy your bath."

Joanne blew her a kiss and, a moment later, Kate heard her weary footsteps on the stairs leading to the Manager's Apartment.

In the residual silence, she moved around on autopilot, locking the side doors and tidying away any last glasses or crockery before setting the dishwasher away. Finally, as the clock struck half past the hour, she made for the front door.

As she did, she passed by Joanne's memory wall, with its framed photographs of people she'd known over the years.

Kate paused to look at them again.

She counted every face, and could put a name to many of them, including her own. There were individual and group shots, including ones with her father…in fact, many featuring her father, as he'd been back then; handsome and proud, with his arm around her shoulders or sitting playing chess with Bill.

Her eyes flitted over the photographs again, hoping she was wrong.

She wasn't.

There were none of her mother—Joanne's great friend.

Not a single one.

Kate looked away, remembering the snippet of conversation her mind had recalled in the boathouse earlier.

"All I'm asking is for you to be patient, a little bit longer," her mother had asked of her father. *"She's going through a hard time, a phase, and it'll pass. We're leaving in a couple of weeks, anyway."*

Kate thought of the rumour surrounding her father and Joanne, and of its significance to the police investigation.

It provided a motive for murder, if Bill had known about it.

Except, what if it was all a lie?

What if her father never so much as looked twice at Joanne Hicks? What if he only had eyes for his wife, the mother of his child, whom he loved so much that he'd commissioned a twenty-five-foot luxury yacht in her honour?

What if...

What if Joanne's feelings were one-sided because she was unhappy in her own life, and she'd made a fool of herself, throwing herself at a man who could not and would not reciprocate?

What if Joanne envied her friend's life, and her husband, and coveted both?

A phase, her mother had said. *Be patient.*

What if Alice Ryce had known all about Joanne's misplaced affections and had pitied her—the ultimate insult to a woman's pride—asking her husband to treat her friend gently, no matter how difficult she was becoming, for the sake of their longstanding relationship, knowing they'd be returning to London soon?

It's getting out of control, her father had said.

Perhaps, he'd meant to say that *she* was getting out of control.

Kate thought of what Lucy had told her about the night her parents died, and then she remembered a passage she'd read in the statement Bill had given to the coroner's inquest, at the time.

I was at home in the Manager's Apartment with my wife, Joanne, from around seven o'clock on the evening in question, until the following morning. She stayed with me throughout the night, as I'd been unwell.

On the face of it, man and wife provided an alibi for one another during a key time when somebody could have fitted a hosepipe to the exhaust on her parents' yacht and fed it into their cabin, returning later to remove the pipe, knowing all the while that nobody would be at home.

Their joint alibi only stood up to scrutiny if Bill could account for every hour that Joanne was beside him. But, according to Lucy, he was blackout drunk; so drunk, he was unconscious, and could account for very little.

There was a back entrance to the Manager's Apartment, accessing the road via a set of stone stairs, which would have allowed somebody to slip out at any time, safe in their supposed alibi while the two girls were downstairs in the main bar, along with most of the village.

Glancing back towards the staircase, Kate flicked the lights off and hurried out of the main door, before locking it with shaking fingers. Then, she hurried through the dark streets of the village, running along the pedestrian footpath towards the ferryboat landing, where she'd left her motorboat.

CHAPTER 33

A single light illuminated the landing and Kate hurried to cast off, toeing the edge of the boat away before hopping onboard to come about and begin the journey to Nick's house, where she could talk everything through with him and try to make sense of what her addled brain tried to tell her was irrefutably true.

"You've spotted it, haven't you?"

Kate's heart lurched into her throat, and she turned from the wheel to find Joanne emerging from the little cabin area, holding Ben's file in her hands.

"I wondered if anybody would ever realise," she said. "I might've known it would be you."

"I don't know what you mean."

"No more lies," Joanne said, in a tone that suggested she was disappointed Kate would even try.

"Lucy gave it away, in the bar, earlier. She didn't mean to, poor lamb, but she did—didn't she? Watch where you're going, love."

Kate turned the wheel swiftly to avoid colliding with a boat moored on the estuary, and reduced her speed.

"Just keep going," Joanne said. "Keep going until I tell you to stop."

Her voice held a tone that brooked no argument.

"She was right, of course," Joanne continued, perching herself on the bench beside Kate to look out across the dark waters of the Helford. "It was the night that Bill got himself paralytic on whisky, for the first time. He'd found out, of course, about Rob."

Kate glanced across at her, then back at the open water.

"My father never touched you."

The words spilled out before she could prevent it, her need to defend her father's memory far greater than her own self-preservation.

Joanne's lip curled.

"He was a *coward,* that's all he was," she spat. "He had feelings for me—I *know* he did. He was just too afraid to act. If he'd never met Alice...if she was never there...it would have been the story of Rob and Joanne."

Kate heard the note of hysteria in the other woman's voice, and told herself to stay calm. Joanne Hicks was volatile, far more than anyone could have imagined.

"Bill gave you an alibi that night, didn't he?" she said. "He told the inquest you were with him all night, but you weren't. Were you?"

Joanne didn't answer for a long time, and Kate thought she hadn't heard her above the sound of the waves, but then she answered in an odd, distant voice.

"Bill loved me, I suppose," she said, wistfully. "I think he hoped things could get better. He thought I'd made a mistake, some sort of temporary aberration, and of course I denied any involvement, so he told himself he was doing the right thing in protecting his family. I helped him along a bit," she admitted. "I dropped in a few choice words about Lucy growing up without her mother, which helped him to make the right decision."

She looked at Kate, then, with eyes that were suddenly full of hatred.

"You had to come back, didn't you?" she snarled. "For years, everything ticked along. He drank and drank, but that was fine, so long as he kept his mouth shut and left me to run the pub. Then, you walk into the bar one day looking like your mother's bloody *ghost*, and it brought everything back. I saw, the moment it happened. Bill couldn't stop ranting about it—about you, and Alice and Rob. He couldn't forgive himself, for the lie he'd told, and needed to put things right, he said."

Joanne made a small sound of contempt.

"I warned him," she said. "I told him to let things lie, but he didn't listen."

"You followed him," Kate realised. "You followed him to Frenchman's Creek, the other night."

Joanne nodded. "I had to," she said. "Can't you see that he left me no choice?"

She shook her head in disbelief.

"He was ready to sacrifice the life we'd built…that *I'd* built—and, for what? All because he couldn't live with himself any longer, couldn't stand wondering if his wife had a hand in your parents' death."

"Did you?" Kate asked her, outright.

Joanne seemed to toy with the idea of lying, then shrugged it off.

"It's just us two," she said, and her lips curved into a smile that turned Kate's stomach. "So, I'll tell you. Yes, I was the one, Kate, and, as far as it goes, I'm sorry for your loss. But *you* must understand *my* loss. Your mother robbed me of the future I might have had with Rob, the children we could have had together. Because of *her*, I was forced to settle for Bill Hicks, and watch the pair of them sail around the Helford looking like cover stars for *Cornish Life*. It was sickening. As for your mother—"

She spat over the side of the boat.

"I've spent a lifetime pretending to be that woman's *friend*," she said. "Mourning her loss, to the outside world, but inside...*inside,* Kate, the moment she was gone, I felt free. While Alice Carew was alive, I felt second best, second rate. She was a constant reminder of everything I didn't have, and never would have. I felt nauseated seeing them together and...God, when she was pregnant with *you,* I can't tell you what I suffered."

"You must really have hated her," Kate said, in an emotionless voice, as she reached down to turn on the boat's tracker.

"That word doesn't begin to describe what I felt," Joanne said, no longer attempting to hide her vitriol, long past keeping up appearances.

"But you say you loved my father," Kate said, blinking salty tears from her eyes. "Why did you kill him?"

"He betrayed me," Joanne said simply. "He betrayed his heart—his *true* heart, no matter what he might have told anybody else. I remember the first time Alice brought him to the Helford…did you know that? Oh, yes, I was there when she introduced us all to her new beau from London."

She sucked in a breath and her voice became coquettish.

"He might have been sittin' with her, but I knew…I *knew* the first time I laid eyes on him that he should have been mine, and he knew it too."

Kate heard the madness, the sickness, but felt no pity; only a terrible, burning anger towards the pathetic creature sitting beside her, one she could happily have thrown into the sea.

"So, you killed them both," she said flatly. "Your husband lied for you, because he was weak and afraid, and spent years mired in guilt, until the day he tried to confess his mistake—which is when you killed him, too."

"Let's not forget that meddling investigator," Joanne pointed out. "Now, surely, you'll thank me for that one."

Kate was horrified.

"Why would you kill a stranger? What did he have to do with anything?"

Joanne made a dismissive gesture with her hand.

"No, not that way, Kate," she said. "Make for the open water, please."

Kate followed her direction, veering away from the safety of Nick's house which shone like a welcoming beacon from its peninsula on the western shore of the estuary and did as she was told.

"Well, it was bad luck for him, really," Joanne carried on, once they were bobbing towards the mouth of the estuary. "He happened to see Bill and me on the pathway the other night, and the greedy little so-and-so came to me, lookin' for a pay-out. I'd have thought he was already onto a tidy earner workin' for your husband, but it's never enough for some people, is it?"

She tutted, just two old friends again.

"Anyway, good riddance to bad rubbish, that's what I say."

CHAPTER 34

Nick popped his head around the door to Jamie's bedroom and, finding him fast asleep, made his way back through to the kitchen where he checked the time—again.

Madge loped in behind him.

"Where d'you think Kate could be?" he asked her. "It's well past midnight, and she should have been home, by now."

He didn't stop to question how easily 'home' slipped off his tongue in relation to Kate; when he thought about it, he'd designed his house with her in the very back of his mind, whether he had realised it or not. Why else would he have asked the architect to add on a tower room with windows on all sides, to take advantage of the best light? He certainly didn't use the space himself, but it was crying out to be somebody's art studio, one day...

"She isn't answering her mobile," he continued. "But she might not have any signal. It's patchy, around here."

Madge cocked her head at him, and then eyed the telephone sitting on the kitchen island.

"You're right," he said. "I'll call The Ship's Mate, just to be sure. It can't hurt, can it?"

He snatched up his phone and keyed in the number for his local, and waited impatiently as it rang to voicemail.

Hello! You've reached The Ship's Mate. We're sorry we can't take your call, just now, but if you leave your name and number...

Nick tried a second time, then a third, with the same result.

"Somebody should be there," he said, and panic began to flutter in his chest.

This time, he keyed in Pete's number, which answered on the last ring.

"Nick? What time d'you call this? I'm a bit busy, mate."

"Sorry to disturb," Nick said, without any remorse whatsoever. "Is Lucy with you?"

"Ah—"

"Put her on the phone."

There was a brief, hushed conversation, and then Lucy's voice sounded down the line.

"What's up, Nick?"

"Sorry to call so late," he said. "I've been trying to get through to someone at The Ship's Mate but nobody's answering. Is anybody at home?"

Lucy frowned towards Pete, and sat further up in bed.

"Mum should be there with Kate, although she's probably at home with you by now," she said. "Nobody's answering? That's very strange."

"That's just it, Kate hasn't made it home."

Lucy relayed the information to Pete, who understood his friend's concern.

"I'm sure she can't be far," she said. "Have you tried her mobile?"

"Yes, and no answer there, either."

"I'll try calling my mum," Lucy said.

"Already tried that, too," Nick said. "Nobody's answering."

"Which boat is Kate using?" Lucy asked him. "It'll have an AIS."

She referred to an 'Automatic Identification System', which all modern vessels had.

"She has Ben's motorboat," he said. "I'll get onto the coastguard now. What about your mum?"

"I'll try her again," Lucy said, starting to worry. "I can't think where she could be, at this time of night."

"Keep in touch," Nick told her, and rang off.

Pete put a gentle hand on Lucy's back, and asked what the matter was.

"They're both missing," she told him. "Kate hasn't made it back to Nick's place, and my mum isn't contactable anywhere. I remember her saying she wanted a hot bath…maybe she's just turned her phone off?"

"Maybe," Pete agreed, and then waited a beat or two. "Look, why don't we take a turn around the water, see if we can spot either of them?"

Lucy nodded, already pulling on her clothes.

"It's probably nothing," she repeated, for her own benefit. "But, after everything that's been happening lately, I think—"

"Yes," he agreed, pulling on a thin sweater. "Can't take any chances."

Nick held a tense phone call with the local coastguard and harbour master who, after some none-too-gentle persuasion, agreed to look for Ben Carew's boat on their Vessel Traffic Service, a monitoring system similar to air traffic control, which used AIS, radar and VHF radio to keep track of all the vessels coming in and out of range. It was a public system designed to prevent boat collisions, but it wasn't fool proof; AIS systems could be turned off so that boats moved around without appearing on any official radar.

In this case, they were lucky.

"I'm picking up a transmission from that vessel just off the coast of St Anthony," the coastguard said, referring to St Anthony-in-Meneage, not far from the mouth of the estuary. "It's heading for open water."

Every one of Nick's instincts went on high alert.

"You need to get a response team out there, right now," he said.

"We haven't received any pan-pans or mayday signals," the coastguard pointed out. "As far as we know, that vessel is in no state of urgency or distress, whatsoever."

"I'll make a donation to the RNLI," he almost shouted. "Take my word for it, will you, Pippa?"

The coastguard heaved a sigh.

"All right, I'll launch a boat within the next few minutes," she said. "But, if this ends up being a waste of time—"

"You have my word, the RNLI Christmas Party will want for nothing," he said.

"The things I do," she said, and made the call.

"They'll be on their way soon, I'm sure."

Kate looked across at Joanne, who was smiling again.

"Who will?"

"The coastguard, obviously," Joanne said. "I know you turned on the AIS, Kate. I could easily have disabled it, if I wanted to."

"Why didn't you, then?"

"It'll be too late, by the time they get here," the other woman said. "You'll have already fallen overboard, after a desperate tussle in which you tried to kill me. Fearing for my life, and in self-defence, I pushed you. It broke my heart to do it, but that's the way the cookie crumbles."

"You've really got a taste for killing now, haven't you?" Kate remarked. "If you want me overboard, you're in for a tussle, all right."

Joanne laughed. "You're so like your mother," she said, with a degree of admiration that was quickly overtaken by hatred. "Just then, you reminded me of the time she came to the pub to speak to me, to tell me to back off her husband and stop embarrassing myself, before Bill found out. Can you believe the bitch said she *pitied* me?"

Joanne tapped a finger against the edge of the motorboat.

Tap, tap, tap.

"This'll do," she said, and reached across to pull the keys from the ignition so that the boat came to a spluttering standstill. All around them, the waves buffeted against the edges of the little boat, which was not made for open seas but for the gentle waters of the river.

Joanne threw the keys into the water, and Kate knew then that her reason had completely gone.

"Here we are, Kate," she called out, across the din of the sea spray. "This is the end of the line."

Joanne reached into her back pocket and produced a pocket-knife, which she flipped open.

"We can do this the hard way, if you like. As you said, I've got a taste for it now, and I'm not afraid to do what needs to be done. Nobody will remember you, after so long, Kate. They'll recall a woman they used to know, but what have you really left behind as a legacy?" she challenged. "A sad history of domestic violence and a four-year-old son who probably misses his father—whereas I'm a local lynchpin. Where would half of the people in these parts be, without me? Without The Ship's Mate?"

Kate heard her words and perhaps her old self might have listened and believed some of the poison poured into her ears. Not now, though; not the woman she was, that day, and the one she hoped to become, tomorrow.

"How dare you place a value on a human life," she shouted. "It isn't for you to play God, deciding who gets to live or die on a whim—and, all because you were rejected. How humiliating for you, Joanne! How that must have burned your pride to know you weren't only second best, you didn't even make second place, at all! I remember my mother and father talking about you, feeling sorry for you, and do you know what my mother said, Joanne? She asked my father to have patience with you, because you were a pitiful wretch going through a tough time. They knew all about you, Joanne, and the only reason they didn't cast you out of their lives was because they felt it would be like kicking a stray dog, when it was already down!"

As Kate finished her tirade, Joanne charged forward, fingers curled into talons, knife glinting in her right hand.

In that moment, she saw her life pass in front of her eyes, and thought of Jamie and Nick, of Ben and all the people she was yet to meet. She saw her mother's face, smiling at her as a child, remembered her scent and the sound of her voice.

All this and more flashed through her mind, and she side-stepped at the last moment. At the same time, Fate lent a hand, sending a wave crashing against the side of the little motorboat so that it tipped up on one side, falling low on the other.

For Joanne, it was a perfect storm.

Her body flew overboard, her cry lost on the wind, enveloped by the water which filled her lungs—just as the carbon monoxide had once filled those of Kate's parents—so that she could no longer breathe.

Even if she had wanted to, there was nothing Kate could have done to help her; in the pitch blackness, she saw nothing more of Joanne Hicks, whose body would eventually wash up on the rocks a few miles further south of their position.

Kate was left alone on the disabled motorboat with the might of the sea tipping the boat back and forth, and she put a desperate 'mayday' call through to the coastguard, who, it turned out, was already on her way.

CHAPTER 35

Two days later

"Mummy! I can't sit still for much longer, I'm st—"

"Let me guess," Kate interrupted him, not taking her eyes off the canvas she was working on. "You're starving?"

"Well, it's been ages since breakfast, and I've been sitting here forever."

Kate looked at the clock on the wall.

"Breakfast was less than an hour ago, and you've been sitting on that stool for twenty minutes," she said, but knew when to call it a day. Outside, the sun was shining, and Nick was strumming a guitar somewhere in the house, which called to her son like a siren song.

"Okay, run along," she said.

Sitting back, she looked at her work in progress with a critical eye. Once, her style had been very precise, every stroke intentional, placed with a steady hand. Now, she had a more fluid style that, remarkably, she was learning to love, and which seemed to create images that were imperfect but more 'real'.

"I love it."

Nick made his way up the spiral staircase to the watchtower, where he'd set up an easel and fresh canvases as a present following her ordeal with Joanne. He thought it would be cathartic for her to express herself through art, and he'd been right. However, rather than creating a series of dark, disturbing images of death on the high seas, Kate was producing a series of portraits of people she loved, beginning with her son.

"You've captured the mischief in his eyes," Nick declared, handing her a cup of tea.

"It isn't hard to miss," she said, and leaned back so he could plant a kiss on her mouth. "Where's Jamie?"

"Playing on the piano," he told her and, sure enough, they could hear the delicate sounds of a four-year-old's fingers jamming against the ivory keys of Nick's antique Steinway.

Since he was out of earshot, she was able to speak freely.

"My solicitor rang, earlier."

"Oh?"

"Yes. He said that Will is abiding by his injunction, as far as they can tell, and he's currently working on a new project at a film studio in London, which should keep him tied up for some time. He's been served with the divorce papers, as well as the civil and criminal proceedings, so he got a triple whammy yesterday morning."

"I almost feel sorry for him," Nick drawled. "Then, I remember, he's an asshole."

Kate laughed, spluttering her tea.

"The bigger argument will be over Jamie," she said, not relishing the prospect. "He doesn't care about him, but he cares about his pride, so he'll put up a fight. He'd rather have Jamie, and send him to an expensive boarding school, than let him stay with me and be loved."

"We'll cross that bridge when we come to it," Nick said. "Hopefully, the other cases against him will be successful, and they'll demonstrate his bad character when it comes to the main argument."

She nodded. "I was never a strategic person," she said. "It would never have entered my mind that I'd need to think like this, one day. He brought this upon himself. If he'd shown any kindness, any consideration at all, I'd have wanted Jamie to have a relationship with his father, but I know his true colours now, and I'll do everything in my power to keep his influence away."

"You're Jamie's greatest champion," Nick said quietly. "If his own mother won't protect him, and have his best interests at heart, who will?"

She turned to look at the picture she'd begun to paint of her little boy, and raised her brush to dab a few more strokes of colour here and there.

"Ben's due out of hospital tomorrow," she said, changing the subject. "I was thinking of throwing a 'welcome home' party for him, at Frenchman's Cottage."

"He'd love that, I'm sure," Nick said. "I'll throw some meat on the barbeque…it'll be great."

"What is it with men and barbeques?" she asked.

"Programming," he explained. "We like making fire, most of us like meat, and we like to eat. Perfect combination."

She chuckled.

"Fine. You can be Master of the Barbeque."

"Please," he said, holding up a hand. "I'll be 'Grand Barbequer of the First Order', if anything."

She shook her head. "Good thing you're so humble about your meat-cooking skills," she said.

"It's true, the Force runs strong in this one," he said. "Now, about the buns—"

"That can be your department, too."

"For the best," he said, and made a note to place a bulk order with the local bakery for enough buns to feed the five thousand.

"I wondered whether to ask Lucy," Kate said. "She must be devastated."

Nick sat down on the stool beside her, and heaved a sigh.

"I spoke with Pete yesterday," he said. "Lucy was inconsolable, when she heard the news about what happened. She's in shock, mainly, and a bit of denial, but she's coming around to the realisation that her mother wasn't the person she thought she was."

"Joanne wasn't who any of us thought she was," Kate pointed out.

"Yes, but Lucy also feels responsible," Nick said. "She blames herself—for the family connection, for not having been able to prevent what happened.

She feels somehow to blame for you having lost your parents."

"That was Joanne's doing," Kate said. "Nobody else."

Nick agreed. "It's going to take some time," he said.

Kate was thoughtful for a minute or two, and then came to a decision. Life had taught her many useful lessons, so far, but one of the main ones had been to grasp every opportunity, and to treat each day as if it was the first and only day. She would not hold grudges against people because of who they happened to be related to; she wouldn't condemn an old friend to a life of secondary guilt and shame. She'd experienced both the good and bad that could come from a community as close as theirs, and she wouldn't wish its wrath to fall upon Lucy, who had done nothing wrong.

She surprised Nick by reaching for her phone, and leaving a message for Lucy to meet her at The Ship's Mate, later that day.

"She's decided to sell up," Nick told her. "I don't think Lucy can face it, after what Joanne did."

"We'll see," Kate said, and plopped a dash of blue paint on the end of his nose.

"Oh," he said. "That's how it is, eh?"

"Uh-oh," she said, as he reached for another paint brush. "Now, Nick, be careful—"

A small shower of green paint splatted on her face, and she began to laugh.

In the living room downstairs, Jamie looked at the dog seated by his side and shook his head.

"They're worse than I am," he said, sagely, and went back to composing his next masterpiece.

CHAPTER 36

Later that day, the three of them journeyed to Truro to visit Ben, who looked and felt far better than he had a couple of days ago—not merely because he was recovering from his procedure, but because his heart was lighter than it had been in fifteen years, knowing that the suspicion he'd held all along had been vindicated.

"I knew there was ought wrong with that boat," he said, for the hundredth time. "As for Bill, lying like that—" He crossed his arms. "May the Lord have mercy, that's all I can say."

"I would never have guessed Joanne was responsible," Kate said. "I never knew she carried so much hatred. Listening to it coming out of her on that boat journey...I don't think I've ever hated anybody as much as she seemed to hate my parents. I don't think I have it in me."

Ben nodded. "She was warped...something was broken inside that one."

"It's Lucy I feel sorry for, now," Nick said. "Pete's doing his best, but she's talking about moving away, where nobody knows her."

"It wasn't her fault," Ben said. "Poor girl. She lost a mother and a father, too."

Kate hadn't thought of it, that way, but he was right. They'd been friends, as girls, and as women they now shared a different kind of bond; one that came from losing both parents.

"She needs good friends around her, at a time like this," she said softly. "I tried running away, once, when I thought I'd lost everything, but I left behind the most important people in my life."

"We're still here," Nick said, and pressed a kiss to her temple.

When they arrived back in Helford, Nick and Jamie took themselves off to the village store so that Nick could collect a parcel he was expecting, and Kate wandered down towards the sea wall in search of a girl she used to know.

"Lucy?"

She spotted her old friend sitting on the edge of the wall wearing another dress of her own creation, this time in a pretty floral print.

"Hi, Kate."

She looked up briefly, then back out towards the water, where a family of ducks coasted along the water searching for lunch.

"I'm glad you came."

Kate crouched down beside her, so their legs swung over the edge of the wall, as they used to do when they were younger.

"Feels like yesterday, doesn't it?" Lucy murmured. "All of us together, larkin' around. It'll never be the same, again."

Kate shook her head. "Only this morning, Nick splattered me with paint," she said.

Lucy couldn't help but laugh. "Come to think of it, Pete turned my shower cold this morning, just to hear me shriek."

"I don't know what we see in those two."

"Must be the sex," Lucy said, deadpan.

Kate grinned, and stole an arm around her friend's shoulders. "It wasn't your fault, Luce," she whispered.

Tears spilled from Lucy's eyes, and she nodded. "I know," she said. "But, I can't forgive my family, for what they did to you, Kate. What they took from you."

"They took from you, too," Kate pointed out. "Neither of us had the parents we should have had."

Lucy wiped the tears from her eyes, and lifted a hand to clutch Kate's fingers. "How can you be so forgiving?" she asked. "If it were me—"

"You'd be the same," Kate said. "I know you would."

Lucy hoped that was true.

"I don't believe in that old saying about apples not falling far from trees," Kate said. "If it were true, my son would grow up just like his father, but he won't. I'm going to make sure of that, if it takes me a lifetime's effort. We're our own people, Lucy, and always have been. Sometimes, it's hard to see, when you're caught up in the drama of other people's making."

Lucy rested her head on Kate's shoulder, in silent thanks.

"I never thought I had much going for me," she said. "Oh, I'm a hard worker, I'm cheerful enough, and not bad to look at. But I never thought I had any talent—"

"Did you make this dress?" Kate asked her.

Lucy looked down at herself.

"Yes," she shrugged. "But, anyone can do that."

"I can't."

"I'm sure you could, if you tried."

"I'm sure you could paint, if you tried," Kate said. "Or write music, or run boat tours, or many a thing. Our choices determine our pathways, but 'talent' is overrated, as far as I can see. It needs hard work, alongside it, or it's just an empty well of potential."

Lucy thought about it, and found she agreed.

"I used to nag Pete about being his own man, finding his own path and all that," she said. "But, the truth is, so long as he carried on working for his dad and being unhappy, it gave me a kind of license to carry on being unhappy and directionless, too. Now, he's picked himself up, dusted himself off and gone out to make himself happy—and he is, already, I can see that."

"Good for him," Kate said. "Now it's your turn."

"I wanted to design clothes," Lucy said. "I took a course at university, learned all about fashion design, but there were no jobs when I left, so I came back here to work for my parents. I suppose I'm good at running the pub, too—"

"Everybody loves you," Kate said, truthfully. "All the locals enjoy chatting to you, Lucy, because you're warm, and you make people feel special. Seniors in the village might feel lonely, if they didn't have somebody who takes the time to spend an extra couple of minutes chatting to them, or introducing them to other people just like them, so they can make new friends. It's a talent, in its own right."

Lucy felt fresh tears threaten, but they were not unhappy ones, this time.

"You—you really think that about me?"

"Of course, I do, you daftie," Kate said. "We all do."

"I'll bet nobody thinks that now," Lucy said. "Not after what's happened."

"I wouldn't be so sure," Kate told her. "Why don't you try re-opening the pub tomorrow, and see how it goes? I think you'll be surprised. Besides, I was planning to throw a 'welcome home' party for Ben, and I was hoping you'd let me have it here."

Lucy had already heard from Pete that they'd planned to have the party at Frenchman's Cottage. However, it was Kate's way of extending the hand of friendship, and offering an opportunity for the whole village to come out in support of one another, in a public way.

That gesture alone was worth more to her than anything else.

"We'd be glad to host the party, Kate," she said, and gave her friend a hard hug. "Thank you."

She drew back, and rubbed the mascara from beneath her eyes.

"Now, which of us is going to break the news to Nick that he isn't going to be 'Grand Barbequer of the First Order', after all?"

Kate raised an eyebrow. "How did you know about that ridiculous title?"

"He's infamous," Lucy said, and rolled her eyes.

"As well as being 'famous'?" Kate said. "Lord, help me."

CHAPTER 37

Long after visiting hours had ended, Ben Carew sat atop his hospital bed feeling healthy as a horse, unless you counted chronic boredom as a medical complaint.

"News is comin' on," his ward companion called out. "Turn the volume up, will you?"

Ben acquiesced, and leaned back to listen to the national news. It was all depressing tales of foreign wars, pandemics and untrustworthy domestic politicians, until the final news story turned to more frivolous 'magazine style' reports of celebrity dramas.

"The actor, Will Irving, who had recently landed the coveted role of Superman in an upcoming, big-budget rendition of the franchise on a popular streaming network, has today been sensationally dropped from the role, following salacious reports that his wife, Kate Irving, has left him amid allegations of widespread

domestic abuse, and has issued divorce proceedings. Irving's representative could not be contacted for comment..."

"Kate Irving...'ere, isn't that your granddaughter?"

Ben looked across at the old man, who'd been in for a hip replacement, and nodded.

"Aye," he said, worriedly.

Then, after a second's thought, he swung off the bed and grabbed his clothes from the chest of drawers.

"Thought you weren't gettin' out until tomorrow!"

"I'm not," Ben said. "I'm checkin' out early."

He tugged on his chords, and began buttoning a striped linen shirt, his fingers fumbling the buttons in his haste to get going.

"Where's the fire?" the other man called out.

"Hopefully, there won't be one," Ben told him. "But there's a man out there who's lost everything, and he isn't the type to take it lying down. Everything that matters to me is out there, beyond these hospital walls, and I'm not about to stand by and let him destroy it."

With that, Ben snatched up the rest of his personal effects and made his way down the corridor towards the main exit, and the taxi rank beyond.

If he hurried, perhaps he'd be home before nightfall.

"I wonder if we should head home to Frenchman's Cottage, before Ben comes back tomorrow," Kate said, as she and Nick made dinner together and Jamie watched a few minutes of cartoons, before bedtime.

"It's getting late," he said. "Why not stay here, tonight?"

He gathered his courage, and went a stage further.

"In fact, you know…I've been thinking. What if you and Jamie stayed here a bit longer?"

"Really? How long?" she asked.

Forever, his mind whispered.

"As long as you feel comfortable," he answered. "As long as you like."

She smiled, and reached up to kiss him.

"Are you sure we wouldn't be intruding? You have your own work, your own lifestyle."

"You mean, tinkling on the piano from time to time, and hosting the occasional celebrity visitor?" He shrugged. "They're overrated, as I'm sure you know."

She laughed, at the dark humour.

"You've been wonderful with Jamie," she said. "And with me. But are you sure this is what you want, Nick? We come as a package deal, and Jamie can't be messed around—by me, or by anyone. At the moment, he thinks we're very good friends, and he considers you his friend, too. If I tell him it's more than that, it's much harder to step back from there."

Nick turned to her, a smile in his eyes.

"You can depend on me," he said, clearly. "I've been a bachelor, Kate, but that's because a wise woman once told me I hadn't found the right girl, yet. Actually, I had, but she got away from me, and I had to wait for her to come back."

Kate couldn't help but smile.

"Jamie's wonderful," Nick said. "Any man would be lucky to have that kid as a son."

"Not every man realises it," she said.

"This one does."

She looked into his eyes, thought of all the mistakes she'd made in her life, and worried about making any more. Once, she'd looked at another man and misjudged his character, but, this time, she had a man who'd been vetted and approved by half the county—none of whom were shy in pronouncing judgment.

"Let's say we'll spend half the week here, and half the week with Ben," she said. "He needs my help just now, while he recovers, and it'll give Jamie a chance to get used to the new living arrangements, over time."

It made good sense, so Nick agreed. "Hey, do you have any bad habits I should know about, before I go 'all in'?" he asked. "Ever leave the toilet seat up, or forget to flush?"

She giggled.

"No, but Jamie might."

"That makes two of us, then."

"Charming."

CHAPTER 38

Ben Carew paid off the taxi and hurried along the pathway to his front door, wondering why there were no lights burning inside the cottage. The whole house was in darkness, other than a couple of security lights which had blazed into action when he'd activated their sensors.

Kate and Jamie must have decided to stay on another night at Nick's house, he realised.

It was a relief to know they were safe and sound, but the first thing he planned to do once he let himself inside was to drop a line to Nick and let him know the latest news about Will Irving. It was possible the man would stay away, if he chose to follow his solicitor's advice, but he wasn't known for taking instructions from anyone, nor caring about the consequences of his actions, so there was an equal chance he'd make his way to Helford in search of his wife and child with the sole intention of snatching them back—or worse.

These troubling thoughts circled Ben's mind as he opened the front door, and, for the first time in his life, he wished he'd installed an alarm system. Sixty years spent living in the same area and he'd never once suffered a break-in, or any other kind of intruder, so there'd never been a need for one before.

But, at that moment, with the night wind whistling in his ears and darkness closing in, he wished he'd taken extra precautions.

The front door opened, and he bolted it behind him, glad to be within the four walls of his home once again, surrounded by all that was familiar.

He moved through the house turning on lights as he went, making for the kitchen where he planned to make himself a cup of tea.

Ben reached for the kettle, but found it missing from its holster.

"Wh—?"

It came crashing down behind him, hard and fast, connecting with the side of his head.

Will Irving watched him fall, set the kettle back on the counter, then crouched down beside Ben's inert figure.

He didn't check for a pulse, or worry about the thin trickle of blood on the old man's temple, but began rooting inside his pockets until he found what he was waiting for.

Mobile phone.

"Thanks, Grandad," he said, and used the old man's thumb to open the keypad.

He spent a couple of minutes scrolling through old messages, then typed one to his wife:

Just got back to Frenchman's Cottage. Worried there may have been an intruder—place all messed up. Can you come and help, please? Love, G x

Pleased with the authenticity of his effort, Irving pressed 'send', and sat back to await a response.

"Nick, look at this message."

Kate hurried into the living room, where she found Nick reading a book about the life and times of Cole Porter.

"What's up?"

She read out the message she'd received from her grandfather.

"I didn't know Ben was planning to come home early," he said, taking the phone to re-read the wording. "I thought he wasn't discharged until tomorrow."

"He isn't," she said, and pulled a face. "But never mind that, now. He says there's been an intruder, Nick. I have to go across and fetch him here."

He stood up, in a quandary as to what to say, and what to do.

"I wasn't going to mention this tonight," he said. "You've been through so much lately, I didn't want to worry you—"

"Mention what?" she whispered.

"It's Irving," he said simply. "He made the news today—apparently, the studio has dropped him from the role of Superman because of rumours circulating around the state of his marriage, and the reason you've left him. They don't want the negative publicity."

"Oh, God," she said. "On top of receiving all the paperwork…Nick, he'll be furious."

"Which is why I took the liberty of alerting DS Keane to the fact," he said. "I was going to talk to you about it after the party, tomorrow, and make a plan."

"It looks like your plan will need to be moved forward," she said.

"I don't want to leave you alone here with Jamie," he said. "This place is a fortress but it's also isolated. I'd feel better knowing I was here to look after the pair of you."

"What about Ben?" she said, unhappily. "I can't stand the thought of him being frightened and alone, especially in his condition."

Nick snapped his fingers.

"I'll put a call through to Sophie," he said, reaching for his mobile. "She could send a squad car out to check on things."

Kate waited while he made the call, but the news was not what they'd hoped to hear.

"She says she'll get a car out there as soon as possible, but there's been a big pile-up on the main road leading down into Helford. Apparently a mobile home collided with a delivery van and they're having terrible trouble getting either of them moved. It's forcing all traffic to go around the long way, and most of her units are deployed to the accident site and on traffic duties. The best she can do is get an officer out within the hour, but it might be longer."

Kate sympathised with the competing demands placed upon their local police, but, selfishly, wished more could be done.

"He's only a ten-minute boat ride away," she said. "Fifteen, at worst. You or I could be there and back in half an hour, if we really hustled."

Nick thought of his friend sitting alone, jumping at shadows, while they enjoyed the warmth of a cosy hearth.

"All right," he agreed. "I'll head over there and bring him back with me. While I'm gone, I want you to keep all the doors locked, okay? I've already shown you how to use the system—do you need me to show you again?"

"No, I remember," she said. "I can check any of the cameras in the security room, downstairs, and I know the code for the keypad."

He nodded, still feeling torn.

"I'll be back before you know it," he said. "Lock up behind me."

CHAPTER 39

Kate sent her grandfather a text message to reassure him Nick was on his way over, and then checked all the outer doors were securely locked. She watched the monitors, which showed Nick reaching the pier, then casting off in his small motorboat belonging to the fleet of 'Teen Spirits' he kept moored on the estuary, leaving one small motorboat he kept in case of emergency use.

The house was airy and light, during the day, but, now, it carried a different sensation. The spacious rooms now felt cavernous and the lighting garish as she wandered from room to room, watching the clock.

Five minutes, then ten...

Jamie was asleep in one of the spare rooms, and she was about to wander over to check on him again, when the security lights blazed into life outside.

She ran to look at the monitors, thought she saw the flash of a figure rounding the far corner of the house, and her heart stopped.

Then, re-started again, pounding hard against her chest.

Will.

Will was here, she knew it.

No sooner had the thought entered her mind, than the house was plunged into darkness.

Kate shrank back against the wall and held a hand across her own mouth to stop herself screaming, so she could listen. She heard nothing but her own breath, at first, deafening in the surrounding silence, then the low hum of the fridge and the whirr of an air conditioning machine on the first floor.

Then, at the far end of the house, somewhere beside Nick's office, she heard the unmistakable sound of a window being smashed.

Slipping off her shoes, she hurried to Jamie's bedroom and scooped him up, whispering for him to stay silent, holding his head against her chest as she crept towards the door. Risking a glance into the corridor, she saw nothing, and took her chance, running barefoot across the tiled floor in the opposite direction until she reached the patio doors leading out into the garden.

She set Jamie down for a moment and fiddled with the locks, which were still unfamiliar, stealing glances along the darkened corridor.

"Daddy!" Jamie's voice rang out into the shadowed hall and, heart pounding with fear, she looked up to see his dark figure walking slowly towards them.

"There you are," he rasped, and Kate's eyes were drawn to the quick glint of a metal blade he held in one hand.

"Jamie," she said. "Come with me, please."

"I want to see Daddy," he said, and she could have wept. "He's come to see us!"

"Yes," Will said, in a funny, teasing voice. "I have, haven't I? Come over here and say hello to me, Jamie."

"Jamie, don't go," she said.

The boy stopped dead, caught between the two of them.

"I said, come *here!*"

Will lunged forward and grasped the boy's arm in a painful, bruising grip, and Jamie cried out. All fear forgotten, Kate ran forward, shoving Will hard against his chest so that he stumbled backward, the knife he held clattering onto the tiled floor.

Jamie ran into her arms, terrified, confused.

"Why does he have a knife?" he asked. "Why did he hurt my arm?"

Kate put herself in front of him, and began inching backward towards the outer door.

"When I tell you, I want you to run," she whispered. "Go down to the pier, and get on the motorboat. Okay?"

Jamie nodded, his eyes wide and frightened.

"Where will you be?"

"Right behind you," she said, watching her husband rise up again, and reach for the knife.

Still shielding her son, Kate grasped the door handle and swung it open, then told Jamie to run. A moment later, the little boy's footsteps rang out into the night, then disappeared into the gardens beyond.

"I'll find him," Will snarled. "I've told you before, Kate, there isn't anywhere you can run to. I'll always find you. You're *mine*. Never forget it."

"Put the knife down, Will."

"This?" he spun it around in his hand, a little bit of pageantry he'd learned for a film role, once. "I don't want to have to use this. I don't want to hurt you, Kate, especially not your beautiful face, but it's clear

I need to label what's rightfully mine, so that others will know."

He stepped forward, brandishing the knife, and she spun around, slamming the door behind her before running out into the night to find her son.

When Nick arrived at Frenchman's Cottage, he found Ben coming around on the floor of the kitchen.

"What happened?"

He hurried to help him up, and was already keying in the number for an ambulance.

"Irving," Ben said, shortly. "It was Irving, it had to be."

"You said there was an intruder, in your message—"

Ben looked confused, and then felt around his pockets for his mobile phone, which was missing.

"I didn't send any message," he said, urgently. "Nick, I never sent any message."

It took less than a second for Nick to realise what had happened, and curse himself for being a fool.

"Go!" Ben told him. "Hurry back! I'll phone the police—"

Nick left the house at a run.

THE CREEK

Kate had only a few seconds' head start, and she used it to sprint down the pathway leading from the house to the boathouse, whipping through the trees and bushes she'd so admired, their leaves trailing against her skin like tentacles.

She spotted Jamie sitting in the motorboat, just as she'd told him to.

"Quickly," she told him, reaching for the line to cast off the boat. "When I tell you to, turn the key in the engine. You remember how to start it?"

Jamie nodded, and then made a small sound of terror, his finger raising to point at the figure that approached them in the darkness.

Kate threw the line into the water and, without a second thought, jumped in after it, shoving the boat away from the pier until it reached the right depth, then trying desperately to drag herself onboard while she called to Jamie to start the engine.

It came to life with a smooth growl, seconds before she was dragged back under the water by a strong pair of hands that she recognised oh so well.

When she resurfaced, she said the only thing uppermost in her mind.

"Make for the village, Jamie! Follow the lights! Go on—"

She thrashed against the hands that held her, kicking and biting, scratching and clawing with a ferocity that took Irving by surprise and gave her enough room to kick away from him with powerful strokes, fuelled by a burst of adrenaline that was pure fight or flight.

"*Bitch!* You'd better come back here!"

Jamie and the boat were too far away for her to catch up, but Kate swam into the shadows where Will couldn't find her, using her superior knowledge of the terrain as an advantage against his superior strength.

It was all she had.

Pete was crooning to Lucy about the beauty of the moon and stars, when he spotted a passing motorboat which, at first glance, appeared to be unmanned.

"Bloody hell," he muttered. "That looks like one of Nick's."

Keeping a sharp eye on it, they noticed it was weaving, albeit very slowly and carefully, between the rows of moored yachts.

"It's going the wrong way," Pete muttered. "Must be in need of help."

With that, he hopped down into his own little dinghy and fired her up, blowing a kiss to his beloved.

"Careful on the water," she told him.

Lucy watched him race out to catch up with the little motorboat, swerving expertly between the others dotted on the water, until he came up alongside.

"*Jamie?*"

Pete could hardly believe it.

"Jamie, reduce the throttle!"

The little boy remembered what his Grandie and Nick had taught him, and carefully pulled the throttle towards himself, so the boat slowed right down.

"Great! Now, turn the engine off!"

Pete slowed his own engine, to keep pace, nudging Jamie's motorboat away from any obstacles as they approached the lights of Helford Village.

Eventually, the engine cut off with a splutter, and Pete jumped onboard to catch the boy up into his arms.

"Where's your Mum, lad? Where's Nick?"

"Daddy's got Mummy!" he wailed, tears coursing down his cheeks. "He's going to hurt her again! He's got a knife!"

"Good God," Pete whispered. "All right, son. All right. Let's get you to your Aunty Lucy, and we'll get straight onto helpin' your mum."

Before he had a chance to say anything else, Pete caught sight of the Teen Spirit II hopping full-pelt across the water, in the direction Jamie had recently come, and knew it was Nick at the helm.

"Nick's on his way to help your mum," he told the boy. "Don't you worry, now. We're all goin' to help."

"Hurry," Jamie said. "Please hurry. My daddy thinks he's Superman, but he isn't. He isn't, anymore."

Pete tugged the boy in for a hug, and brought he motorboat around.

It was a hard day when a boy found out his father wasn't all he was cracked up to be, and he knew all about that.

CHAPTER 40

"Where d'you think you're going now, Kate?"

Will's voice rang out across the water, and echoed around the forest.

"You think you can hide forever, is that it?"

Kate heard him approach, and willed herself to stay strong.

"I must admit, Kate, that you've surprised me, lately," Will continued, as he moved through the trees lining the edge of the water, stopping now and then to listen. "I like this new side to you—it's very exciting. I'll look forward to enjoying whatever other surprises you've lined up for me, since you've been away."

He fell silent for a while, and her heart beat heavily against her chest like a wingless bird.

She heard a twig break somewhere nearby, and she told herself to keep breathing, keep steady, and not to fold.

"Boo," he said, and she swung around with the branch she'd been holding, its bark connecting hard with his muscled torso.

It buckled him for precious seconds, but no more.

Soon, he rose up again.

"I've been training for several hours every day," he bragged. "D'you really think that would make any kind of dent?"

He ran after her, while, in the distance, he heard the sound of a motorboat approaching.

"I think your lover has returned," he called out. "I must go and welcome him, and congratulate him on his good taste."

Kate stopped running, no longer fearful for her own safety, but for Nick.

"Leave him alone!"

She raced towards Will, this time—no longer running but attacking, ready to put herself in front of a good man, a man she loved, to prevent him coming to harm.

"Touching," Will snarled, and delivered a sharp, back-handed slap across her face, sending her sprawling back against the hard floor. "Keep out of this."

He ran back towards the pier, so he would be ready and waiting when Nick Pascoe landed.

Kate dragged herself up again and called out to Nick, waving her arms to warn him.

"Turn back!" she shouted. "He's waiting for you, Nick! Turn back!"

But Nick heard nothing above the sound of the water, and raced towards the pier, bringing his boat alongside.

Kate saw him land, watched him turn his back to tether the line, and saw her husband creep through the shadows of the trees like a predator, waiting for his moment.

"*No!*" she shouted, and her voice echoed through the trees. "*I won't let you!*"

She sprinted after him, hurling herself against the man who'd once been everything to her, but had made himself less than nothing.

He threw her off easily, but the tussle had drawn Nick's attention, and he hurried along the headland to help her.

This time, she needed no help.

Rising up like a phoenix, Kate bared her teeth and launched herself at Will Irving, wrestling and kicking so that they fell to the floor, bruising her skin, tearing it from her body, but she didn't care. All she knew was that she couldn't allow him to win, not this time.

Never again.

They rolled to the edge of the waterline, his hands gripping her throat as they tipped over and slid down the bank to the water's edge, where the silty riverbed rose up to meet them.

Irving struggled to stand, writhing against the mud, his feet sinking deeply into the moist ground. Kate, who grew up playing in those muddy banks, knew how to crawl across them, commando style, until she reached the bankside, where Nick waited for her.

"Kate! Here, take my hand," he said, and hauled her upward. "Are you hurt?"

She thought of the cuts and bruises, then of the bruises on her heart.

"Nothing that won't heal," she said. "Where's Jamie? Did he make it to the village?"

"Pete has him," Nick said, having received a message on his journey back. "He's with Lucy, and they're looking after him."

"What about Ben?"

There was no need to answer that, for at that very moment they heard the sound of another boat approaching, and in a few moments the man himself arrived on the pier in his ferryboat, with four police officers as passengers, including DS Keane and PC Turner.

They made their way across to where Nick held Kate securely in his arms, and then looked down at the man who writhed in the mud, hurling obscenities.

"Give me a minute with him, eh?" Ben asked.

Keane inclined her head, and nodded towards two of her officers, who made their way down to pull the man out of his own filth.

Irving was unrecognisable, by the time they raised him up.

"Hey, pretty boy, remember me?" Ben said, cheerfully. "Last time we saw each other, you were attackin' me from behind, like a bloody coward. Well, here I am, Big Man."

Ben spread his hands. "Fancy tryin' again? See if you can throw a punch while I'm lookin' you dead in the eye."

"I don't hit old men," Irving spat.

"Didn't seem to bother you before," Ben baited him.

Irving sprang forward, throwing off the two officers who tried to hold him, and swung out with his fists.

Ben dodged him easily, and drew his own fist back to land a punch squarely in the man's face, breaking his perfect nose with a satisfying *crack*.

"Not so big now, eh?" Ben muttered.

They watched the police cart him off, heard him whine about assault and miscarriages of justice, then Kate turned to her grandfather.

"How's your hand?" she asked him.

"Not as sore as my head," he said. "I could use a cuppa, but I'm not sure I'll be able to look at a kettle in the same way again."

EPILOGUE

The party was a roaring success.

People turned out from all corners of the estuary, both in celebration of their ferryman's recovery and recent bravery, as well as to christen The Ship's Mate having come under new ownership. Laughter and bawdy humour were the orders of the day, the latter being supplied chiefly by one Fred Lorne, Esq., who was more than delighted to regale the company with tales of his many adventures on land and at sea.

"Sorry, Blondie, but it's time to say 'goodbye'."

Nick looked at Madge with genuine regret, and wondered whether she had a sister he could move in, so Jamie had a dog to call his own.

"You've got your own family, back in Carnance," he said, referring to a nearby cove on the Lizard

Peninsula. "They miss you, so it's time for us to say 'farewell'."

"Talk about the 'long goodbyes'. Why not just write her a song, for pity's sake?"

Luke Malone approached the table where his friend was seated and, with a happy *yelp*, Madge ran over to greet him, showering his face with slobbery kisses while her furry body shook with delight.

"I missed you too," he said, laughingly. "Alright... alright...there, now, sit down."

Madge sat, resting her head on Luke's foot as he took a chair next to Nick and fed her a treat.

"Thanks for looking after her," he said, reaching down to rub the dog's fur. "Did we miss much?"

Nick smiled, and shook his head.

"Nah, nothin' much," he said. "Same old, really. Oh, there's somebody I'd like you to meet. Where's Gabrielle?"

"She got chatting to one of the women up there," Luke said, with a shrug. "She had a little boy—"

"He goes by the name of Jamie," Nick said softly. "I'm hoping to adopt him, one day."

Luke looked across at his friend, then back at the throng of people.

"I thought you only ever had eyes for one woman… the one who got away? What was her name, again?"

Nick smiled, and watched her come down the terrace stairs beside Gabi, who happened to be discussing the need for more illustrators in children's fiction.

"Kate," he said softly. "Her name is Kate Ryce, and she's a wonderful artist and human being."

Luke recognised the look on his friend's face, followed his line of sight to where his wife was chatting to an attractive woman with long, red hair, and took a thoughtful sip of his beer.

"You're a goner, mate. Take it from one who knows."

Nick grinned, and raised his own beer in a toast.

"You said she was an artist?"

He nodded.

"I might have some exhibition space coming up," Luke said. "D' you think she'd be interested?"

"Ask her yourself," Nick said. "She's a woman who knows her own mind."

At that moment, Kate turned to look across the crowd of familiar faces and smiled at him, as she'd done since they were children. He saw his past, present and future in that smile, and knew there was nowhere else he'd rather be.

AUTHOR'S NOTE

The story of *The Creek* came about, in part, from the many years my family has visited that special part of Cornwall and come to think of it as a home from home. For a period of eight years, my parents lived on the north shore, just around the corner from St. Ives, and whenever James and I visited them from London (where we were living and working at the time), we managed to steal day trips to other parts of the county, including the Helford estuary. Years later, when we had our own children, James and I returned to the Helford to rediscover its hidden pathways and lush gardens, borrowing some of its peaceful atmosphere to take home with us, until we were next able to visit. There are countless photographs of our son playing on the beach at Helford Passage, walking along the South-West Coastal Path from there to Durgan and beyond, or munching his way through a pizza baked in the oven outside the real-life Shipwrights Arms pub in Helford. At this juncture, I will reiterate those hackneyed words so often used by authors the world over, which is to say that, in my story, The Ship's Mate is an entirely fictitious entity, as are its staff. I have, of course, taken inspiration from the setting of the real-life inn, which is perched beautifully on the edge of Helford Creek, and would recommend a visit to anyone who happens to be in the area!

Frenchman's Creek is another name so well known to readers, including myself, thanks to the wonderful storytelling of Daphne du Maurier. The wonder of a beautiful landscape is that it can inspire so many works from creatives such as myself, those who have come before and those who will, no doubt, come after. We look upon the same view and see very different things, which makes for even more stories that readers can enjoy; many more paintings that viewers can admire, and so on.

The story of Kate is both an everyday one, and an extraordinary one. Deliberately, I made her husband a well-known face with a humdrum habit, so that his celebrity is meaningless in the mind of the reader; the message being, of course, that it doesn't matter what you do for a living, it only matters who you happen to be as a *person*. From an emotional perspective, this was a complicated book to write, and required a degree of self-restraint when it came to character development; after all, almost every character could have been developed more and more, until this story was two or three times the length it happens to be, now. However, character development can be the enemy of good pacing, and, for a summertime thriller, that must be borne in mind. The beauty of writing a 'world' of summer suspense based around Cornwall is that, in future books, I can revisit the lives of past characters—much as I have done with Luke and Gabrielle, who made a cameo appearance in this novel but enjoyed their own main story in *The Cove*. In the same way, I look forward to developing the lives of Nick and Kate, of Pete and Lucy and of Sophie Keane in stories to come, as they interact with new characters and continue their lives in and around the beautiful land and shorelines of Cornwall.

Thank you to my readers for making *The Creek* another UK #1 bestseller on the Amazon store, I am always blown away by your kind support of my work and it brings me great pleasure to know that so many of you are made happy reading the stories that I write.

Until next time...

LJ ROSS
JULY 2022

New for 2026

Order now!

***There's nothing so deadly as the sea, and
the man who survives it . . .***

Clara Enys was finally living the dream. After years of grafting, she was the proud owner of Cornwall's newest restaurant, The Lizard, named for the peninsula upon which it sat, perched high on a clifftop overlooking the sea. When she wasn't whipping up culinary feasts, she volunteered at the nearby lifeboat station, serving as crew with a team who risked their lives regularly to save others. With no immediate plans to settle down, life was pretty much perfect.

When a distress signal comes through one stormy night from a luxury yacht, Clara is ready to answer the call. Too late to save the vessel, they search raging seas for survivors – but find only one . . .

A man with no name, no memory, and the capacity to turn her world upside down.

If you enjoyed this book, why not try the bestselling Alexander Gregory Thrillers by LJ Ross?

Atmospheric thrillers featuring forensic psychiatrist and criminal profiler Dr Alexander Gregory. Loved by readers for the fast-moving and page-turning plots, international locations and shocking twists, with psychology adding fascinating depth to the stories.

LOVE READING?

JOIN THE CLUB...

Join the LJ Ross Book Club to connect with a thriving community of fellow book lovers! To receive a free monthly newsletter with exclusive author interviews and giveaways, sign up at www.ljrossauthor.com or follow the LJ Ross Book Club on social media:

@LJRossAuthor

@ljross_author

ABOUT THE AUTHOR

LJ ROSS is an international bestselling author known for her atmospheric mystery and thriller novels, including the DCI Ryan series which has sold over 12 million copies worldwide. Her debut novel *Holy Island* published in 2015 and reached number one in the Amazon UK and Australian digital charts. Louise has since released over thirty novels, most of which have been UK number one digital bestsellers. She is also the creator of the bestselling Dr Alexander Gregory series and the Summer Suspense series. Louise is a keen philanthropist and proud to support numerous non-profit programmes in addition to founding the Lindisfarne Prize for Crime Fiction, the Northern Photography Prize and the Northern Film Prize.

Born in Northumberland, England, she studied Law at King's College, University of London, then abroad in Florence and Paris, and worked as a lawyer before pursuing her dream to write. She lives with her family in Northumberland.

If you would like to get in touch with LJ Ross on social media, please scan the QR code below – she would love to hear from you!